THE INN-SITTER

The Inn-Sitter

Heather Mihok

First edition, October 2022

Proofread by iWordyNerdy on Fiverr.com

Cover art and design by Marie Muravski

ISBN/SKU 979-8-9865249-1-7
EISBN 979-8-9865249-2-4

For Kimberly -
to keep you up at night.

One

The wind pushes against my back, cold and blustery, as my temporary knight in shining four-wheel drive disappears back down the way we came. He'd told me his name when I climbed into the passenger side of the SUV, but I can't remember now. The mantra in my head must've buried it. *Please don't kill me, please don't kill me.* Because that's what happens to hitchhikers, right? It's Stranger Danger 101: you hitch and then your body ends up in a ditch somewhere, mangled beyond recognition.

Imagine getting this far just to end up in a body bag.

I squeeze the lapels of my denim jacket over my fuzzy pom-pom scarf, shielding my neck from the icy blasts. The urge to shout for him to wait, to jump back in that car and keep going, pulls at me with the strength of a weightlifting champion, but instead, I focus my attention on the building before me. My safe haven. My sanctuary. The place I'll call home for the next seven days.

The Keystone Mill Inn looks just like it did in the ad. The two-story building sits at the top of a hill packed dense with Virginia pine. It's modest in size, made of whitewashed stone, with a charming balcony atop a wraparound porch. A long set of stairs lends to its impressive entrance.

The wooden steps creak beneath my heavy boots, bowing under my weight. A weather-beaten rocking chair to my left sways back and forth in the breeze.

I take a moment to gather myself, not sure what to expect. As grateful as I am for this much-needed opportunity, I have to wonder . . . what kind of person invites a stranger to stay in their home unsupervised, let alone watch over their business?

The front door opens just as my knuckles make contact with the wood.

A woman appears on the other side of the threshold. I don't know what I was expecting – maybe a colonial grandmother type with a long dress and hair curled up? This lady isn't it. Her hair's pulled into a frizzy ponytail, more gray than brown. Leathery skin spattered with age spots suggest a life hard-lived, as do her worn-out jeans and baggy sweatshirt.

She looks at me expectantly.

"Hi," I say. "I'm . . . Hazel Hopewell." The lie tastes funny on my tongue, and my heart constricts. I shouldn't have used Mom's name, but it's too late now. "We talked on the phone?"

"Well, hello there, Hazel."

Her voice is deeper than I remember, tobacco-roughened and drawling. We shake hands, her calloused palm pressing tight against my fingers; the grip of a woman with something to prove. Her eyes flit around my features, as if counting the stress pimples on my face.

There are more than a few. The last few days have taken their toll on my complexion, culminating in an overnight eruption of hard, red bumps swarming my chin. A year ago I would've been embarrassed by the state of my skin, but now there are more pressing things on my mind.

She stares so long I wonder if she can see the bruise, long gone a sickly yellowish-green, beneath my concealer.

"Now, Hazel. That's a name I haven't heard in a long while. It's nice seeing young ones with older names. Makes me think you're more mature than your peers, more trustworthy. And you aren't gonna let me down, are ya?"

She grins, showing a mouthful of yellow teeth.

She steps back and I enter the front room. It's a small space, just big enough for a slim coat rack, a mud bench, and the two of us. Her body heat warms me as she squeezes by, and I get a strong whiff of wood smoke and stale potpourri chips, like the kind my grandma used to leave out in an etched crystal dish. She died when I was seven, so my memories of her are few and faded. But from what I remember, she had large arms that encircled me and pulled me into her warm, smushy breasts, a sensation of life-affirming comfort my little kid brain didn't fully grasp at the time. My heart, already pulled tight with longing, cracks, and I have to carefully tighten my face to avoid showing emotion. If grandma were alive, I wouldn't be here. I would've sought her out instead.

We move through the claustrophobic mudroom and stand directly in front of a hallway with a narrow staircase running up alongside the wall. Bright sunlight illuminates the foot of the stairs from the left, where I assume some type of living room awaits.

I unbutton my jacket and unknot my scarf, catching the movement in a small, antique mirror on the wall. I quickly scan my appearance – light brown skin made darker by the aged glass, round cheeks mauve from the cold, concealer still in place, thank God – and tame my windswept curls by tucking them behind my ears. I don't want her to think I'm self-absorbed, so I quickly turn back and give her my full attention.

"I'm Raina Marshall but you prob'ly already figured that." The woman takes my outerwear and drapes them on the coat rack. "My husband, Bob, is around here someplace. Bob?" She hollers down the hallway, her voice cracking like twigs scraped against the wall. She turns back to me, and her eyes land on my neck. "Now that's a pretty necklace you got there."

I didn't even realize I'd been twisting the silver pendant between my fingers. I clutch it, covering the script-style *T* with my thumb. I hope she didn't look too closely. Maybe she'll think it's a cross. "Oh. Thanks."

"What's the 'T' stand for?"

Crap. Hoping never does any good. "Oh, uh, my dog. Um, Tia."

Another lie.

I can't tell her it's my initial, not when she thinks my name is Hazel. I really didn't think this through, did I? Disappearing is not as easy as they make it out to be in movies. Especially at the last minute. I should've taken more time to prepare, to invent a detailed persona that Mrs. Marshall can trust, especially since I'm supposed to be looking after her place. But if I'd waited any longer, who knows how much more violence I'd have to endure?

She tilts her head as if waiting for more. I guess it is kind of weird having a pendant of your dog's name.

I think quickly. "It's . . . in memory."

"That's a shame. Tough losin' the fur babies, but it's a fact of life. We're simply meant to outlive 'em."

My body dissolves with relief. That was close. I'd forgotten all about the necklace. It was a gift for my thirteenth birthday, and I never take it off. At this point, it's a part of my body. I can't even remember the last time I unclasped it. It'll be hard but I have to put it away – can't have any more questions like that.

After a couple of deep, phlegm-filled coughs, she shouts again. "Bob, come here and meet the girl!"

An elderly man shuffles in behind her. His handshake is the opposite of hers, gentle and doughy. His skin is translucent, and tangled clusters of dark veins are visible beneath his delicate, puffy skin.

"Hello!" His voice is as soft as a freshly baked roll – everything about him reminds me of carbs. His eyes, the kind of cloudy blue that indicates vision impairment, roam over my body from behind thick glasses, and I wonder how much of me he's actually taking in.

"My," he says, "aren't you a pretty one?"

My cheeks flush with warmth. It's not often I get compliments, and I'm not sure what to make of this one. "Thank you."

"First time in Fox Valley?"

"Yeah."

"Raina tells me you're comin' from up north. D.C. That right?"

"Kind of." I rub behind my ear. "A town just outside it."

"All them nasty politics, don't know how you can stand it. And you're studying to join the hospitality business? That right?"

I smile and let him take that as a yes.

"Well, you won't get much practice here, I'm afraid. I'm sure she's told you."

She did. When I called to inquire about the gig, she explained that during low-season they don't mind closing up shop – and I wouldn't have any guests to mind. That was a relief. I was prepared to fake it, but I really wouldn't know how to handle stuff like guests. Obviously, that's not what I told her on the phone, but it's nice to know I won't have to pretend with anyone else. If I'd had more time to plan, I wouldn't have bothered with any of this, but with such short notice, my options for getting away were limited. It was either this or go for a sugar daddy, and at this moment in time, I am so done with men.

"Now," says Raina, "it might not look like much, 'specially compared to the fancy digs you prob'ly got up north, but it's our home and our pride and joy. My family's owned this building since nineteen forty-three, but it was built nearly a hundred years before that. There've been more than a couple of renovations, but that's to be expected after so many years. Hard keeping things in their original shape. Take my mother, for instance. She installed pull-down stairs for the attic when I was a little girl. A glorified ladder! Land sakes, what good does that do anyone?"

She sighs and rolls her eyes.

I nod in sympathy, unsure what to say.

"Well, enough chatter." She clasps her hands in front of her. "Like I said on the phone, we're havin' a bit of a family emergency. That's why we need someone like you to come out here and help us for a bit. Bob's ma had a stroke, and the doctors aren't sure she'll be around much longer, so we're headed to Raleigh to say our goodbyes."

"Oh, that's awful. I'm so sorry."

"Yes. It hasn't been easy. Granted, the woman's nearly ninety years old, so . . ."

She shrugs in a way that suggests she's not as upset as she's making out to be. As someone still riding the soggy coattails of grief, I'm not entirely sure I understand her reaction.

"Let's get down to brass tacks, shall we?" she asks briskly. "We're gonna be gone for a week, maybe two. You're available if we need you longer?"

I nod.

"Good." She gestures I should follow as she walks down the hall. "Well, now I'm sure you'd like a tour of the place."

Two

<hr>

The hallway would be well-lit if the brass sconces on the wall were actually turned on, but milky sunlight filters in from a window at the very end of the hall and it's just enough. A worn rug with a traditional floral pattern softens our footsteps, and deer heads line the walls on either side, their majestic antlers reaching for the ceiling. As we pass each one, it feels like their black, glassy eyes follow us. With the dim lighting, musty smell, and dead animals, this place gives off major creepy vibes. But it's nothing scarier than what's waiting for me back home.

Raina stops abruptly, and I nearly bump into her ample behind.

She turns around, face scrunched in a puzzled expression.

"That all you brought?" she asks, indicating my purse.

It's only a cheap tote, but I cling to the straps as though it's worth millions. She can't know what's inside it, there's no way. And then – feeling truly stupid – I realize she's asking about a suitcase. My cheeks burn as I scramble for a believable excuse.

"Oh, I – uh . . . shoot, I must've forgotten it in the cab. I'll have to call the company and hope no one took it."

"Mercy! You should've said so before lettin' me ramble on. Let's call 'em now before he gets too far. You don't want to be left without your things, dearie. Come this way, which company did you use? Mountain Transport?"

They have real taxis out here? What are the odds?

"We do business with them on occasion – they do long hauls for guests sometimes. These roads can be tricky, and some people aren't comfortable driving them. We can phone 'em up, I'm positive your things are safe –"

"No, no, that's okay." I can't let her know I hitched my way here. It might raise flags. I'm supposed to be a competent inn-sitter, right? She'll ask questions – and if she learns I'm a minor, she'll send me packing. Then I'm back to square one.

"It was . . . someone else. I'll call after the tour."

"Oh." She looks bewildered by my response, eyes wide. "Oh, right. Well, if you're sure?"

I nod so fast my teeth clack together.

"Yeah, no worries," I say. "There's no rush. Like you said, my things are in good hands, right? It can wait a few. Honest."

She hesitates, deliberating.

Adrenaline leaks from my heart and snakes down my legs with a cold, twitchy energy. If this is the lie that blows my cover, I don't know how I'll execute another plan. Clearly, I'm not cut out for this.

The seconds stretch into infinity. I curl my toes inside my boots.

"Alright-y then." She shrugs. "It's your stuff so's up to you. Let's start this way."

My eyelids flutter and I fight the urge to close them in relief.

Raina leads me deeper inside, and I get my first real glimpse of the inn.

"These rooms here are the downstairs bathroom, linen closet, mine and Bob's bedroom, and our office."

She shows me each one, opening doors for about three seconds before closing them with a firm click.

"Sometimes the handles stick, so you really gotta twist 'em." She demonstrates, the dark iron knob squeaking in protest, eliciting the same tight pull at the back of my throat as nails on chalkboards.

"All the guest bedrooms are upstairs. They won't need servicing, but you can have your pick of beds."

She backtracks toward the mudroom before walking through an archway into what I had previously guessed was the living area.

More deer heads decorate the walls, as well as other, smaller creatures like squirrels and raccoons, frozen in a sick mime of their times alive. I skirt my gaze around them and take in the rest of the room. Two plaid sofas pushed together in an L-shape frame an old TV, the kind I've only seen in period dramas. It has a bubble screen and an honest-to-god antennae. A coffee table displays colorful brochures about the area, fanned out across the rough-hewn plank. Bookshelves line the perimeter of the room, but there aren't many books – glass figurines of shepherds, angels, and cherubs, as well as mismatched picture frames, take up every spare inch of space. A massive grandfather clock looms in the corner, lazily ticking every other second as if time doesn't matter here. Thick blinds obscure the windows.

Like the hallway, the room is dimly lit, but it's a cozy vibe, I guess. I can easily tuck myself away here for a while.

A doorway at the back of the room leads to a dining room, nothing fancy, just a heavy looking walnut table and six maroon dining chairs.

Through yet another door – the place is laid out like a nesting doll – is the kitchen. It's smaller than the dining room but appears to be equipped for basic meals.

Raina stops and puts a hand to her chest.

"Mercy," she says. "You must think I'm a terrible hostess. You want somethin' to drink? A snack? You must be famished after your trip."

It would be rude to decline, so I accept a glass of water as she talks.

"The interior's fine," she explains. "My main concern is my dog, Skippy, as discussed on the phone, and frost in the garden. Just 'cause we're approachin' spring don't mean a good March frost won't damage my seedlings. I need the garden ready for wedding season come May."

"I bet it's really pretty here in the spring."

"Long as we're vigilant. Now, forecasters predict another big cold front coming in the next few days, so I'll need you to keep an eye on the weather and cover my garden as necessary. I'll show you where the tarps are before we leave. And we've had problems with pipes freezin' this winter, and I'll need you to prevent that so it don't cause damage – repairs are hell on the purse. Just let the taps drip overnight and turn them off in the morning – that should do the trick. If not, I'll leave you the number of our plumber in town."

"Got it. No problem."

I sip my water.

Something tickles my lip.

I pull the glass away from my mouth, and a thick, brown spider nearly the size of my palm gracefully maneuvers its sinewy legs over the rim.

I drop it in shock, the glass shattering at my feet. Mortified, I glance up just in time to see a shadow, four feet tall and stretched horizontally, dart past the doorway behind Raina.

Sweat licks my palms. Was that the dog? Wouldn't I have heard the patter of its paws as it scampered away?

Between the spider and the quiet shadow, my senses run overboard, and I rub my arms as if I can brush away the discomfort along with the dust of glass.

"Goodness!" Raina exclaims. "What's the matter?"

Did she not see the massive arachnid crawling toward my face? Where did it go? I survey the rubble of glass on the linoleum, sharp islands rising from the sea of tap water. It's nowhere to be seen.

"I'm sorry," I gush. "I'm so sorry. My fingers just . . . slipped."

"It's alright, just watch your feet."

I help her clean up the broken glass and ask, "So, how many pets did you say you have?"

"Just the one, Skippy. He's outside. Why?"

I could've sworn the shadow was an animal. What else could it have been? I shake my head. All the stress must be getting to me.

We backtrack once more, toward the hallway, going up the narrow staircase to the bedrooms. I run my hand along the railing, feeling the dips and curves in the natural wood. It's almost like someone took a wizard's gnarled staff and mounted it to the wall.

"You can stay in any one of these," Raina says. "Take your pick, don't matter which."

Five rooms in all and each one looks nearly the same, save for the colors. There's a green room, a red room, a yellow, blue, and a white room. Patchwork quilts dress old-fashioned, four-post beds, and I hum in acknowledgement as she explains how the quilts were hand sewn by her grandmother and ladies at her church. Everything else is as you would expect – wooden dressers stand guard over the rooms, and antique mirrors with ornate brass frames add a surprisingly decadent touch.

I select the blue room for my stay, since blue is supposed to be calming and I need all the help I can get. It's the last room at the end of the hall and not much different than the others, but, being on the corner, it has two windows and gives me a better sense of space. The windows look out over the inn's private road on one side and the woods toward the back on the other.

Nature. Freedom. No one knows I even left. He won't find me here. A sigh escapes my lips, and it feels like, maybe, I can breathe again.

At least for a little while.

"Folks come here to get away from it all," says Raina, as though she can hear my thoughts. "To disconnect from their fast-paced, technology-run lives. No phones in the room, no Wi-Fi-fiffery nonsense. Mobile phone reception is weak in these parts. It helps guests get back in touch with nature and other human beings. We actually talk around the dinner table, none of this texting nonsense. We hold civilized conversations."

"That sounds nice."

And I'm sure it is. But that's not why I'm here.

A whisper brushes across my left cheek. *"Don't . . ."*

I turn toward Raina. "Sorry, what?"

She lifts her eyebrows.

"I just – I didn't catch that."

She slowly shakes her head, bottom lip curled out. "I didn't say nothin'."

Oh.

"Now," Raina rubs her hands together, "money talk. Five hundred, as agreed, correct?"

"Um, yes. Correct."

"Two-fifty, upfront, the rest upon our return. Of course, you'll have free reign of the place and total access to whatever food's in the pantry, but if you need more, here's an extra fifty in addition to our agreement. Just take this to the Value Green grocer, it's about eight miles down the road, but you can use the truck out back. Keys are on the hook in the kitchen."

Her fingers snap so suddenly I jump and step back.

She sizes me up with a long, squinty-eyed stare.

"I'm a trusting person, but I should've asked – you got a valid license?"

She'll want to see it, won't she? She'll see I'm seventeen, and then I'll be screwed.

"Yeah, uh, yes. I have one. I only took a cab 'cause I don't have a car."

"You city kids with your subways and taxis. Here in the real world we chauffer ourselves. Well, alright then. Just checkin' – gotta make sure everything's in order here."

I lower my gaze. She's so gullible. I feel really bad about taking advantage like this.

After showing me the minutiae of the daily tasks for upkeep, she sighs and brushes herself off. "I suppose that's it. Got any questions for me?"

I shake my head. All I really care about at this point is settling in, alone.

"As far as ground rules," Raina says, "there ain't much. We welcome you into our home and want you to be comfortable, but I must ask a couple'a things from you besides the wee bit of maintenance. Firstly, the liquor cabinet is a no-go and the office is hands off. It's locked, but the keys are marked on the ring so please keep the door shut."

She probably doesn't want me snooping around for financial information. As if they're not paying me enough already.

"That's fine," I assure her. "No problem."

"And the shed, well. It's a mess. Just stay out of there. I don't need you trippin' on a box and fallin' on a rusty nail or something. Hospital bills are *not* part of the agreement, hmm?"

"Sure, okay."

"I need more than a 'sure,' my dear."

"Yes. I understand. No shed."

"And since we're on the topic, I suggest you don't take to wanderin' too far around these parts, seein' as there's bears and other wildlife I assume you city folk don't got much experience with. Better safe than sorry."

"Bears? Really?" I gulp. "But aren't they hibernating?"

"With the spring comin', you never know who's wakin' up. Just stick to the garden and you'll be fine."

"Okay."

"*Don't...*" A chill ripples down my back.

"I'm really sorry," I say. "But what? Don't do what?"

Raina squints. "You need tellin' twice?" Her voice rises in pitch, and I fear I'm upsetting her. Better not push my luck.

"Nothing, sorry, just thought you said something. Never mind. I must be tired from the journey. Or something." I'm rambling. I need to get her back on course. "Anything else I should know?"

"Nope." She shakes her head. "That'll be it. You're ready for the keys."

Three

Raina and Bob drag their suitcases outside and shove them in the back of a faded green, slightly dented SUV.

Raina shakes my hand, thanks me again, and ensures that I know where her cell number is kept on the fridge. It's stored in my phone, but I don't have it with me.

I smile and wave as she hops into the car, spry as a kitten despite her advanced age. Bob honks the horn, three quick beeps. At the sound, a streak of yellow fur enters my peripheral vision as Skippy comes around the corner, the Labrador bounding toward the car.

My hand flashes out for his collar. The nylon burns my palm as he jerks forward, trying to break free. He perks his ears up at me, then looks plaintively at the car as the taillights disappear into the trees. His ears fold back and he whimpers.

"Sorry, buddy," I mumble. "You're stuck with me for now."

I gaze at the trees surrounding the property. They bend and sway, rustling as they whisper secrets to each other. Besides Skippy's whine, it's the only sound for miles. I breathe deep, tasting fresh pine in the back of my throat, and close my eyes.

I'm free.

A real smile tugs at the corners of my lips for the first time in ages. I never thought I'd get away, but I did. This is only temporary, though – a place to lay low and get my bearings. But earn some extra coin while hiding out?

I'll take it.

I leave Skippy to wander the grounds as I go back inside. Without Raina's voice filling my ear, I notice how quiet it is. Even the ubiquitous hum of electronics seems to be absent here.

The muscles in my neck relax, and my shoulders slowly drop. I didn't realize how tense I'd been. The things I went through . . . I shudder. Can't think of the past, it's behind me now. I need to look forward and make a plan.

Time to finally take inventory.

I get my bag from where I left it and unzip the hidden inside pocket.

A wad of cash stretches the cheap polyester lining like a pregnant belly waiting to deliver. I didn't dare check it until I was finally alone – it wouldn't take much for someone to knock me over and run off with it. Getting away was my first priority, my only focus.

But now?

I squeeze my fingers into the opening and grasp the bundle, the plastic teeth of the zipper scraping my knuckles as I wiggle it out. The pocket was clearly not meant for such bulk.

Kneeling at the coffee table, I loosen the wad with my fingers, the captive bills unfurling as if sensing freedom. My heart pounds.

It's a lot.

I could live off of this for a while. I could . . .

Wait a minute.

A couple of hundred-dollar bills peel away to reveal something that makes my heart sink.

A flash of pink paper. Then blue. I scatter them across the table.

No fucking way.

Pretend money, like the kind children use to play shop. Worthless paper cleverly concealed by the two hundred-dollar bills that, now upon closer inspection, may also be fake. Pretty sure Ben Franklin didn't have a grill.

I slam my fists on the table. My breath comes shallow. There should have been a few thousand here.

I've been played.

The *one* time I take action for myself. Of course. Pressure builds behind my eyes, and my vision blurs. How could I let this happen? Not only did I seriously mess up, but I've been purposefully made to look like an idiot. Because they knew *I'd* be doing the drop. It was my first time. My nerves were thrumming, so I just took the money and left. It's my fault, all because I didn't check.

And what if I had? Would I have been brave enough to do what needed to be done? I couldn't put the fear of God in a toddler, let alone a couple of thieving dealers. Why would anyone trust me to deliver such a large order? Obviously, no one knew I was bolting, but did he seriously think I could get the job done? I was in such a hurry to get out of there – and now I'm screwed, in more ways than one.

My heart picks up as I remember the events that played out just the night before, the way my breath fogged in the cold night air as I waited for the delivery, the way I automatically rubbed my hands together, despite adrenaline running warm through my veins. Standing alone, I imagined the police rolling up in a cruiser, blipping their siren – that's how it always goes on TV, right? If I got caught, I'd be wearing an orange jumpsuit behind bars for a long time.

The alternative wasn't much better. The only thing getting me through was my plan.

I shifted the backpack full of incriminating evidence from one shoulder to the other, steering my mind away from its contents, the addictions it would fuel, and the lives it could ruin.

Flicking my gaze around the darkened parking lot behind a rundown strip mall, I checked for cops, witnesses, or worse – spies. Prison time is preferable to the consequences doled out if my plan got discovered by some brown-nosing associate. It's not unthinkable to have someone watching me, reporting back my every move. My plan would be screwed.

I'd never get away.

Some of the streetlights were burned out, casting shadowy spots on the cracking asphalt. I guess that's why they do their shady business there. The empty storefronts and graffiti kept most people away with their depressing aesthetic.

I exhaled slow and steady, a vain attempt to calm my racing heart.

Remember the plan, Temperly, I told myself.

This was the risk I had to take for my reward: freedom. Freedom from Mrs. Shapiro and her group homes, freedom from *him* . . .

A car pulled up and stopped, but it wasn't the cops, though the silhouette alarmed me at first. It could've been a retired cruiser, based on the shape and the way my body instantly felt the urge to run.

A large guy climbed out, followed by a crew of about three lanky soldiers. They all bore the familiar mark of their gang – a swirly tattoo running up the lengths of their necks, signifying the initials of the park they call their own. I dropped my gaze from the ink to what was in his hand.

My heart leaped with hope at the sight of the duffel he carried. This was really happening.

"Oh, shit." His voice matched his body – large and looming. "Whatchu doin' here, doll baby?"

I cringed at the name. So gross.

"He sent me," I said with as much authority as I could muster.

"Yeah?" he said before bobbing his head from side to side. "Yeah, we was told. Just making sure you for real. Alright. So you got it?"

He eyed up my backpack.

I nodded and slipped the strap off my shoulder, avoiding eye contact with his crew.

He came closer, brandishing the duffel bag.

"This should be easy," he assured me. "Long as it's all right and good, should be no problem."

"It's right," I said. It's always right. When it comes to money, he doesn't mess around.

The exchange took all of five seconds. The buildup in my head made it seem like it should've been longer.

I held out the backpack, my arm trembling from the weight of it.

He handed me the duffel and crossed his arms.

One of his guys slipped the backpack from my fingers and peeked inside. Nodded his approval.

The large boss guy uncrossed his arms and smiled without showing his teeth. "Pleasure doin' business with you," he said.

"Sure. Yeah."

I turned, nice and slow, fighting the urge to run. Not yet. I couldn't raise suspicion.

"Tell Monster I said 'hey.'"

That stopped me in my tracks. It shouldn't have, but the nickname sent shivers down my spine. Was this code? A trap? Did he know what I was up to?

I looked over my shoulder at him and forced myself to smile sweetly, despite the grinding of my teeth behind closed lips.

"Will do," I said with a false cheeriness I hoped he couldn't see through.

"Tell him hey," I mumble angrily now. I shake my head at the thought. Fat chance. If all goes well, I will never see that bastard again. The anger dissipates as quickly as it came, replaced by a gnawing fear. I hunch over the table with my head in my hands.

This is all wrong. I was counting on that money. Now what am I going to do? This inn-sitting job was supposed to be a placeholder, a chance to catch my breath before pushing on to phase two. Five hundred dollars is a lot, yes, but not enough for what I'd had in mind. It might get me across the country, but it won't last long enough to keep me there, to build a life on my own . . . away from *him*.

Now what will I do?

I get up and pace around the coffee table. The wooden floorboards creak beneath an antique rug with every step, tightening my nerves. As I circle the room, I examine the items around me. Is there anything of value I could pawn for more cash? It's not like the Marshalls have my real name – they couldn't charge me from afar. Judging by appearance, the picture frames and tchotchkes might be old but they're far from valuable antiques. I pick up a glass figurine of a shepherdess herding sheep. A yellowing price tag on the bottom says it was purchased for 4.99 at Kmart. I could probably hawk it for a quarter, if anyone actually dealt with coins anymore. I put it back.

My mind whirls, desperate to create a plan of action while my legs take me around the living room and into the kitchen. I half-heartedly open and close the walnut cabinets until I stumble across a box of hot chocolate.

Memories flood my mind, not unwelcome, but bittersweet.

When I was little, I drank hot chocolate every winter. It was my favorite after-school treat, a little pick-me-up before doing homework. Mom put extra marshmallows in the mug; she called them little clouds. I believed I was literally sipping heaven, and my fingertips tingled from holding the warm cup.

I rub my sternum so hard I imagine that, beneath my T-shirt, the skin's peeling right off my chest. But I don't care. A familiar pang in my heart erupts whenever I think of her, and I'm desperate to get rid of it.

God, I miss her so much.

A little childhood comfort might soothe the pain, so I rip open a packet and pour it into a chipped, earthenware mug that says "I'd Rather Be Fishing." Stirring in some milk, I nuke it in the microwave until it forms a slippery skin. Not waiting for it to cool, I gulp it down in eight blistering swallows. At least the pain is in my mouth now, a welcome distraction from the usual, chest-lurching grief. Warmth fills my stomach and I quickly make another cup, vowing to savor this one as much as my damaged tongue will allow.

Plucking a magnetic notepad off the fridge, I carry it along with my mug to the dining room and sit gingerly at the table. Wincing, I shift on the hard seat to alleviate the soreness in my backside. It doesn't help. God, sitting still hurts. Adrenaline masked it for a bit, but now that I'm settled it's wearing off. And, just like that, the memory comes in flashes.

Voicing my doubts about the so-called "errand." Not wanting to embarrass myself in front of our friends, I mimicked the confident tone of influencers – everyone loves a boss babe, right? I thought that was how I should act. Besides, my questions weren't unreasonable, considering the shady aspect of the job. I was new, inexperienced, couldn't someone else make the drop and I'd get the next one?

He likened my excuse to that of a kid dodging homework. He pulled me to his lap and, in one swift move, bent me over his knees for a playful spanking. Only it didn't stay playful for long.

Our friends averted their eyes.

Now, fresh waves of humiliation warm my skin. It wasn't the worst thing he'd done – not by a long shot – but it was the most public. Jesus, how was that only yesterday?

I flip over the sheet with Raina's number on it to a fresh, blank page.

Taking a fortifying sip of cocoa and chewing on the lingering dehydrated marshmallows, I think about what to write.

Where can I go from here? When the week is up, I'll be out on the street again. I need a destination.

I think of family members near and far, hazy names and faces that I can't recall. If I reached out, would they even remember me?

Maybe family is a bad idea – it would be too easy to track me down through them. Depending on who found me, I'd either end up in the system . . . or put their lives at risk. Because he'll believe the money was real, as I did, and likely seek punishment for taking it. I can't bring that to innocent people.

I should give up. What if I stopped fighting the inevitable, went back home and turned myself over to social services? Here I am thinking I'm all grown, but it's too much. Wouldn't it be nice to let go and have someone else be in charge of my life for a while? It might be a relief having someone else do the thinking and planning for me.

When Mom died, a caseworker showed up in the form of Mrs. Shapiro, a buttoned-up, pasty-faced woman of middle age and no sense of humor. She reeked of cinnamon gum chewed too long. Because I'm a minor, she tried putting me in a group home for kids without parents. She said it would be temporary. But Monster told me horrible stories about those places, experiences he'd had growing up without his parents. He convinced me that my life is not government business and welcomed me into his little apartment with open arms. The idea was to lay low until my eighteenth birthday, when I'd be free from Mrs. Shapiro and her control.

I never thought I'd be escaping his too.

I push the notepad away, frustration coiling my shoulders once again. I can't go back. I'd be too easily found with a paper trail like that. I thought I would get as far away from the east coast as possible. California, maybe. But can I afford it on my own? Even if I hitchhike across the country, there's still going to be rent, food, utilities – these things add up quick. Full payment from the Marshalls might get me started, but I'm still underage for almost a year, with no job, no money, and no references. I never thought this would be easy, but I didn't expect it to be so hard.

And I need a change of clothes. As much as I would love to have a suitcase full of stuff waiting for me at a taxi depot, that's a luxury I'm never going to have.

Scratching at the door breaks my train of thought. It's a raspy, uneven sound.

Shk shk shk.

I stiffen. What is that?

A muffled whimper follows the scratching, and I let out a sigh. It's only Skippy, ready to come inside. I let him in after wiping the mud off his paws with a ratty towel.

"Did you leave me a gift in the yard? Huh, boy?"

He nuzzles my hand, and despite the cold, wet doggy snot on my fingers, it's a comforting gesture.

He wanders off to God knows where and I'm alone again.

Choosing to focus on the here and now, I scope the kitchen for food and take stock of what they have. Basic ingredients, mostly – spaghetti noodles, cans of soup, and frozen vegetables. I can work with this, but I'm not sure how long it will last.

There's only half a loaf of fresh bread, and only about a quarter of a gallon of milk. Maybe I should get a few things from Value Town, or wherever Raina said to go. I'm not looking forward to that – I don't want to leave this place any more than I have to. It's better to stay hidden. But starvation won't help anything, so I pick up the pen and click it a few times before making a list.

Perishables. Bread. Milk. Maybe some fruit like oranges for the vitamin C – can't afford to get sick now.

And more hot chocolate, for my nerves.

I look at the meager list I've created. So I need a shopping trip. I'm only doing it once because gas is expensive and I'm not wasting a single dollar. I'm young and independent now; it's time to be frugal. But I'm not going anywhere today. Today, I'll get my bearings.

I swallow the rest of my cocoa, but it's cooled and most of the powder has settled at the bottom as sludge. Skippy wanders back in and butts his head against my arm, demanding to be petted. I pat the top of his head – the fur is silky and smooth to the touch.

The vanilla scent from the marshmallows earlier lingers in the air and floats through my mind as I fall back into memories of Mom.

It's only been a few months since she passed. If she were alive, I never would've left. My life would be so different. My chest constricts with longing. I wish she were here. I miss her smiling face, with her one crooked tooth in a mouthful of otherwise perfect teeth. When she grinned, you couldn't help but smile with her.

Rubbing my face, I groan into my hands. She's not here. Get a grip. I can't be wallowing like this.

I need to toughen up if I plan on surviving.

Four

I'm standing in the room I've chosen for myself. Heavy clouds blot out the sun, giving the light through the windows a grayish cast. Everything is decorated in shades of the palest blue, so there's a sense that everything's bleached of color. I flick the wall switch, turning on a lamp next to the bed. The lampshade has a doily design on it and fills the room with a warm glow.

I turn in a circle, surveying the room.

An upholstered chair sits at an empty desk that might have once been a sewing table. A small trio of framed embroidery on the wall above it display Bible verses about love, faith, and trust. Again, I think of my grandmother. She had a massive wine-colored Bible next to the potpourri. Maybe she and the Marshalls would've gotten along, been friends. Maybe this is a sign that I'm on the right path, that I've done the right thing after all.

But I can't bring myself to settle in yet. That word "don't" keeps playing on a loop in my mind, in a voice that's not my own. Why? I couldn't say, but it's left me uneasy and restless.

I turn off the light and back out of the room.

Downstairs, I perch on the couch in the living room, taking it in. Walking sticks, roughly four feet high and made of gnarled wood, poke out from a bronze container etched with a giant bear fishing for salmon, its claws poised for a strike. The phrase "Virginia is for Lovers" displays on the wall in hand-painted script across a circular slice of tree trunk, the rings showing its age. A pile of folded quilts in a wicker basket adds a level of coziness to the room. It's not my style, but the inn has a certain charm to it. I could imagine having a romantic weekend here with my boyfriend.

My boyfriend. Because I still have one, don't I? It hasn't been ended, not officially. But it won't take long for him to catch on to the fact that I've left him if he hasn't. Thrill prickles my heart, equal parts relief and terror.

I know what happens when you double-cross him. I've seen it firsthand, once. Once was enough. Snapped fingers, like crab legs at a seafood restaurant, were just the appetizer of this feast of pain. An unimaginable experience for the offender, his bloody face scrunched up tight in agony so his features blended together, indistinguishable, like scrambled eggs with ketchup. The cruelty went on for what felt like ages, but I couldn't walk away. I couldn't even turn my head to vomit at the sight of such brutality. The horror of it dripped over me like hardening glue, keeping me silent and still until it was over and the poor victim passed out in a pool of his own blood – enough to send a warning to anyone else thinking of stealing from the monster who runs the streets.

And yet, here I am. What will he do when he realizes I'm not coming back?

I grab the remote and power on the TV. Maybe I'll find something entertaining enough to take my mind off things.

Rippling static assaults my senses, and I frantically jab the buttons until the volume goes down.

Right away it's obvious they have no cable. Channel surfing proves depressing. A local news station lamenting a tax hike. A cartoon for preschoolers learning the alphabet. Not much else, mostly white noise.

I turn the TV back off and stand up, considering the bookshelves.

Picture frames stand as makeshift bookends, wedged between spines. Younger versions of Raina and Bob smile up at me from a boat, looking smoother and softer around the edges as sunlight glints off the water surrounding them. Their hair, rich and full of color – hers, brown, and his, a dishwater blond – blows behind them in the breeze. They look happy. Finding someone and actually growing old with them is a sweet thought. I smile as I move on to the other photographs. Every frame holds a photo of them – no one else. Huh. That's kind of weird. Is that normal? No captured memories of family and friends, just the same two faces slowly aging over the years.

Browsing the book titles doesn't fill me with hope for stimulation. Fishing guides, a wildlife encyclopedia, cookbooks, and one dog-eared romance novel with yellowed pages. It might be the most entertaining thing in this place.

How will I occupy my time? There has to be something I can distract myself with. Anything.

I stand at the foot of the stairs, looking down the hallway. There might be something in the office, but I promised not to go in there.

I touch the handle and wiggle it anyway – locked.

I take a few tentative steps down the hall. There are no sounds inside the house, other than the odd ticking of the grandfather clock. It's kind of an eerie place. All I wanted was to be alone, but now I'm not so sure. I didn't realize how oppressive isolation can be.

It's better than the alternative.

I touch the wall, the planks cool and smooth, and drag my fingers across them as I head toward Raina and Bob's bedroom. I know I shouldn't. But I need clothes, and I don't have enough money to blow on new items at the moment. At some point, I'll have to find another way to earn, but for now, I'll just borrow and hope something of hers will fit me. It's not like anyone's gonna see what I look like anyway.

I open the door, wincing as it creaks, and my cheeks flush with embarrassment. Why did I wince? Who's gonna know except Skippy?

Their room is bigger than the ones upstairs. I bet originally it wasn't even a bedroom; they just hauled a bed in here and made it their own. It's dark though. The blinds are drawn and the angle of the room doesn't get much natural light filtering in.

I stroke the wall for the light switch and turn it on.

Much, much bigger.

And there's a TV – a hi-def flat screen mounted on the wall across from the bed. Jackpot. They've been holding out on their guests. I spy the remote on a nightstand by the bed and smile inwardly. I'm technically staff so . . . I flop on the bed and turn the TV on.

Basic cable.

I never thought I'd feel so happy to see a limited channel plan in my whole life. I try not to feel too creeped out about being on their bed, try not to think about them laying here, sweating in their sleep, spooning, cuddling . . . ick, no. I can't do this.

I get up and brush myself off, as if to rid myself of the uncomfortable thoughts.

I can't stop fidgeting, looking around, checking my surroundings.

The accordion-style door of their closet opens wide like a yawn. Flannel shirts and cargo jackets dangle from wire hangers, a dark palette of army green, black, and navy. I spot one ugly Christmas sweater with Rudolph's bright red cherry nose. I pull down a plaid flannel shirt, and the strong scent of detergent hits my nose. It's a little big but should be comfortable to wear around the inn.

I hesitate only for a moment before pulling off my grimy T-shirt.

"Don't . . ."

I whip around. My fingers slacken, dropping the shirt to the floor.

A face in the mirror, eyes wide looking back at me.

My heart jackhammers inside my chest, trying to escape.

But, like some parody of a scary movie, it's just my own reflection.

A chuckle rises from the back of my throat, uncontrollable, turning into a full-on belly laugh as my pent-up stress releases in the form of humor. Oh wow, I think. Wow, that's embarrassing. So dumb. Kind of funny, though.

I want to tell Mariah, my best friend back home, about my stupid moment, but of course I can't, and the laughter slowly dies with that thought.

I scoop my T-shirt back up before tossing it in the hamper. I shake out the flannel and slip it over my skin. The worn-in material feels soft and comforting. The sleeves hang down over my hands, so I roll them up, an easy fix.

What else is in here?

The dresser drawers squeak terribly on their tracks, and I wince at the grating sound.

Jeans. The woman wears nothing but jeans. They're all huge around the waist, so I leave them be. Shirts are one thing, but pants are personal on a whole other level.

Turning out the light, I leave the room, fully intending to come back later to watch TV and lose myself in some reality competition show.

Skippy's laying on a plush doggie bed in the living room and lifts his head, regarding me as I come back to the couch. He lowers his head, resting it on his paws, eyes drooping. Must have worn himself out running around outside.

I stretch out on the couch and watch the dust mites swirl in the air. In a daze, I reach up to touch them. The flannel sleeve drifts down my forearm to reveal the ugly tattoo marking my skin, the ink black, raised, and new. I never wanted one. The idea of permanence always scared me into indecision. I rub it, not for the first time, as if I can magically erase the squiggly letters "M+T" inside a heart that looks as if a child fisting a crayon drew it. His brand. My stomach roils whenever I see it, and I swallow the hot, sour bile that bubbles up in my throat. A friend of his purchased a tattoo gun and "needed the practice." I fought back, recoiling at the idea of being permanently marked with a needle, by an amateur no less. My hands blurred back and forth in front of me, a physical interpretation of my frantic "no, no, no's," and the sound of skin slapping skin filled the room as he reached for me anyway. Despite my efforts, he gripped my wrists tight and held me still. Gave his friend the go ahead, who hesitated, but only for a second. I don't blame him; when it comes to Monster, no one needs telling twice. I stopped struggling in case my jerky movements made the end result even worse. "Make it all fancy," he'd said, laughing. "Like her necklace, here, see it?"

Now I raise my hands to the back of my neck and brush the hair aside. Fumbling for the clasp of my necklace, I dig my thumbnail into the latch. Undone, the delicate chain slithers into my palm.

I won't need it anymore. I'll be using a fake name from now until forever. Still, my heart weighs heavy as I place it gently on the coffee table.

That girl is gone now. That life, behind me.

I am totally, completely alone.

Five

Black. That's all I see. One round spot of darkness, a tunnel that will consume my soul.

Laughter echoes around me, reverberating off the walls. "It's just a little fun!" his voice taunts. "You like fun, don't you, Sweet Tea?"

A drop of sweat traces a slow path down my back, only to be wicked by the fabric of my shirt. The sound of his breath, quick and excited, meets my ears.

I'm sure I hear the squeak of the trigger.

"Mom!"

I awake with a gasp.

My pillow is drenched in cold sweat, and I wipe my face, taking a moment to cover my eyes. I rustle the sheets with my legs, shaking away the remnants of the dream.

Even apart, he's always with me.

Pressing fingertips hard against my eyelids, I will myself to forget the nightmares that once plagued my life and now interrupt my sleep. With every heartbeat, they fade further away, until all I'm left with is my new reality. I'm here, alone.

Safe.

I force my breath to slow, calming my racing heart. It's all good. No one knows where I am, I made damn sure of that.

Instinctively, I reach for my phone, only to remember that I left it behind, just in case. Couldn't risk him tracking me. Now it feels like a phantom limb, a missing body part that still itches to be scratched.

Rubbing my eyes, I sit up and contemplate my surroundings. The clock radio on the nightstand next to the bed glows angry red numbers at me – 8:07 am. I'm not much of an early riser, never have been, except when necessary, like for school.

But I can't sleep anymore. It could be the unfamiliar surroundings, or, more likely, my nerves. I keep wondering what's happening back home. The tension has me wound up like a coiled spring.

Opening the bedroom door, I find Skippy sitting on his haunches in the hallway.

He stares at me intently.

"What?"

His ears perk up but he doesn't blink. He's kind of tripping me out.

"What do you want?"

It's like a game of hot or cold. Every time I speak his eyes brighten, but his ears droop back down. I wonder if he's made a mess in the house, and it occurs to me he hasn't been out since last night.

That's when I discover the magic words.

"Wanna go outside?"

It's as if I've asked a child if they'd like candy for breakfast.

A firework shoots off inside of him, and he leaps down the stairs and scrambles to the front door, nails clicking on the wooden floor. He waits for me, panting and bouncing up and down on his front legs.

I let him outside, where he immediately marks a shrub with the world's longest pee. I feel bad that I didn't realize his need much sooner.

I make my way to the kitchen where I have toast with butter and jam, along with some hot chocolate.

When everything's eaten and cleaned up, I let Skippy back inside, taking care to wipe his paws first.

Then I tackle Raina's daily checklist.

Check the weather.

I turn on the news and wait for the forecast. Partly sunny, high forties. No freeze in sight. Excellent. The garden will be happy. It's mostly wispy tendrils of greenery, and Raina told me I'd have to protect them with a plastic tent if there was a frost advisory. "The plastic tarps are just inside the door there," she'd said as she pointed beyond the garden to a shed, "but it's a damn mess, and if you can avoid going in there as much as possible, that'd be great." The shed itself is clearly handmade, consisting of graying wooden planks and a flat tin roof streaked with copper-colored rust. It looks spooky as hell, like the kind of place a serial killer would hide, so I'll heed her advice.

Feed Skippy.

In the kitchen, I bury a measuring cup into the gaping mouth of the massive bag of dog food, plugging my nose to the salty smell, and pour the hard, brown nuggets into Skippy's plastic bowl. He buries his nose in it, making snuffling sounds as he eats, and I suddenly understand the phrase "wolfing it down."

I collect a feather duster, a microfiber towel, and a can of Pledge and proceed to lightly dust and wipe the windowsills and hard furniture until I'm sneezing from the effort.

I sweep Skippy's hair up off the floor and dump it in the trash in the kitchen and watch the clumps of yellow fur float to the bottom of the wastebasket. I place my hands on my hips. Well, now what?

I'm itching to keep moving. I could do the shopping, but it might be better to wait a little bit just to make sure I don't forget anything, because I plan on going only once. If only I didn't need the money, I'd be off already with the three hundred *and* the truck, as terrible as that sounds. I need to keep heading west, to get away from here, but to do that I really need the whole amount, especially now that my drug money is literal trash. The moment the Marshalls are back and the rest of my payment is in hand, I'm out of here.

* * *

Two days in, and I'm padding into the kitchen for some lunch when something splatters beneath my feet. My socks swell up with ice cold water. Hissing from the sensation, I step back and survey the scene. What happened in here?

I'm standing in about an inch of water, flowing out from directly beneath the sink. How long has that been leaking?

Grimacing, I tiptoe through the water to check it out. The curvy pipe underneath the basin oozes water from a crack, the liquid snaking a wet, gray trail down to the end of the rod where it drips, fast, to the floor.

My stomach clenches as I realize it's up to me to fix it. Only I'm not sure I'm cut out for this kind of responsibility. What's the name of that plumber again? Raina must've forgotten to write it down like she said she would. I pluck her number off the notepad on the fridge and look around for a phone.

For the millionth time, I ache to use mine.

There's a clunky, gray and black telephone standing up on the counter. A cordless. My grandma had one just like it. I've never used a landline before and, for a second, I wonder it if will electrocute me in my wet socks.

Hopping up on the counter, I peel off my socks and drop them to the floor, just in case. *Plop, plop.*

I dial Raina's number and press the plastic speaker to my ear. The connection rings once, twice . . . voicemail. I hang up. What should I do? Just sit around, waiting for a response? I try calling her again, but it doesn't go through.

I survey the water. It's spreading, slowly but surely. How long should I wait for her to call me back? Until the whole place has flooded? And what if there's damage to the floorboards, or the sink itself? Would that come out of my pay?

I can't risk it.

That plumber's number has got to be around here somewhere. There must be a phonebook. I reach down and pull open drawers, careful to keep my balance on the counter. Silverware, measuring cups, aha. A junk drawer. That's where Mom used to keep our old one. But no luck here, it seems. I slam the drawer and suppress a groan.

The office. It's the next logical place, right?

Sliding off the counter to a standing position, I gingerly splash through the water to the counter opposite me, where a ring of keys dangles from a brass hook on the wall. They've gotta be for the off-limits stuff, like the liquor cabinet and the office.

I grab them and tiptoe out of the kitchen, drying my feet on the rug as I cross through the living room.

I pause by the office door. Raina said not to go in there, but that doesn't change the fact that I need the name of her plumber. I flip through the keys until I find one marked "office" and shove it into the lock.

I turn the handle.

The room is dark, with a single window blocked by a large filing cabinet. There's a desk against the wall closest to me, on top of which sits an ancient computer and another landline.

A metal box, taller than me, looms in the corner, a momentary distraction. It's shiny and black, simple in design but impressive in stature. There's a door cut into the front of it, marked only by a combination padlock and a silver handle.

I've never seen anything like it. Is it a bank safe? If this were a cartoon, it would be the kind of thing that falls out of the sky and smooshes the bad guy. If I were animated, dollar signs would be popping out of my eyes right now. Maybe that's my ticket out of here. The Marshalls are nice and all, but I need to get moving.

Guilt weighs on my heart and my shoulders droop. They really are nice and gullible, aren't they? At the very least, I should get a plumber in here. I can't dwell on this when the kitchen literally looks like a tsunami crashed into it.

Making a mental note to return to the safe once the kitchen is clear, I go to the desk and start pulling open drawers and rustle around the papers inside, looking for a list or a business card or . . . aha! This must be it.

Foley's Plumbing.

I pick up the phone and dial, waiting as the line rings.

My nervous hands fiddle with items on the desk. A bottle of nail polish, sky blue, finds its way into my palm. The bottle feels cold and smooth. The back of my mind wonders when Raina would ever wear this color. Maybe it belongs to a grandchild? But wouldn't there have been photos of the child?

"Hello?" a man answers, and I set the bottle down.

"Hi, yes, I need a plumber?"

As I explain the situation, my fingers flit over the clutter on the desk – tangling up in a silver charm bracelet. The dainty individual charms – a ballet slipper, the Eiffel Tower, an A+ – tinkle softly against the wood. It must belong to the same girl that wears the nail polish.

The man on the line asks for my address, and when I give the name of the inn he says, "Oh, is that you, Raina? Didn't recognize yer voice!"

"Um, no actually."

Awkward.

"I'm, uh, just taking care of the place while she's away."

"Huh? Oh, I didn't realize. Sorry, it's just we've done work at Keystone before. Raina's not there, you say?"

I pinch the bridge of my nose. Questions aren't good but can't be helped in this case. Guess I'd better explain, especially if they do regular business.

"No, I'm afraid not. Family emergency."

"Sorry to hear it. Hope things get better soon."

"Thanks, I'll tell her you said that. Can you get here soon? It's just that the kitchen is turning into a swimming pool."

"Someone'll be there within the hour, you can count on it."

"Thanks so much."

"No problem, sweetheart. You stay dry, now."

* * *

I stand in the kitchen doorway, arms tightly crossed.

The plumber they sent lies on his back, his head beneath the sink, apparently unbothered by the water soaking into his jeans. He seems nice, but I'm still uncomfortable with him being here, no matter how necessary his plumbing skills are.

When I opened the front door, he spoke before I could even say hello.

"I hear you're taking care of the place for a while." He shifted his toolbox to one hand and reached out to shake mine. "I'm Brian Foley."

"Oh," I couldn't stop my mouth, "you're . . ."

"I'm . . . ?"

Young.

Based on the voice I'd heard on the phone, I was expecting an older person. But this guy looks fresh out of high school. Built like a footballer, with short, auburn hair and eyes the color of gingersnap cookies – every cell in my body craves to get closer, alarming me with the sudden attraction.

I fight it down with a swallow and take a deliberate step back to remind myself why I'm here.

"Um, different. From what I expected."

"Which is?"

His eyes crinkle around the edges when he smiles, full of charm.

Crap, I totally put my foot in it.

"You sounded different on the phone, is all."

He laughed at that.

"You probably spoke with my dad, I can see how that'd be confusing."

I needed to get off this awkward train.

"Anyway, Brian," I said. "I'm . . . Hazel."

"Pleased to meet you, Hazel."

His smile would disarm an assassin.

I averted my eyes and showed him the kitchen where he whistled low, assured me it'd be "done in a jiff," and set to work.

I'm not sure what to do with myself, that's why I'm standing in the doorway, watching him. Occasionally he grunts, and the clang of a tool hitting metal rings out. I have no idea what he's doing but that's okay, just as long as he does.

He scoots out from under the sink and sits upright, wiping his face with a cloth.

"Busted pipe," he says. "I patched it, but you'll want to let Mrs. Marshall know it needs replacing soon, otherwise it could leak again."

"And we don't want that."

He chuckles.

"No, you don't want that. We'll send a bill for the service. Usually, we expect payment upfront, but Dad says the Marshalls are having family troubles? So it's an exception. Hard when loved ones suffer, ain't it?"

My smile feels flat.

"Listen, I don't know how long you're gonna be around, but Fox Valley is a small town and there's not much here in the way of entertainment. If you get bored or hungry one of these days and want something a little different, I know the best spot for a chicken-fried steak, grits, and a slice a pie. Not all at the same place, but don't let them know I said that."

He winks.

My belly swoops without warning.

Is he simply being nice, or did he just ask me out? Obviously, I can't say yes, but I don't know how to respond. Too receptive, and it'll be harder for him to get the hint. Too cold, and it might attract even more unwanted attention. Aren't small town people notorious for gossip? Imagine what they'd say about the hermit babysitting an inn. Rousing the curiosity of the locals is the last thing I need.

"Don't . . ."

I shake my head against the word that keeps rattling around in my brain, touching my forehead as if I can press it away. His smile fades like a sunset, all brightness gone. Did he hear it too? Or am I the only one losing my mind? He hesitates and ducks his head, suddenly shy.

"Just a thought," he says, formality creeping into his tone. "Anyway. If you need anything else, don't hesitate to call. We're around twenty-four seven."

"Thanks."

I watch him leave through the window, parting the curtain.

He climbs into a pickup truck with Foley's Plumbing painted on the side and starts the engine.

He looks up and, for a split second, our eyes meet.

I drop the curtain and step back. Better to let the sweet boy go and find some townie with less baggage.

It won't be long before I'm gone anyway.

Six

The sun sets a little later each evening, hinting that spring is close. Even still, the sky goes dark long before I'm ready.

Night on the mountain brings a level of darkness I never thought possible. Without dense civilization, the familiar orange glow of ambient lighting is nonexistent. The sky presses down on the inn, quietly smothering it. I flick on every single lamp, saturating the house with as much light as possible. Who knows what could be lurking in the shadows?

Brian left hours ago, and I've been mopping up the kitchen to the best of my ability. My stamina's not that great, and my muscles ache from pushing the heavy, water-logged mop back and forth, periodically wringing it into a bucket. It was tedious work, and now my body screams for a hot bath.

I take another long flannel from Raina's closet and go to the bathroom. It's pretty typical. White tub, freestanding sink, and check pattern linoleum floor with a spidery crack running through the middle of it. A ruffled drape covers the tiny window for privacy.

Even still, I'm struck with the sense of being watched. It's a weird feeling, like tingles down my back.

I look over my shoulder to see if maybe Skippy has snuck up on me, but the room and hallway are both empty.

I close the door, but it doesn't help. The feeling hasn't gone away.

"It's the solitude," I say out loud to bolster myself. "You're just losing it a little. You're fine."

Running the bath dispels some of the creepiness, as the rushing sound of the water fills my head and drowns out any lingering concerns. Steam builds up around me like a warm blanket until I'm comfortable enough to peel off my clothes.

I swipe my hand beneath the running water and make adjustments to the temperature. When it's perfect, I let the tub fill up some more before twisting the knob back. I need soap before getting in, so I turn around, looking for a bar or a bottle of suds.

I freeze.

A shadow lingers outside the bathroom, the light between the door and the floor blocked in such a way to suggest a pair of feet.

I cover my mouth, quelling the urge to scream. The last drops from the faucet plop into the tub, and each *drip* is like a bomb going off.

I can't look away from it. Could it be Skippy, waiting for me to let him out?

I put my clothes back on.

Heart pounding a bruise inside my chest, tongue heavy in my throat, I slowly pull the door open.

No one.

I go out into the hall and look both ways. Keeping my steps light and quiet, I tiptoe from room to room, thoroughly examining the place for an intruder.

Still, nothing.

Was I just imagining it? What is *wrong* with me?

A small sound, quiet at first, then rising. Glass rolling on wood – a marble. No, not a marble. I stiffen as the tiny bottle of nail polish rolls its way toward me down the hall, its label spinning in the sconce light. It stops a few feet away from me. I pick it up. The glossy bulb chills my hand, like it's been refrigerated.

My nerves pull taut. There's only one reason that bottle would be rolling out of the locked office, and that means I'm not alone.

Someone's messing with me.

Steeling myself, I march to the kitchen, footsteps loud and defiant, where I scan the counters for the knife block. The heavy wooden cube sits next to the toaster, black handles sticking out just begging to be touched. I wrap my fingers around the thickest one and pull – the overhead light glints off its gleaming, silver blade. For a moment, part of me feels silly for taking it, but another part, the quiet place inside of me that senses things aren't right, applauds.

Experimentally, I touch the edge of the blade.

It's sharp. It will do.

If he's found me, then I'm ready for him. I won't go down easy, I swear. "Stop playing and get out here!" I shout. "Come on!"

I tilt my head, listening. The house is soft with night. All I hear is the thumping of my heart.

Lifting the knife high, I search the rooms again, poised to strike at first glance. I double-check the locks and peer out of the curtains into the dark, squinting, but nothing seems out of the ordinary.

I sit on the couch for an hour, letting my muscles soften with the realization that I've made a mistake. Who knows? Maybe I carried the nail polish out of the office with me when I was distracted by the plumbing? I could've set it at a funny angle somewhere and it finally tipped over, making it roll? It's a stretch, but I don't know how else to justify it if I'm actually alone here. My sigh is long, heavy. Tired.

I carry the knife into the bathroom with me and rest it on the edge of the sink, an arm's length away from the bath.

Just in case.

* * *

I can't sleep. The solitude is way too eerie. You know that feeling of being watched? I just can't shake it. The little hairs on the back of my neck prickle and stand upright as I search the place for the hundredth time, but I'm definitely alone. My paranoia's getting out of hand. My eyes stay wide as I settle back into bed, and I keep the light on because my imagination has cranked into overdrive. I picture eyeballs floating in the window beside the bed, somehow seeing me with X-ray vision through the blinds. I don't consider myself a wimpy person, but I've never been totally isolated like this.

Back home, even if I was alone in the apartment, there was still the sound of life outside the building. The whoosh of vehicles on my street, dogs barking, the whistle of the commuter train less than a mile away. It was a comforting ambience I took for granted, because no matter how scary a few people can be, the majority aren't so bad.

Here, though.

My ears strain to pick up any familiar sounds, but there are none. An owl hoots and I jump, my shoulders tight against my ears. God, that's spooky. Occasionally, the wind curls around the roof, whining. But mostly there's silence. The silence is the loudest thing I've ever heard. A vacuum of nothingness, absorbing the environment and myself with it.

If I can't hear anything, do I even exist?

I roll onto my side, pulling the blanket up to my chin. Without distractions, my thoughts drift to him as they always do.

We met the way old people used to before the internet, by chance.

My friend Mariah and I needed a place to hang, so we began our quest for a place to call our stomping ground. We tried restaurants, but that required us to order food, which burned through our wallets faster than we liked. The mall security guards were always on us to "keep it moving," and we got tired of walking real quick.

That's when we found Skeeter's. It was a dingy pool hall with questionable nachos and warm, foamy beer that smelled faintly of dirty dishwater. The owner prided himself on his obscure record collection, often playing ancient rock or metal at unholy volumes. Low wattage bulbs hanging from the ceiling gave off a surprising cozy glow, and, after the initial shock of grunge, it felt warm and inviting. And because they were so lax about checking ID, we often found ourselves there after school.

One day, after a few weeks of wasting afternoons in the stale, muffled cocoon of Skeeter's, I saw a bunch of guys loitering by our favorite pool table. It was the only one without a crooked slant, so we could actually try playing the game. One guy seemed to have a hold on the others – obviously the alpha of the pack. But he was smiling as they gathered up cues, and I couldn't take my eyes off him. His wiry body thrummed with energy, and his blond hair, shaved close to his head, showed off flame tattoos crawling up his neck. I nudged Mariah as we got closer. "Hey. Who's that?"

"Oh, him?" she said. "He was in my sister's class a few years ago. That's Monster."

"Why?"

"What?"

"Why'd you call him a monster?"

She laughed.

"That's not really his name?"

She laughed so hard she couldn't respond other than to clutch my arm, her pink acrylics pressing into my sleeve.

"No, serious. What kind of name is Monster?"

When she caught her breath, all she said was, "You'll have to ask him."

Her sly grin did nothing to calm the sudden racing of my heart. Monster didn't sound like a good name. But Mariah walked confidently up to the guys and stood with a tilted hip, her go-to stance when she was ready to flirt. I came up behind her as she greeted them with a hello and a hair flick.

"Mariah," Monster said. His voice had that roughened edge to it that smokers get. "Kendra let you out to play?"

She lifted her chin.

"I'm a senior. I don't need my sister's permission to do anything."

"That so?"

"Yep. So bring me a beer."

The guys laughed, but Monster didn't. He pursed his lips, as if considering. His gaze traveled down the length of her body. Something about that made my stomach shifty.

Then he looked over her shoulder at me. "Who's your friend?"

Mariah turned to glance at me. "She's a little thirsty. So you can call her Sweet Tea."

"Mariah!" I hissed, ducking my chin to hide my blush.

"It's okay." She winked. "He'll buy you a drink too. Won't you?"

He snapped his fingers, and one of the guys jumped up and headed for the bar. I hate admitting that I was impressed by that. He didn't even have to say a word. None of the guys at school had that kind of magnetism. I never once questioned his authority or why the guys were so eager to please him. At the time, I had stars in my eyes. What if I'd pressed for a little more info? What if I'd known what he was like? Would I have stayed the hell away or continued with my silly infatuation?

I rub my face, scrubbing hard with my palms as if to erase my thoughts. No point in thinking about what ifs. All that matters is right now.

And right now, I need to sleep.

BANG.

I squeeze my eyes shut, and my heart forgets to beat.

What was that?

It came from overhead. There's nothing up there but the roof. Did a tree branch break off in the wind? Is it an animal leaping onto the roof in search of some nocturnal eats? Or something less easily explained?

There's no way I can check. You couldn't pay me enough to get a ladder and climb up there to poke around in the dark. It's just not happening.

My eyes flick back and forth behind my dark eyelids as I listen, finely attuned to any sound above.

Nothing.

It doesn't happen again, but that doesn't stop my pulse from hammering, my eyes glued open. For the next hour I lay still, listening.

Seven

It's early morning, still dark, and I'm planning on reading a little bit in bed before getting up. But I can't find the romance novel I'd started. I left it on the bedside table last night, but when I wake up, it isn't there. I check the floor beneath the table – clear. Flipping the blankets, I hope maybe it'll shake free of the rippling fabric. It's not fallen into the bedcovers, nowhere.

I get up and ransack the entire building, even the office, with no luck. I ask Skippy if he took it for a chew toy, but he just licks my wagging finger.

The book doesn't seem to be simply misplaced – it just isn't anywhere.

I know it's silly, but it was an escape from reality, from memories that keep taunting me. The crushing solitude will get to me if I'm not careful, and that book was the only thing keeping me occupied.

I go back to the bedroom and there it is – right where I initially had left it, on the nightstand.

I press my fingers against my eyelids, hard. I must be losing my mind. This isn't the first weird thing to happen in the three days I've been here. I've started smelling random things. The most frequent scents being nail polish and cocoa butter, tinged with rotten eggs. The blue nail polish hasn't been touched since I locked it back in the office, not even once, though I was tempted – I haven't painted my raggedy nails since last summer. Besides, the rim of it was so crusted over with dried lacquer it'd be impossible to open. I've checked and double-checked the fridge and all the eggs are fine. And Raina certainly doesn't have any cocoa butter around here. Believe me, I've checked. She uses some ancient plumeria-scented crème circa 2001 with a dusty lid – it's so old the ingredients have separated inside the jar. Even if she did have some decent lotion, say, in the bathroom cabinet, why would the scent suddenly drift past my nose while I'm watching TV?

I pick up the romance novel and flip the pages. As I do, a new smell seems to rise from the pages.

My stomach clenches. No. It has to be my imagination, from lack of sleep.

Bringing the book to my nose, I take a tentative sniff, expecting the usual musty, wood pulp odor synonymous with aged paper. But my nose is met with the worst odor I can think of. It bothers me even more than the rotten eggs. I stand frozen, dissolving into panic, as the smell grows stronger, filling the room and clogging my nostrils.

The fragrance is unique to hospitals – liquid antiseptic and the sharp, sour tang of illness. It's a fragrance associated with endless corridors, a twisting labyrinth of white walls and linoleum that squeaked beneath my boots each afternoon when school let out. I held my breath as long as I could, taking little nips of air through my mouth only when the need for oxygen became unbearable. I learned to hate that stench, associating it with the oncology department, crippling fear, and uncertainty, but it couldn't keep me away from Mom's side.

Whenever I smell it, I remember. When I smell it, I shatter all over again.

My life. My world. Reduced to brittle bones and a near-constant grimace of pain only her fellow patients could understand. She passed with my hand in hers – delirious, drugged up, and numb. It was better than having her awake and racked with pain – it cracked my heart to see her like that.

* * *

Later in the morning, after my chores, I'm propped up on the couch flipping through the romance novel, trying to stop these memories from assaulting my mind. It doesn't work. I sigh and toss the book on the coffee table, not bothering to mark my place. The sun gradually lightens the windows with a soft glow, and I watch as the sky turns from inky blue to bubblegum pink.

Then, a voice in my ear. A breathy sound that tickles the delicate skin behind my earlobe, sending goosebumps up to my hairline. It's so quick it's already a memory.

I don't even know what it said. But I heard it – the intonation of a sentence against my eardrum, as if someone's right next to me. Except no one's there. Clearly, the solitude is getting to me if my brain is creating imaginary conversation.

I stand and make my way to the bathroom.

After washing my hands, I stare at my face in the mirror, losing myself in the reflected image. My pupils swim in a pool of melted dark chocolate. The bruise on my cheek, thankfully, has nearly gone. My hair, mixed, can't decide if it's going for curly or straight, so it settles for wavy.

Each freckle on my face looks like splatters of dirt. When I was little, I used to scrub at them in the bath for what seemed like ages, thinking I was dirty. I remembered how devastated I was when Mom told me they were there to stay.

There are features I do like, however. My eyes are large and doe-like. My lips are full and naturally mauve. I know for a fact that women will pay ungodly amounts of money for a pout like mine.

Water splashing into the basin breaks me from my thoughts. The faucet's running again, but I didn't turn it on. My hands are still hanging by my sides.

I step back despite mushy knees, confused and more than a little freaked out. The water rushes hard, its noise filling my head as I look at the handle – it's definitely turned to the "on" position.

Hand trembling, I push it back to stop the flow and wait to see if it starts up again.

It doesn't.

I turn the water on and off, on and off. It works just fine. Maybe I only imagined it.

But even now, I keep hearing a faint dripping sound. I'm not sure where it's coming from. It's not the overeager spigot, and the pipe under the sink is dry. The tub isn't dripping either.

I can't seem to pinpoint exactly which direction the sound is coming from, almost as if it's a phantom noise in my own head. When I check the kitchen, the plumbing is still sealed up the way Brian left it.

But I hear it, I do hear it, the gentle *plip-plop* of water hitting a puddle. I try ignoring it. What else can I do? The sound follows me around as I start my morning chores.

* * *

When the sun has burned away the fog of the morning, I put on my jacket and take Skippy outside. He bounds around, aimless and happy, while I do a perimeter check around the house, trying to discover the cause of that loud crashing sound last night.

I crane my neck but can't see the top of the roof, so I scan the trees instead, looking for the telltale signs of a broken branch.

Thing is, the trees are so clustered and the branches are of all lengths and sizes that it's impossible to tell if one is broken or just plain stumpy. I bet there's a ladder in the shed. I could drag it over if I'm brave enough. Do I really need to know what's on the roof?

I think about another sleepless night, and the answer is obvious.

Yes. Yes, I do.

The shed holds a variety of tools and equipment, most of which I don't know the names of let alone the purpose for. Boxes stacked precariously fill the space as far as I can see. Sawdust tickles my throat. If I needed anything other than the tarps or the ladder, I'd have to wade further into the shed, which could be dangerous – a person could get tetanus just from *looking* at some of these rusty tools. I can see why Raina doesn't want me messing around in here.

Thankfully, I don't have to look far for what I need – there's a ladder hanging sideways on some hooks, and I wrestle it down to the ground. It's awkwardly shaped and must weigh, like, fifty pounds.

Dragging it to the house proves to be a workout, but I manage. I have to know what's up there. It can't have been my imagination. I lean the ladder against the back wall, next to my bedroom window. The extension slides up, doubling its size, and I grip the sides.

It occurs to me that I don't actually know if I'm scared of heights. Guess now's the time to find out.

The first step creaks when I put my weight on it.

I step carefully on each rung, using my legs to lift myself up.

As I get closer to the top, I realize there's quite a lot of space between the ceiling in my room and the actual rooftop. Space that's just a bit larger than needed for insulation. I run my hand over the brick. It's rough and my fingers come away with a fine layer of grit that I wipe on my jacket. It must be the attic. Of course it would be the attic. There's no basement here.

I glance down. Skippy looks so small from up here, like a puppy. The trees that seemed so tall from the ground bend and sway toward me, as if curious about what I'm doing up here.

So, it turns out I'm not afraid of heights, but I can't say I much love them either. I've come this far, though. I keep climbing.

When my eye line meets the gutter, I pause, suddenly nervous.

I take three deep breaths, letting them out in noisy gusts to psych myself up for what I'll find. A dead squirrel perhaps? A bear? They climb trees, right? I wouldn't know what to do if I saw one, except maybe pee myself. The most ferocious wildlife back home are gray squirrels and pigeons. The ladder doesn't actually reach the top, so I have to stand on my tippy toes.

The wind blows my hair back as I take a moment to balance myself.

I peek over the rim of the gutter.

The roof is flat and filthy, covered with a slimy layer of rotting leaves that look like spoiled chocolate icing. My gaze roams from left to right, seeking out something large enough to make a sound that carries through a layer of attic. It would have to be something pretty big and obvious, right? There's nothing like that up here.

The ladder tips a bit to the right, so I shift my weight to steady it, abandoning the view. The metal rattles beneath my feet, and I've had enough. I'm done.

Taking my time, I make my way down the ladder and have never felt so relieved to be on solid ground.

Well, that solves it. It was only my imagination. I guess being in isolation like this would do that to a person, but I was so *sure* it was something.

A horrible thought occurs to me. What if the bang didn't come from the roof, but inside the attic? What if something got into the house? Like a mouse . . . or something bigger? My stomach sours. I have to go check, don't I?

Eight

After meeting Monster for the first time, Mariah and I haunted Skeeter's almost every day. He was always there. I'd drink iced tea while everyone else got tipsy, then we'd waste time playing pool, talking and laughing.

Ultimately, it was the laughter that hooked me. Is there anything more addictive than the shared experience of a full belly laugh?

One day, Mariah texted saying she couldn't go out. I felt bad for her, but I also felt disappointed about not seeing Monster. He was taking up a lot of space in my brain lately. He was all I could think about during classes, and I couldn't focus on my homework. I didn't know if Mariah would be upset, but I went without her anyway. I couldn't face a long, lonely evening at home or another night in the hospital when I could've been laughing and having a good time with him.

I took a deep, fortifying breath to steady my nerves before opening the door of Skeeter's. I never went anywhere without Mariah – she was the leader and I always followed.

But not that night.

Monster's grin when he saw me melted away my jitters. He was my friend now, not just Mariah's sister's old school mate. He always bought me sugary iced teas, and I looked forward to them.

He knew how old I was but didn't seem to care. We started hanging out, just the two of us. He treated me like an adult and I liked that, it made me feel grown up. So we went out a couple of times, nothing major. To a movie. A club. And we danced. For hours we danced. There was a definite connection, a vibe, whatever you want to call it. Something nameless, shapeless pulled us together.

The first night he kissed me, his lips were so soft and tender it felt like I'd come home. Until his hand caressed my neck, his palm sliding up beneath my chin. It wrapped around my throat and squeezed. He sucked the pitiful wheeze from my mouth. I didn't enjoy it but wanted him to like me, so I moaned a little, a deep purr I'd never made before, hoping he'd think I did. His throaty hum in return felt as if I'd leveled up. I got him to want me. So I let him crush my throat as his lips demolished mine with the sort of passion lacking in my short romantic history, warm and confident and hungry. He loosened his grip, breaking the kiss, and I gasped – for air, for life.

I never told Mom about him, of course. She wouldn't have approved. I let her believe I was just spending time with friends from school, and that was that. Even though she was always working, and then always in the hospital, he never came over to my place. I didn't want to risk a neighbor seeing and blabbing to Mom.

Maybe if I'd told her, things would've been different. But no matter how hard I wish I could go back in time and smack some sense into my younger self, I can't.

That's the hardest part. Knowing I made a mistake and paying for it now. That's what I'm thinking about as I stand by the ladder for what feels like hours, my nose going numb with cold, working up the nerve go back in the house.

What have I gotten myself into?

Propelled by fear, I force myself back through the kitchen entrance, where I search every drawer I can find until I come across a flashlight. Shoving the handle of it into the waistband of my jeans, I walk the length of the upstairs hallway, neck craned as I look for the telltale outline of a pull-down ladder.

I spot a ring pull near the end, but I can't reach it. I get the chair from my room and drag it underneath so I can stand up on it.

I pull the ring and, with a squeaky groan, the hatch lowers. A wooden ladder, folded up accordion style, lies nestled in the hatch. I slowly stretch it out to the floor, my heart reverberating inside my head.

No qualms about heights this time, but a different sort of dread weighs me down like the wet mud Skippy enjoys playing in. I creep up the ladder and peer over the top rung. It's not a normal attic, the kind you imagine from children's storybooks with light and space and magical things to discover packed away in old-fashioned trunks.

It's a crawlspace.

I can barely see, it's so dark up here, but I can sense the roof is only a few feet above my head.

I pull out the flashlight and click it on, sweeping the soft beam of light around. Wooden crates line the narrow space on either side. It smells gross up here, like something died. I cover my nose – the stench, like rotting, unfound Easter eggs, is unbearable. In the weak circle of my flashlight, I notice a few brown pebble-like things – mice or rat droppings for sure.

Something tickles the back of my neck. I clap my hand to the base of my skull, looking around, careful not to lose my balance on the steps.

I look up at all the cobwebs drifting lazily from the beams. That's all it was, a fluttering web. Creepy, but harmless.

Movement in the far back corner catches my eye.

A shadowy mass slithers from along the wall, low to the floor, and my skin prickles in response.

Blood rushes to my limbs, begging them to move, but instead of climbing back down I shine my light over there, holding my breath. Only boxes appear in the beam.

I squint, hoping to see it again but also kind of hoping not to. Frozen, I wait for something to jump out at me.

I'm not sure how long I stare at the corner, hardly blinking, eyes stinging from the dust swirling in the air. Nothing.

I let out a slow, shaky breath. This place is getting to me. My imagination hasn't been this active since I was a kid and it is, without doubt, in full working order. I click off the flashlight and climb down.

Folding the ladder back up, I gently push it toward the ceiling. The springs do most of the work, and the hatch closes seamlessly in place.

I don't know if I can take this. My anxiety ramps up again, my head dizzy with a surge of blood. I can't stay here. But how can I leave without the rest of the money? I have a terrible image of myself pleasuring truckers across the country, just to get by.

Then I remember the safe in the office and my mind takes a devious turn. I can't help the thoughts that arise, but are they any worse than what I've already done? Though it wasn't as lucrative as I'd hoped, stealing from *him* didn't feel like a crime.

This would be different.

So very different.

Raina and Bob are generous people, letting a stranger come into their home, their place of business, and trusting me to look after their precious pup. They aren't expecting any harm. And from the general look of this place, they aren't exactly rolling in the dough.

But curiosity blots out reason. Why would they need a locking box that huge if it isn't full of cash, or jewelry, or something of value?

My original plan could still work. Maybe California's not off the table. With resources, I could get a bus and somewhere to stay until I find proper work. It'd be a whole lot easier to figure out with cash on hand.

Sidling up to it, I reach out and touch the metal. It's cold and smooth. My fingertips leave sweaty prints, faint but visible, and I use the sleeve of my shirt to rub them away. The lock has a rotating dial surrounded by a ring of numbers.

Hmm.

What would the code be?

Looking around doesn't yield many ideas, but when I take both hands and run them up and down the sides of the box, I feel a wispy bump, thin as a strand of hair. A piece of paper, taped to the side. If I hadn't been searching for something, I wouldn't have noticed it.

Bingo.

Carefully, using my fingernails, I scrape and peel the adhesive away from the metal. The paper strip beneath the tape is small enough to fit inside a fortune cookie, and on it, instead of my future or a cutesy phrase about success, are three numbers. 15-24-10.

My fingers tingle with anticipation.

I turn the lock to those precise numbers and it clicks.

It's open.

I let out a shaky breath, feeling woozy all of a sudden. The door swings wide with ease.

Disappointment leaks into my gut, softening my belly, while unease tiptoes up my chest and tightens my throat.

In front of me are not bags full of money or jewels, not even bank information. Instead there are weapons. Rifles, I believe, or maybe shotguns, their elongated barrels gleaming in the light. Above them is a shelf with another, smaller box on it. Like the safe, it's metal, black, and intimidating.

With trembling hands, I pull down the box and open it. Two handguns lie nestled in foam that's been custom-fitted to their shape.

Of course. This is the country. I've even seen the results of Bob's hunting dotted around the inn, furs and antlers and stuffed creatures. But seeing them, part of me just assumed they were purchased for decoration. Isn't that what people do? I should've realized that, in the mountains, people go after their décor in a different way.

My lips press together so hard they tingle. I might not be a country girl – far from it, in fact – but this isn't my first time seeing a gun. That was a cliché, of course. The seven-year-old finds a pistol in her parent's closet, and thank God the safety was on. I pretended I was aiming at a bad guy, little arms straining under its weight, just as Mom walked in. She flipped, naturally, and I never went in her closet again. It wasn't until I was older I learned she kept the gun in case my dad came back sniffing around.

The second time I experienced a gun was much more recent, and I try not to dwell on it too much. It's part of why I'm here, after all. How does that quote go about apples falling from trees?

I lock everything back in place.

I guess I'm staying here after all. I can't believe I thought I could steal from such nice people. What is wrong with me?

Resigning myself to a few more days here, I search for mouse traps in the supply closet. They have one box with only a single wood-and-metal contraption left inside, which tells me this is not an unusual problem. But when I go to set it by pulling back the metal snap, it turns out the spring is broken, a useless, dangly coil.

I could just let it be. So there are mice. Okay, big deal. I can suck it up for now, right? I'm not staying here forever. But as the day goes on, all I can think about are their pink tails trailing along the floor, their beady eyes and long, sharp teeth. What if they chew through electrical wires and start a fire? I saw that on the news once. Or what if, while I'm sleeping, they actually nibble on my toes?

It's time I made a visit to town.

Nine

As I'm fetching the keys to the truck, Raina calls on the landline.

"Looks like it might be a little longer 'fore she bites it," she said, her voice crackling down the wire. "I really hate to ask, but think you could stay on another couple'a weeks? There'll be a bonus in it, make it worth your while. Whadd'ya say? Help us out?"

I hesitate. Bonus? It's hard saying no to more cash in hand. But could I really put up with the strange happenings for two more weeks?

"What kind of bonus?" I ask.

"Well, let's up it to a grand per week. Including this past one. Would that suffice?"

Shit, that's a lot of money. How can they afford it? Nothing about the inn screams financial success on that kind of level. But she offered, and that would definitely give me a leg up on my plans.

I rub my forehead, thinking about all the weird stuff that's happened. It's not like it was anything particularly dangerous, right? I just got a little worked up. And when I think of the bigger picture, of Monster, there is no safer place for me right now than Fox Valley.

"Um," I say. "Okay. Yeah. Let's do it. Anything to help out."

"Wonderful, thank ya kindly, darlin'. You're an angel."

Two more weeks. Fourteen days. It's not that long, really. But still, I need groceries. A change of clothes that actually fits. A new book to read.

And, I shudder to think, mouse traps.

* * *

Skippy hears the jingle of the keys and comes running like his tail's on fire.

"You're staying," I tell him. Bringing him with me will only draw attention. I just want to get in and get out, unnoticed by anyone save a cashier. "Stay."

His ears drop back and he whimpers, disappointed.

The truck could qualify as an antique. The chipped, flaky paint was probably once a classic cherry red but time and exposure to the environment have faded it to a rusty orange. Smudges cover the passenger side window with what I'm guessing is Skippy's snot. I imagine him happy to ride along, nosing the window until Raina or Bob rolls it down so he can feel the wind.

The inside of the truck smells like stale smoke and, strangely enough, mud. I never realized mud has a very distinctive smell of its own, different from plain old dirt. I check that my hand-written list of necessities is still in my pocket before starting the engine.

The key needs a couple of turns before the truck reluctantly grumbles to life. Once the engine warms I turn on the heat, setting it to full blast, wishing I had gloves. The steering wheel is cold as ice. Using the office computer (shame on me), I Googled the address of Value Green, assuming most of the shopping is in that general vicinity, and wrote down the directions. It seems pretty straightforward, just time-consuming, travel-wise. Which, considering how long and empty my days have been, isn't necessarily a bad thing.

The winding road snakes precariously through a tightly-knit forest of trees. On the way here I was too shaken with adrenaline to notice my surroundings. But now, as the driver, I am forced to see just how remote Keystone Mill really is.

Ten minutes of nauseating twists and turns later and I finally pull onto a main road. It's long and straight and there's not much to see on either side other than trees.

I turn on the radio for the illusion of company, spinning the dial for a decent station. It's mostly static. Then country music bursts through the speakers with a twang.

I listen for a while, trying to enjoy the plucky guitars and warbling voices, but the music fades as I drive on, followed by more static. The dial finds only a religious station, from which booms a particularly aggressive bible-thumping sermon. After a few minutes of damnation and hellfire – sounds like I'm going straight to hell for all my lies and deception, according to this guy – I turn the radio off.

I'd rather have silence.

The sky weighs heavy with moisture – the forecast called for rain later. I bet in any other season this drive would be nice. Peaceful, even. But I just want to get there and back as quickly as possible.

The road yawns before me, wide open and lonely. Maybe I should've let Skippy ride shotgun after all.

The first real signs of life crop up after the longest stretch of the highway.

First, a trailer park, followed by small houses with dilapidated siding and overgrown lawns.

Then, a neighborhood one could almost call suburban.

And then I arrive.

The truck lumbers down an old-fashioned Main Street lined with quaint shops on either side. If were they cleaned up a bit with a fresh coat of paint, they could belong on a movie set. There's a hardware store and a post office, a café and feed store. A church steeple rises high above the row of sleepy storefronts.

I stop here, pulling the truck in front of a secondhand store. The engine clicks as it rapidly cools. The sidewalks are clear, not a person in sight. Even still, I chew the inside of my cheek, the tissue soft and malleable between my teeth. No one knows me here. It should be okay. There won't be any spies around, waiting, watching, ready to report my every move. I'll be quick – in and out and back before the morning's over.

I can do this.

I consult my list before stepping out onto the pavement. Mouse traps, groceries, and some basic clothing, perhaps a travel bag to carry them in. I definitely need some new underwear. I can't keep washing the same pair every day. But my goal is to save as much money as possible, so I'll ask Raina to reimburse me for the traps since it's a business expense.

The hardware store will be my first stop, and I look both ways unnecessarily as I cross the street. A string of sleigh bells hanging from the door handle jingles when I open it, and the mixed smell of metal and sawdust clogs my nostrils.

At first the place seems empty. A country love song plays softly from a little radio next to the register. I go in search of mouse traps, up and down the narrow aisles crammed full of hammers and nails and shovels and rakes and firewood.

"Fancy meeting you here."

I whirl around to see Brian Foley standing behind me, his cinnamon eyes lit up with surprise. I'd forgotten how his cheeks dimple when he smiles.

"Sorry." He runs his hand over his head, tousling his rust-colored hair. "Didn't mean to scare you."

"I'm not scared." I shrug, feigning indifference. "I mean, um, how are you?"

"Good, thanks. Needed some new ratchets."

He holds up a plastic case. The lid is clear and inside is a row of metal tools that look like wrenches, only they have circular tops instead of claws.

"Well, just one – this size here – but they only got the set. So now I guess I'm really set!"

He laughs at his own corny joke. I let out a mediocre "heh" in response.

"Anyway," he says. "What about you? What'cha doing down the hill?"

"The hill?"

"Yeah, uh, that's what we call it when Keystoners come to town."

"Keystoners?"

"Yeah, the Marshall's inn is technically in Keystone County, though the address is Fox Valley. You notice how thin the air is up there?"

"I get it – from being 'up the hill.'"

"Yeah." He rubs the back of his neck. "I guess that sounds a little silly to a tourist."

I'm quick to correct him. "I'm not a tourist."

"Right."

A few awkward seconds pass. So I fill it with the only thing I can think of.

"We have mice," I blurt out. "I'm looking for some traps."

He nods, unfazed by my random outburst.

"Little demons. And the Marshalls not got a cat or anything, right? They're dog people if I remember."

"Yep."

"I think the traps might be over this way."

He beckons to a shelf with an array of dusty boxes with ancient price stickers peeling off the fronts.

"Here you go."

He hands me a box with a faded picture of a skull and cross-bones superimposed over a hissing rat.

"How many do you need?" he asks.

"How many do they have?"

Chuckling, he hands me two more.

"This should cover you. Unless it's a major infestation we're talking about, in which case Mrs. Marshall should call pest control. Johnny's the guy – she have his number?"

"Uh, probably. But I don't think it's as bad as all that. Yet."

"Maybe this will head off the problem. Nip it from the get."

"Maybe. Thanks."

I take them to the register with Brian trailing behind me. No one's there.

"Hello?" Brian calls over the counter. He leans over it a bit, accidentally knocking over a display of outdated "how-to" magazines. "Amos? You back there?"

A grizzly old man swings open a backroom door and comes toward us, scowling.

"Why didn't you ring the bell?"

He taps an old silver bell on the counter. Somehow I missed it among all the clutter.

"Didn't think you actually wanted to be called like a maid, Amos."

Amos harrumphs and then looks at me.

"You buyin' that?"

I nod, dropping the boxes on the counter.

He tallies it up on the giant cash register, each button producing an ungodly chirrup that echoes for days. I hand him a twenty-dollar bill – some of the precious food money Raina bestowed upon me. He thrusts the change and receipt in my direction which I hastily stuff in my pocket as he puts my merchandise in a plain brown paper bag.

"Thank you," I say, repeating it again to Brian when he steps up to pay for his ratchets. He didn't have to help me but he did. He at least deserves politeness. But I'm not here to make friends.

I'm already pulling open the door to leave when Brian says, "Hey, wait."

I pretend I don't hear him and let the door close between us.

I hurry across the road, fumbling for the keys. The bells jingle again, faintly behind me, probably happy to get so much use in one afternoon. Crap. He's coming right for me. This is what happens when you're too nice to people – they won't leave you alone. I should've run down the street rather than going for the truck.

"Hey," Brian calls. "Hazel."

Sighing heavily, I turn around.

"Before you go back, I wanted to ask you something."

"I'm a little busy," I say. "Things to get, a crazy long list. You know how it is."

He nods quickly, a living bobble head.

"I do. Yes, sorry. I was just wondering what you had planned for the rest of the day. Seeing as you're here it might be kind of nice to show you around. There's more to see than you'd think."

"I don't know, I should really go, it's such a drive . . ."

"Exactly. Which is why I would feel terrible sending you back on an empty stomach. At least stop and have lunch with me."

"I don't even know you."

His blue eyes pierce mine.

"Then get to know me."

"Are all you country guys so forward?"

"No." He smiles. "But sometimes there's need for an exception."

I can't suppress the dart of excitement that pricks just below my ribcage. I am completely unprepared for this.

I look at the truck. A few specks of rain hit the hood, the window, and then my face, icy pinpricks.

The paper bag crinkles beneath my white-knuckled grip. I'm not supposed to make connections here – I'm supposed to lay low and then disappear, no leads left behind. I still have purchases to make, but my stomach rumbles at the idea of a hot meal that doesn't consist of buttered noodles. As if he can sense my inner struggle, he takes a step closer.

"Just lunch. Or coffee. It's not fancy, but at least it's quick if you end up hating my company. Up to you. Your choice."

"I know that."

My words come out sharper than intended, and he rubs the back of his neck.

"Didn't mean to offend," he says. "Look, if I'm bothering you then I'm real sorry. I just thought it'd be nice to offer. But you don't have to worry – I'll leave you alone now."

He turns and starts walking away before I even give him an answer. How can he assume what I'll say? That's not for him to guess. I think of all the times Monster called the shots – and how I blindly went along with it.

That swings my decision.

"Okay," I say. "Yes. To lunch, not just coffee."

He stops. His nose has gone flamingo-pink from the cold, his toffee-colored eyelashes impossibly long. He blinks as a raindrop hits his cheekbone.

"Really?" He grins. "Great! What are you hungry for? As I've said before, I know a great place for chicken-fried steak."

"Um," I cough. "What is that, exactly?"

His eyes widen. "You're not serious?"

"Never had it."

"No kidding? Well, you're in for a treat, you can count on that."

Ten

Turns out chicken-fried steak is pretty tasty. I fork another mouthful of battered beef and hum as I chew.

Brian, sitting across from me in the booth, sips his iced tea.

"You like it?" he asks.

I speak around a bite of meat. "It-sh sho good."

"Glad you're enjoying it."

He picks up his burger and takes a large bite, ketchup and pickle juice running down his chin.

I gesture with my fork. "You got a little . . ."

"Oh." He takes the napkin and dabs it up. "Thanks."

We lapse into silence as we eat.

Chewing, I take in our surroundings. We're in a diner, but not the cute, retro kind, despite the unoriginal half-moon crackling in the window in a garish shade of radiation. This place probably once considered itself cool back in the 80s or something. Yellow and brown are the primary color scheme. The placemats are laminated and sticky, likely drenched in several decades' worth of artificially flavored maple syrup.

I've only seen two people running the place, but surprisingly, a large handful of patrons keep them busy. My Coke takes forever to get refilled. But after tasting this steak, I can't even be mad about the wait.

The sky spits icy droplets at the window, picking up speed. Water streams down the foggy plate glass.

"They're callin' for hail later," Brian says.

"Guess I should cover Raina's garden. She's terrified of frost."

"If it's cold enough to hail it's cold enough for frost."

He bites his lip as if aware of how obvious that statement is, and my eyes are magnetically drawn to his mouth. I never noticed he has a snaggletooth.

"Are we really talking about the weather?"

"Looks that way." He wipes his hands and leans forward on his elbows. "We can change the subject. Why don't you tell me about yourself?"

I swallow my steak and instantly start coughing. Damn, way to play it cool.

"You okay?"

Alarm colors his expression.

"I'm fine."

Only I'm not. The piece of meat is lodged at an uncomfortable angle and, to my horror, I begin hacking like a spikey demon's trying to crawl out my throat. My coughing fit takes a life of its own, and my eyes water from the effort.

"*Hack* – sorry."

"No reason to be sorry, just as long's you're okay."

I nod to reassure him.

He offers me his tea and, bypassing the straw, I take three deep pulls. It's thick and sweet as syrup. It does the trick.

"I'm making a habit of thanking you," I say, relieved that my breathing's returned to normal.

"No problem. I'm here to help."

I wipe tea from my upper lip before it can stain. "So, what, you're like my knight in shining armor?"

"I get the feeling you're not exactly a damsel in distress."

Funny, it seems to me that's the only position he's ever seen me in. Needing the sink fixed, needing help finding the traps, needing a proper lunch . . . what other humiliating situation will crop up next?

I don't know how to reply, so I don't.

He shrugs, looking sheepish. "It's just that, you don't seem that way. That's all."

A woman comes over to our table and I reflexively hold up my glass for another refill, but she is not our waitress. Her frizzy hair is dyed the kind of red that looks more orange, and an enormous smile reveals coffee-ravaged teeth that look like they haven't even *heard* of whitening gel, let alone used any.

She beams at my lunch companion. "Brian! How are you? It's been too long."

"Mrs. Rhodes!"

Brian scoots across the vinyl seat and stands up. He towers over the lady and leans down to wrap her in his arms.

She clutches his back, clearly very happy to see him.

"I heard you were back in town," he says. "How was Florida?"

"Hot, like you wouldn't believe. And gators everywhere."

"You're kidding."

"Well, maybe if they'd remembered their sunscreen, they wouldn't look quite so leathery."

She winks and Brian makes a face like "ooh, you got me!"

What's with the cheesy humor in this town?

I try sinking down in my seat, hoping to avoid an introduction, but no luck. Her gaze falls on me and her smile widens.

"Who's this?" she asks. "I'm sorry, how rude of me to interrupt your meal."

"No trouble at all!" Brian gestures toward me. "This is Hazel. Hazel, meet Mrs. Rhodes. She was my elementary school teacher."

"So nice to meet you, darling."

She shakes my hand, her skin tissue-soft and slippery in my grip. I'm afraid if I squeeze too hard it will slide right off her bones like sausage casing.

"Hazel's from out of town, so I thought I'd let her experience the finest dining Fox Valley has to offer."

"Is that so?"

I want to melt into my seat and become one with the vinyl. In lieu of liquefying my body, I smile-grimace at Brian, silently hoping he'll take the hint and leave it at that. Despite what it looks like, I'm not trying to make friends here.

Oblivious, he keeps talking, oversharing.

"Yep, she's house-sitting the inn for Mr. and Mrs. Marshall while they're out of town."

"Goodness, you're running it all on your own?" She looks astonished. "It's just you look so young to be managing a business."

I'll never admit there aren't any guests right now, because then they'll know I'm alone and vulnerable.

"I'm twenty-one." The lies never stop.

Mrs. Rhodes purses her lips. "Like I said."

I prickle.

"Twenty-one, huh? You like them older then, don't you, Brian?"

My face lights on fire, my freckles likely dissolving and bleeding together in the spreading blush.

"What?" I can't stop myself. "How old are you exactly?"

"Eighteen last July," he admits, ducking his chin before taking a long sip of tea.

"Don't . . ." Mrs. Rhodes whispers.

My attention whips back to her. Did she just say what I think she said? A beat passes but she doesn't finish her sentence. Did she really say it or am I hallucinating outside of the inn now?

Curiously, her gaze turns unfocused. It's as if she's staring right through me. Her forehead crinkles, the untamed hairs of her eyebrows pulling together in unity.

Brian looks alarmed.

"Mrs. Rhodes? Are you alright?"

He touches her shoulder.

She tumbles forward, one hand on my shoulder, the other scrabbling for purchase in my lap.

"Oh, Jesus!" I steady her by the arms. "What's happening?"

She blinks, head drooping.

"Goodness, I'm sorry." Her voice is muted, as if she's speaking into a pillow. She pats my hand. "I don't know what came over me. It must be a senior thing. Try not to get old, sweetie."

But that's exactly what I'm trying *to* do.

"Are you sure you're fine?" Brian asks. "Here, take my seat."

He hovers like a worried parent, but she waves him away.

"It's okay, dearest," she insists. "Thank you. I'm just a little tired."

Her gaze snaps to me so quickly I jerk back as if slapped. The sudden clarity in her eyes unsettles me.

Then, just as quickly, she looks away.

Smiling at Brian she goes in for another hug. "I best be going. It's good seeing you again, kid. Come by the shop and see me sometime."

"Will do that."

She turns to me, no longer meeting my eyes.

"Again, nice meeting you, Hazel. Take care, now."

She walks away.

Brian sits back down, the bench squeaking as he does so.

"Well, that was weird. I sure hope she's okay. I haven't seen her in a long while," he explains.

"She seemed nice."

"She was my favorite teacher. The best. I was so lucky to have her." He sighs, contentedly patting his stomach. "Dessert before you leave?"

"I should really get going."

I had been eyeing up the cakes in a glass display, but it's clear I've overstayed.

"Thanks for this," I say.

"You're welcome. I hope it was good enough to tempt you out again soon."

He seems really nice and I don't want to hurt his feelings, but it's time to put him in his place.

"You know I'm only here for a couple more days, right? Sorry, I'm not looking for anything romantic or physical or otherwise."

"Sure. I just had to take a chance. We don't get pretty girls like you through here every day. So I had to try. Hope we're okay."

"We're cool."

I offer to pay for my meal but he declines.

"Lunch was my suggestion. I invited you. It's the least I can do."

I raise my hand in a small wave.

"Bye, Hazel. Drive safe. The roads get slick."

Why does he have to be so cute? I got out in the nick of time. This is one complication I don't need in the mess that is my life.

Eleven

He wasn't kidding about the roads. The rain turns to sleet on the long stretch of highway, the ice leaving slick patches on the asphalt. On several occasions, the truck veers over the yellow line. I barely know how to drive, let alone in this kind of weather, and my arms ache from the strain of steering against such precarious conditions. Do I speed up to get it over with? Or slow down for better control? I press the brake, wanting control, but instantly learn that's the wrong thing to do. The truck skids at an angle and I course correct, too quickly, and now I'm skidding the other way. What do I do? My head's fuzzy with panic. I pull straight again and thankfully the truck responds. Okay, slow and steady, no slamming on the brakes.

Going uphill is the worst, though. I squint through the yellow headlights to better see the curves in the road. One wrong slip of ice and I'll be over the edge, tumbling down the mountain, smashed by ancient trees that have withstood worse in their time on Earth.

It takes a lifetime to reach the inn.

The hiss of ice fills my ears as I run to the door, shopping bags in hand, careful not to slip on the steps.

I fumble with the keys, my fingers tingling from the cold.

Skippy's waiting for me inside the door, and he licks my hand happily after I've shut it.

I turn on a light – though it's only three-thirty in the afternoon, it's become very dark.

I carry the bags into the kitchen and start putting away groceries.

Then I tackle the mouse traps. They're the old-school type that snap with the lightest touch. I smear them with peanut butter as instructed, cock them, and strategically place them around the inn, including the attic. Let's hope it'll do the trick and stop any crazy sounds from keeping me awake at night.

I close the attic hatch, watching it settle back into place in the ceiling.

I dust myself off, feeling accomplished.

Still full from lunch, I make a cup of hot chocolate and settle onto the Marshall's bed with a DVD. I could use a laugh, so I've chosen a dumb comedy to take the edge off.

Just after the opening credits, a bang rings out upstairs followed by a skittering sound overhead.

I grab the remote and lower the volume, listening.

Rapid thumping, directly above my head, like someone running in place – eight beats in a row.

The ceiling rattles and I'm sure a mouse couldn't do that.

Skippy's been cooped up for hours – he's probably just messing around. I should let him outside. That dog has endless amounts of energy; if I could bottle some, I could sell it and make my money problems disappear.

A whimper comes from the floor to my right.

I look over and see Skippy curled up next to the bed. Has he been there this whole time?

I glance at the ceiling. Not again. This can't be happening again.

Uneasiness growing in my belly, I force myself upright. Despite my numb legs, I go investigate, steeling myself for what I might find.

I check the traps on the first floor. They're all in place, undisturbed.

I creep up the stairs, trying to soften my footsteps. If there's an animal, I want to catch it in the act – not that I'd know what to do if that happens, but I'll figure that out later. I reach the landing.

At the top of the stairs, I flick on the hall light.

A shadow darts across the wall at the end of the hallway, near my room.

I scramble backward, hunching my shoulders, gripping the rail for balance. I sweep my gaze from side to side, trying to catch whatever it was that moved.

I look up and my heart forgets to beat.

The attic door hangs wide open, the ring pull swinging back and forth.

I squeeze my eyes shut.

No. There's no way.

I slowly open my eyes, but there's no question about it. The ladder is still folded up on itself, but the attic has definitely been opened. There's no way a mouse did that.

Which can only mean one thing – there's someone else in this house with me.

Twelve

I 'm not alone.

My arms go numb at the thought.

My mouth sours, and my whole body feels mushy with dread.

Slowly, I slink back down the stairs as quietly as I can. In any other circumstance, I would call 911. I *should* call 911. But if I do that, they'll want my name. Identification. A statement. And then it might make the news. It could send my whole plan into a downward spiral. I'd be too easy to track from here. But what if there's an ax murderer lurking around, ready to hack me into fun-sized pieces?

What if *he's* found me, looking for revenge?

Somehow an ax murderer would be preferable.

My breath comes ragged as I reach the living room. Ducking behind the far side of the couch, I debate my options. I could run to the truck and get as far away from here as possible. But then what? Where can I go? Besides, the weather conditions are worse now than before – I'd skid on the ice and wreck for sure. And how much time would I let pass before coming back? What if the intruder simply makes himself at home, eating my ramen and watching my movies, comfy and content to wait for my return?

I press a fist to my forehead, swallowing a sob.

I strain to hear the telltale footsteps of someone approaching. Silence.

Oh my God, he's waiting patiently for me to come out. That's what I'd do if I were a killer. Let the victim come to their own demise. Save a lot of hassle and effort. There's no way in hell I'm going out there. But how long should I wait? My stiff muscles cramp, frozen with indecision.

I crane my neck around the edge of the sofa. I don't see anything.

Skippy wanders in, seemingly unbothered by anything.

I sit up a little straighter.

He goes to his doggy bed in the corner, scratches at it, and curls up on top, closing his eyes.

If there were a person in here, Skippy wouldn't be so chill. He wouldn't be upset either, but he'd definitely befriend the newcomer.

Cautiously, I stand, listening for unusual sounds. I let out a shaky breath. Maybe I'm overreacting. Maybe I hadn't closed the hatch completely and it simply weighed itself down, opening of its own accord? I rack my brain, trying to remember if I actually saw it snap closed. I really thought that I had. I remember a sense of accomplishment when it did, having checked something off the to-do list before settling in with a movie.

That's when it hits me. The smell. It's back again. Nail polish, sharp and tangy and sour. I shake my head. I can't let it get to me. Not this time. But the scent doesn't go away like it usually does. If anything, it gets stronger. Thick and heavy, like walking into a busy nail salon. I bury my fear so deep I almost can't feel anything at all and start looking for the source. I can't ignore it. It's so strong now, it has to be coming from somewhere.

It doesn't take long to find it.

In the hallway, on the wall beneath the deer heads, are streaks of pale blue. Wet and glistening in the sconce light, written in nail polish, the word "DON'T." Underneath that, at a funny angle, the word "go."

Don't go. Don't . . . go. Is something in this house trying to tell me something? Trying to keep me here? It's the opposite of every horror movie I've ever seen. In those, the ghosts are always saying "get out" or "leave." But "Don't go?"

The polish bottle is nowhere in sight. I half expect it to come rolling toward me like it did before. But nope – the inn is quiet and still.

Wildly, I check around myself but see nothing else out of the ordinary. Going through each room and doing a thorough search proves that I am, after all, alone in this house. That doesn't stop the creepy sensation of being watched. I want nothing more than to hop in the truck and speed like a demon from hell out of this place, but it will be safer to wait until daylight and let some of the ice melt off the roads.

Fetching the large knife from the kitchen, I call Skippy to come with me to Raina's bedroom, where I lock the door from inside. I check there are no cracks in the curtains and pat the mattress to encourage Skippy up onto the bed with me. I wrap my arms around his furry neck, and he licks at my hair. His solid warmth is calming and reassuring.

"You're staying with me down here tonight, boy."

This time I don't feel the slightest bit weird about being in Bob and Raina's bed. It is what it is. I force myself to watch the movie, but it's difficult when even the slightest sound of the house settling or the radiator kicking on makes me jump and takes my attention away from the shenanigans on the screen.

When the movie is finished, I watch infomercials well into the night, unable to sleep.

Thirteen

Monster and I hung out for a week before I finally asked about his name.

We sat on the curb outside Skeeter's while he lazily sucked on a cigarette. I pretended the smoke didn't bother me and held my breath each time he exhaled.

"So, like, how'd you get it?"

My timid voice embarrassed me.

The moon, a thumbnail, dangled in the twilight sky above us. Steam rose from the asphalt parking lot before us as the temperature dropped. Goosebumps prickled my arms, and I rubbed them to bring back the warmth of the day.

"Your name," I prompted. "Were you, like, really into Halloween as a kid or something?"

At that, he laughed, a quick barking sound that ended in a coughing fit. He spit on the ground and took another drag, waving his cigarette at me.

"You're funny, Tea. Halloween. Pshh."

I didn't think it was that funny, but I laughed anyway.

"So then, where'd you get it? Your parents couldn't really have named you Monster."

"They didn't." He paused. "Sure you wanna know? It might scare you."

I pulled my shoulders back. "I'm not afraid of anything."

"That so?"

I nodded.

He lifted his eyebrows, finished his cigarette, and flicked the remains into the parking lot.

He kissed me, long and hard. My brain went fuzzy with pleasure, and I let myself forget about my question as our lips explored each other in the yellow glow of a streetlamp.

He never did tell me. But I understand now. Early on in our relationship people hinted at his darker side, but I thought it was all exaggeration. You know how people like to gossip and build things up to be bigger deals than they actually are. But the first time I saw him punch someone, the air hissed from my lungs as if I'd been on the receiving end of his curled knuckles. Which is funny because when it was my turn, my breath got caught somewhere behind my sternum, as trapped as my dignity.

* * *

The sun shines cheerfully in the morning, burning away the crust of ice and fear that blanketed the Keystone property overnight.

Opening the door, I take in the misty steam of warming earth as Skippy runs past me into the yard. The air, thick with the scent of damp vegetation, coats the back of my throat with a black licorice tang. I've come outside to check the weather conditions, ready to leave if safe. I tap the ground with the toe of my boot, and the sheer layer of ice cracks like burnt sugar and melts instantly into the softening ground. Through a fog of exhaustion, trance-like, I wander over to the garden, cracking ice along the way.

In the terror of yesterday, I completely forgot about tarping the plants. Obviously, there were more pressing things on my mind. The little buds were ravaged by the ice and are now matted to the ground, their wilted baby leaves looking like cooked spinach. I kneel, cold damp seeping into my jeans, and touch one with my fingertip. It's slimy and limp.

Raina's gonna kill me.

I'm too tired to care.

I stare at the plants, my vision blurring with fatigue. I can't bring myself to go back inside. How I managed to get through the night, I'll never know. All I wanted was to leave. But in the gentle light of day, it's harder to justify grand theft auto from an elderly couple, even after the events of last night. The strangest thing is, this morning the message in nail polish was gone. The wall was clean and bare as usual. No odor, no stains on the wood. I can't explain it. So I'm even more confused than before. How do I make sense of this?

The sound of crunching gravel draws my attention, and I turn to see a station wagon pulling up the drive. My heart picks up speed as it approaches and parks in front of the house. I stand up from my kneeling position with a grunt and shield my face as the rising sun pierces the tree line. Who is that? I'm not expecting anyone – at least, not anyone with good intentions. Turning to grab Skippy and duck behind the house, I find that not only is he bounding toward the car, tongue lolling, but I've already been seen.

Behind the windshield, the driver raises a hand. The door opens and a pair of rain boots touch the ground.

Oh no, what if it's a spontaneous guest seeking vacancy? I should tell them we're closed, nothing more to it. I can do that.

I brush my hands on my jeans and roll my shoulders back, projecting confidence as I stride over to the car, meeting them head-on.

When the visitor comes fully into view, I stop in my tracks.

The woman from the diner – Mrs. Rhodes, was it? – comes forward, waving, her multi-colored patchwork skirt flapping in the breeze.

What is she *doing* here? My skin prickles like a shield made of tiny knives, already on the defensive.

"Well, hello!" she calls as she approaches. "Sorry to call un-announced. I'm not interrupting anything, am I?"

"Uh. No. Not exactly."

"I was hoping I could speak with you a moment, that is, if you don't mind. It won't take long, I promise."

I tilt my head, contemplating her request. This woman I met for all of two minutes suddenly wants a chat?

I struggle for a response and her laughter replaces my silence.

"I understand, darlin'," she says. "I'd be wary if I were in your shoes as well."

What's that supposed to mean?

"Please. I do feel it's urgent." She looks around. "Aren't many cars. Slow season, isn't it?"

She's an old woman. What harm could she possibly do?

"Actually," I say, "the inn's closed up right now. Just while the Marshalls are gone."

Her brow creases.

"Ah, that makes more sense. No offense, sweetie. I just can't see Raina leaving her business to anyone but Raina. Shall we go in?"

She nods as if answering her own question and walks toward the entrance.

I hesitate.

She touches the handle and turns to look at me, bushy eyebrows rising like a theater curtain. Her face softens. "Ah," she says. "Is there . . . a problem?"

If only she knew. I shake my head and reach out with my hand, palm up. "Be my guest."

I don't know what I'm expecting when we step over the threshold. Another message? More thumping?

Inside, she slips off her coat and drapes it on the rack.

I keep mine on. It's silly, but right now it's like a comfort blanket, a symbol of protection.

"You said this will only take a minute?" I remind her.

"And it will. I'm just getting comfortable first. When you're my age, you'll understand that comfort is everything. Now, you wouldn't happen to have some tea, would you?"

I stare, incredulous. "Uh, I think so."

"Wonderful."

A beat passes.

"I'll just, uh, go make some," I say.

I venture into the kitchen, silently mouthing "oh my God." Who is this woman and what does she want?

I plop two tea bags in mugs, fill them with water from the sink, and shove them in the microwave for thirty seconds. They don't need to be hot. They just need to be done.

I find her in the living room, settled back on the worn couch, looking around with squinty eyes that soften when she sees me.

"Thanks so much," she says when I hand her a lukewarm mug. Her hands are weighed down with rings of all sizes, gemstones, and colors, and they clink against the ceramic when she wraps her fingers around it. To her credit, she doesn't complain about the lack of temperature.

I take the armchair across the room, looking back and forth. Nothing weird has happened since coming back inside, and maybe it won't with a visitor as a witness. I'm not sure if that's better or worse.

"I know this must seem awfully impolite," she says. "I debated whether I should even come. It's just that I have this pressing sense of urgency."

"Urgency about what?"

She leans forward, placing her mug on the coffee table. Her hands clasp over her knees.

"I have something I need to explain, and I won't blame you if you don't believe me. I'm quite used it."

I swallow.

"What is it?" I ask.

"Well, to jump right in, I have a gift."

"For who?" I'm genuinely confused.

She chuckles softly. "Not that kind of gift."

I catch her meaning and make an "O" shape with my mouth.

"You mean like a psychic?" I ask.

"Like a *medium*, yes. I can sense spirits, auras, and have intuition regarding a person's life path."

Is she for real? "Okay. Sorry, why are you telling me this again?"

Her eyes darken. She blinks and shakes her head.

"When we met yesterday, I felt a disturbing sense of unease. There's no easy way to say this, but there's a darkness around you, following you, and you need to be careful. There are forces at work here that are out of your control."

"What?"

She shakes her head again, her glasses slipping a bit further down the bridge of her nose.

"I'm sorry to come to you like this. Ordinarily, I don't speak up unless a client seeks me out for a reading, but I'm concerned for your wellbeing, young lady. Brian clearly has an attraction for you, so any friend of his is a friend of mine, and I wouldn't consider myself a good friend if I left you unaware of your current, shall we say, situation."

"I'm not totally sure I believe in this voodoo stuff." Although recent events are skewing me otherwise.

"Trust me, darlin', it's not voodoo, or witchcraft. This is something without a name. I've been gifted and I believe it's so I can help people during our earthly experience. Can I ask you something? Have you noticed anything unusual happening since you've arrived here?"

I think of the nail polish, the noises on the roof, the strange shadows, and the attic door swinging on its hinge.

"Maybe."

She considers her words, tapping her lips with her bejeweled fingers.

"I've known the Marshalls for a long time. But I don't know you. So, if it's not too nosy of me to ask, how is it you came into this precious position of caring for the inn?"

I draw myself upright.

"They placed an ad online. Why?"

"I wouldn't ordinarily ask. It's not my business. But if I have a sense that someone's life is endangered, I feel morally obligated to say so whether they want to hear it or not. That way they can make choices knowing everything to be considered."

My heart staccatos against my ribcage. Danger? What danger? Could she seriously know about Monster?

"What are you talking about?" I ask.

As freely as she's been speaking, the fact that she pauses, silent, sends my blood running cold.

I take the tea string and dunk the bag a few times to cover my nervousness.

She gazes down at her hands for a moment, and I imagine she's inwardly gathering strength. At last, when she lifts her eyes, I see they are red-rimmed.

"Dear . . ." She stops and clears her throat, delicately touching her wrinkled neck. "This place isn't safe for you. I feel very strongly that you should leave, immediately."

She looks up at the ceiling. I follow her line of sight, but there's nothing there and no sounds to be heard.

"Mrs. Rhodes?"

"Isabella, please."

"Um, okay. What are you looking at?"

Slowly, as if she's having trouble dragging her attention away from the ceiling, she meets my eyes.

"Nothing at all, if you heed my advice."

I take a noisy gulp of tea, the liquid slurping past my lips as I think of how to deal with this. She's obviously delusional and needs help. Right? But then, what does that make me?

I set the mug on the table with a clunk. "I can't leave. Not yet."

"The inn will be fine."

"Look," I say. "The instant the Marshalls come back, I'm out of here. The very second. So you have nothing to worry about."

"I fear it might be too late by then."

"Why?"

"The spirits here," she whispers. "And there are many. Your presence disturbs them, and they're very angry."

"*My* presence?" My gut twists into a knot. Are they ancestors of the Marshalls, maybe? Do they know I'm a liar, a thief? Are they looking out for them by tormenting me, scaring me into leaving? But the message said don't go. "So what do they want?"

Her answer is simple. "Revenge."

"For what? What did I ever do to them?"

"I'm not sure. They won't show me the details. I'm having a difficult time getting them to open up. Do you mind if I try?"

I shake my head.

She closes her eyes, palms forward on her lap, breathing deeply for a minute. Her eyes pop open. "They don't wish to communicate with me," she says. "They don't care about me. They're only interested in you. Please tell me you can make other arrangements."

"I can't."

"If I brought you proof, would that make a difference? I know someone that can help."

Before I got here, I wasn't sure I believed in ghosts. But now this feels all too real. I cover up my fear with anger and annoyance, even though I'm shaking inside my skin. I don't want her to know how much she's gotten to me. "Look, I don't even know you. And I don't know how things are done around here, but where I come from, people don't make decisions based on the hunches of strangers." I stand, trembling hands on hips. I don't even care if I'm being rude. The woman has overstayed her welcome. "I think you should leave now."

She stands as well, not breaking her gaze from mine.

She reaches into her purse, a handmade beaded thing, and pulls out a business card. She holds it up.

"I want you to call me if you experience anything . . . worrying."

"No thanks."

"Take it."

She thrusts the card at me, and I only grab it to make her leave faster.

"I'm serious. Don't hesitate, *Hazel*."

Did she just emphasize my name? If the spirits know I'm lying, does she know too?

I follow her onto the porch and stand there, arms crossed, as she gets into her car and drives away.

Despite my effort to appear strong, my body thrums like violin strings pulled too tight. Her visit has shaken me in some unexplainable way, and I wish she'd never come. I wish I'd never agreed to lunch with Brian. I wish I could go back in time, back to the innocence of childhood, and snuggle up with Mom beneath our big, fuzzy blanket we'd pull out for movie watching. But there's no point in wishing, especially about the past. It only leads to disappointment when the wish can't come true.

I turn back to the house.

The blinds in the living room window drop as if someone has been peeking out, watching us.

My feet feel like they're stuck in mud. I can't blink. I can't move my stare from the window, the blinds swaying gently.

It was Skippy. It had to be Skippy. Dogs do that, don't they? Watch as their potential for a ride goes away, whimpering, their cold, snotty noses making a mess on the glass?

The only thing is, the glass is clean.

I look at her card. It is plain white cardstock with a painted sun and moon, blue and yellow, thick brushstrokes giving it a childlike quality. It reads "Isabella Rhodes – intuitive spiritual healer, tarot readings" and lists an address and phone number.

I tap it against my palm, letting the sharp, cutting edge of the cardstock prick indignation and bravery back into me.

I march inside and close and lock the door behind me.

Fourteen

My bravery only lasts long enough to search Raina's closet for something heavier than my jacket. I settle on a thick, quilted number, buffalo checked in red and black. It smells strongly of sawdust, but it's not unpleasant. It's weighty on my shoulders, and already I can feel the material insulating my body. Maybe I just need a little break, away from the inn and away from people. Going stir-crazy indoors isn't helping anything, and some fresh air would be good. The weather is perfect for exploring the land, bears or not. Besides, don't people come here for the nature?

Let's see what it's all about.

Outside, the sun shines bright white now, blinding me. I wish I'd remembered my shades.

"Come on, Skip!"

He bounds ahead of me on the path leading beyond the shed, into the woods. There's a clear, trodden dirt path, so I'm not worried about getting lost. Crows caw overhead, beating their wings against the wind as they flock from tree to tree. I kick at the dirt beneath my feet, thinking of all the people who've walked this trail before me. Couples, probably. Holding hands, happily together. Maybe newlyweds. A twinge of sadness constricts my throat as I think about what I will never have. That will never be me. When I left Monster, I left all hope for a happy, normal life behind. I've been delusional for too long.

Skippy's far ahead of me now, barking at some animal I can't see. His legs are already smeared with dirt and mud. I wonder if I'll have to bathe him and how I would go about doing that. Do I put him in the tub? Hose him down outside? Is there a special shampoo made just for dogs, or will Raina's shampoo suffice?

I guess all of these questions mean I'm staying. At what point I decided, I'm not sure. I'm not happy about it, but what's the point of bailing now? I've made it this long; I can handle a few more days.

Beyond the standard outdoorsy sounds – birds chirping, twigs snapping beneath my feet – a new sound meets my ears, soft and melodic. It has a constant rhythm, a soothing effect.

I keep walking and the sound grows louder.

Eventually, I find the source – a river, cutting through the trees and rushing south. It probably feeds a giant waterfall somewhere. I'm drawn to the water and veer off the path to get a closer look.

Skippy finds his way to the bank, sniffing. There must be fish in there.

Huge, weather-beaten stones guard the edge of the river and I climb on top. Their cold and wet damp seep through my jeans as I get higher and higher.

I sit cross-legged on the tallest one, hugging myself for warmth.

The view is incredible. The sun glints off the rippling water, giving the appearance of sparkling diamonds. The water bubbles along until it reaches an island cluster of rocks not unlike the one I'm sitting on, where it picks up speed, bursting into a rush before sending a fine, misty spray into the air.

Watching the water, listening to the hush of white noise, I feel calmer than I have in months. Things have been harder than usual lately, with Mom's recent passing and Monster slowly spiraling out of control, constantly drunk on greed, power, and whatever substances he peddles.

And then, not long after I moved in with him, the betrayal.

I should've seen it coming, it's so obvious in hindsight.

One night, he wasn't at Skeeter's when we were supposed to meet. I waited ages, making small talk with the bartenders and pretending like I wasn't hurt. I kept texting him with no response. Eventually, I gave up and walked back to the apartment.

And that's when I found them: Mariah and Monster, locked in an embrace that put my time with him to shame. Mariah pulled back and looked at me from over his shoulder, her pupils blown, the whites of her eyes practically nonexistent. Her nose was dusted with the telltale powder, the kind I'd seen so frequently on him, now shared with my best friend.

So what did I do after that?

I ran.

I ran and hid, crashing at a mutual friend's house, and I didn't pick up my phone for two days. They both called me repeatedly (after they'd come down, of course). Mariah more so than him, blaming the drugs.

But I was done with her. With them. How could I forgive what they'd done? After upending the fractured remains of my life to be with Monster? I'd even missed Mom's funeral on his suggestion, implying that Mrs. Shapiro would be waiting afterwards to whisk me away to God-knows-where. I never got to say goodbye, and that's on him.

But loneliness is a funny thing. It wears you down and makes you think time spent with cheaters is better than nothing at all.

I went back, of course.

But things escalated.

Nightmares plague me of one horrific afternoon, not too long ago.

I'd been organizing our dresser, arranging my stuff so it would fit. Moving a few of his shirts aside, my fingers brushed something cool and hard beneath the cotton material. A gun, similar to the one my Mom had. Naturally, I freaked out and confronted him. Gesturing to the drawer, I asked, "What is it for?"

"What do you think it's for?"

He snatched it from its nest of clothes and twirled it.

I instantly realized my mistake in timing – he'd been drinking, among other things. It never seemed like much of a problem until after I'd caught him with Mariah. It was like he didn't have to hide his true self anymore.

My stomach sank.

"Huh?" he taunted. "What do you think? I know. Let's play a game. You guess why I have this, and if you're right, I'll treat you to some ice cream. But if you're wrong, we pull the trigger and see what happens. Cool?"

What? He had to be joking. It wasn't funny, but it couldn't be real.

"You're kidding."

"Does it look like I'm kidding?"

I glanced across the room at the door, wondering how quickly I could run.

He noticed.

Stars exploded in my head and I gasped.

Before I could react to the strike, his hand grasped my neck and squeezed. That's when he put the gun to my head. His lips set a hard line, and my face wet itself with tears.

"Now think, Tea. What do I have this for?"

I blubbered, "S-self defense?"

He made a sound like a buzzer. "Wrong! Now let's try your luck."

And he did it.

The horrible click of the trigger is a sound I will never, ever forget.

"Lucky strike," he said. "You get to guess again."

"No, please, I'm sorry, I didn't mean to pry . . ."

"Guess. Again."

He ran the barrel down my cheek and along my jaw, setting it beneath my chin.

"To . . . to hurt someone?"

My eyes were closed and I waited, but the click never came.

"Good guess," he said, pulling the gun away. "Remember that. Those who go against me get this in the end. Betrayal is the last thing they ever do."

I couldn't stop blubbering.

He put his arm around me and gave me a sloppy kiss.

"Relax, Tea! It's not even loaded. It's just a little fun!"

But it wasn't fun – it was terrifying, his laughter and the steel pressed against my skin.

Bullets or not, that game of Russian roulette was my breaking point. It wasn't safe anymore, and there was nothing I could do but run.

I pound my fist on the rock.

It doesn't satisfy my frothing anger, so I hit it again and again, the sound absorbed by the mineral.

Nothing breaks, nothing shatters or screams.

Not like people.

When I'm finished putting the hurt on the rock, the soft fleshy part of my fist is red and sore.

* * *

Tonight, it's time to do what I've been putting off for a week. Not having my phone has been a special kind of torture, but in a way, it was nice because I didn't have the inevitable assault of texts, calls, and notifications coming left, right, and center.

But it's time now.

Time to go through all those messages I've ignored. No phone means no news. No way of knowing what's happening back home. Not that I have a home anymore. Not that *everything* would be shared on social media. But still. Private messages and status updates keep my finger on the pulse of my neighborhood.

I go into the office where the Marshall's outdated computer sits waiting, its square-shaped monitor dark and unused. I turn it on and wait for it to come to life. As the machine rumbles a bit, waking up, I pick up a pen and tap it on the desk a few times. It's printed with the words "University of Denver" and an official looking red and white crest.

Huh.

Did Bob or Raina ever attend college in Colorado? Seems unlikely. One of their kids? But they never mentioned any children, did they? Maybe it got left behind by a guest.

Maybe it's none of my business.

My eyes fall on something glinting in the light, and my stomach lurches. The nail polish is right there on the desk, where I first saw it, despite not finding it anywhere in my search. It's still sealed tight around the edge, crusty with age. It hasn't been used in a long while, yet somehow the fumes keep wafting throughout the house, somehow a message was written in lacquer.

The monitor lights up, catching my attention. Using various combinations of the safe's lock code as a PIN, I breathe a sigh of relief when access is granted.

I bite my lip as guilt curls through me once again for breaking the rules.

I quickly pull up tab after tab and sign into my various social media accounts.

You know that expression about pulling teeth? This is more like wrapping a metal wire around your tooth and touching it to an outlet. Every private message sends a sharp zing of heat down my body, and as much as I'd like to stop this self-inflicted torture, a part of me feels like I deserve it.

My worst fear is confirmed: people are actively looking for me.

According to the police, I'm a missing child.

To the outside world, Monster's presented himself as the worried, dutiful boyfriend, worthy of pity and hope. "Please," he's typed. "The cops won't do nothing. It's up to us to find her, to keep her safe!"

The likes and comments roll in, a tidal wave of support. Thoughts and prayers are harmless, but others worry me. Some would say the hunters he's deployed are even better than the cops at finding missing people. They're loyal and fiscally motivated. They fill my inbox with messages that make me want to curl up into the fetal position. Nestled between the *where r u's* and the *are you ok's* lie the words I've been dreading most.

You can't hide, bitch.

U gonna pay.

And the simple promise from Monster himself: *I will find you.*

I might have left everything behind, but it doesn't erase the fact that he could still show up at the door, demanding his money.

With interest.

And not the cash kind.

He's gathered search teams, pockets of helpers that have been scouring neighboring counties and towns, all in the name of my safety.

If only they knew.

Should I leave a comment? It wouldn't be traceable, right?

My fingers graze the keyboard as I mentally compose a statement. If I tell them I'm fine, would they stop looking?

The internet disconnects.

I try pulling it up again to no avail.

My stomach sinks. Now I am truly cut off from the world.

The screen warps into a rainbow of jittery lines. The computer beeps once, a desperate cry for juice before going out completely.

Punching the power button does nothing.

Knowing full well it won't work, I slap the side of the box anyway.

The lights make a slight *pop* before swathing me in darkness.

I blink – there are no streetlamps or ambient light sources to provide a glow through the windows like back home. Nothing but inky blackness. My eyes provide a bright display of neon squiggles, desperate to make out shapes in the room.

I fumble around for the switch and flick it up and down.

No luck.

I make my way carefully out of the room and down the stairs. Slowly, hand along the wall, I get to the kitchen, where the flashlight already waits on the counter.

Shining the meager beam of light around, I look for the circuit breaker and eventually find it back in the office. I examine the switches, checking to see if they've been tripped. I ghost my fingers down the row of switches, and they all seem to be in place.

Did the bulbs simply burn out? No, that's absurd. Every single one just kicked simultaneously?

A warm glow appears in the doorway, attracting my attention. I look into the hallway and realize a light has turned on in the entry room.

Only one.

It pulses gently, as though taunting me with it.

Then a lamp in the living room. My toes curl as it brightens, and I swear my heart stops beating.

Soft light shines down the stairwell, indicating a lamp is on upstairs too.

Goosebumps erupt down my arms. It takes everything inside of me to remain calm. There has to be a logical explanation for this.

Thumping down the stairs.

Footsteps, heel to toe.

But I'm looking right at the steps – and no one's there.

The sound stops.

Then, whimpering.

I look down to find Skippy next to me, head low, sniffing the ground. He makes high keening noises, clearly distressed. Without warning, he startles and zips off to his dog bed, cowering.

What's possessed him?

Ooh, not a good thought.

I didn't think I believed in ghosts or supernatural beings. But I'm running out of explanations for all the weird stuff that's been happening.

The lights turn on again and the silence returns.

Screw the money. It's not worth it to stay here. I can find another place to hide. Heart pounding, I go back into the office and power on the computer. It works normally like before. With swift fingers, I browse for more ads like the Marshall's. House-sitters needed, pet-sitters too, places I can stay free of charge and make a buck while I'm at it. I'll hitchhike like before. No problem.

I'm clicking on random towns, wondering just how far away they are, when a low growl rumbles in my ear.

I whip toward it, eyes wide.

Nothing.

But I heard it, right *there*. It was right next to me.

I shoot up out of my seat and power walk to the living room to check on Skippy. He's curled up on his bed and raises his head curiously. It wasn't him.

I can't blame this one on the dog.

And that can only mean one of two things: my paranoia has finally gotten the best of me and I am truly going bat-shit crazy, or this place is freaking haunted.

Fifteen

By morning, once more, I'm a wreck. After the phantom growl, I raided Raina's closet and put on the thickest, warmest looking tops I could find. Digging in her dresser, I borrowed three pairs of wooly socks and pulled them on, layering them like cake, planning to walk as far as possible until I could hitch a ride. But then Skippy, curious about my flurry of activity, nudged my hand with his cold, slimy nose and my heart crumpled. He didn't deserve to be left behind, all alone. How would he eat? Who would let him outside? But I also couldn't stay in the house. So, with a long sigh that turned into a frustrated groan, I gathered as many blankets from the bedrooms as I could carry and went out to the truck for a cramped, cold night of restless slumber.

Now I have a painful crick in my neck, a cramp in my leg, and surely a bruise the size of a plum from the gear shift pressing into my hip all night, but as the sun rises and pinkens the atmosphere, my body finally melts into sleep.

It doesn't last long.

Something touches me, waking me up. Pressure on my head, moving down my neck. It repeats. And again. It feels as if someone is stroking my hair, but that can't be.

I shut my eyes tight and hold my breath. My heart rattles against my ribcage, desperate to break free of its prison.

Another stroke.

I jerk wildly upright, banging my hand on the steering wheel.

Predictably, nothing is there, but I definitely felt that.

"What *are* you?" I shout.

When met by silence, I'm torn between fear and feeling ridiculous. Maybe I'm so deprived of sleep and human contact that my body's creating sensations just to stave off boredom. The brain can play powerful tricks – I remember that from psych class. If I'm losing my mind, would I even be aware of it?

I open my eyes, hoping to catch movement or *something* that can explain the things I'm hearing, smelling, and now feeling. I rub the condensation from the truck windows, peering out.

Several minutes pass, but, as usual, there is nothing.

Birds trill, greeting the day, unaware of anything strange or scary in the world. I listen to them chirp their ignorant bliss, pretending for a moment that everything is good and safe, no matter what my mind decides to conjure up.

Then, pressure. On my neck. The weight on my esophagus, pressing down.

My eyes pop open wide and dart around, seeing nothing, but still the pressure's there, increasing with every second.

I gasp unsuccessfully for breath. It's starting to hurt.

I bat at the air, desperate for relief. I can't move my head, let alone sit up. What's happening to me? It feels like someone's trying to snap my neck. Am I dying, suffocated by an invisible threat? How can I fight what I can't see?

Then, just as suddenly as it started, it stops. Its crushing hold on me eases as if it never happened. I sit bolt upright, coughing, catching my breath.

My eyes water, whether from the strain or just plain old tears, I can't say. This has upped the ante. Something's not right.

Electrified by the moment, it suddenly feels as if I've had ten espressos. I need to get out of here.

Now.

Weighing the pros and cons of being in public versus being choked by a spirit – town wins by a landslide.

Sixteen

I walk up and down Main Street with one eye over my shoulder, heading for Mrs. Rhodes' shop. I couldn't leave the inn without some sort of plan. I'll have to be quick to avoid being seen. Those messages replayed in my mind even as I rifled through the trash for her business card and called to set up a meeting.

The sun burns holes through the clouds, scattering warm patches of light onto the sidewalk like a checkerboard. Most of the storefronts are boarded up, abandoned perhaps for places with more foot traffic. One week ago, I never believed a town this small even existed. And unless they get some more enticing shops here, people will continue to stay away. Maybe the locals like it that way. I know that, for now, I like it that way too.

Wait a minute.

I stop in front of a store.

A light shines through the narrow pane of glass, soft yellow, warm and inviting. Painted on the window in curly white script is the name "Crystal Spirits."

I've found her.

Opening the door strikes my senses with the sweet, heady scent of incense. Too much smoke and fragrance in too little space. The store is not fancy. Dark water stains creep down the peeling wallpaper, and there's not much in here except for a couple of bookshelves and worn armchairs with mismatched fabric. I notice only one of them holds actual books. The rest are stacked with displays of crystals, candles, boxes of incense, and herbs. There's a card table in the corner with a tented sign offering psychic – excuse me, *intuitive* – readings. But there's no one here, and it's dead quiet.

"Hello?" I call out. "Mrs . . . Isabella?"

A nondescript curtain against the back wall swooshes aside, the rings clattering against each other to reveal another room and Isabella coming out of it.

She smiles, obviously pleased to see me.

"It's nice to see you again, Hazel."

When she uses the name, my heart prickles with sadness and shame.

"I'm glad you're here." She bustles around the room, tidying up. "Won't you sit? I can make us some tea. It's so cold today, isn't it? Tea will warm you right up. I make it with spices – nature's wooly pajamas for the inside." She winks. I'd rather a hot chocolate but I don't say that. I'm not in a position to be choosy these days.

She takes my arm and guides me to a cushy chair.

Sinking into its plush softness, I worry I won't be able to stand back up without assistance.

"Won't be a moment."

She disappears through the curtain, the fabric fluttering behind her. The hum of an electric kettle meets my ears.

A few minutes later, she returns with a tray weighted down with a teapot and dainty teacups. She hands me a cup on a tiny matching saucer, like something I imagine Victorian ladies would use. I have never been served tea this way, and I fear I'll drop it any second. The cup trembles a little, rattling on the plate, and I touch the handle to keep it still.

"It's herbal," she explains. "All organic. You want sugar? I've got some here."

"I'm fine, thanks. Are you, um, going to read my leaves or something?"

Laughter bursts from her lips, a hearty sound, and I grip my cup to avoid spilling.

"No!" She wipes her eyes. "Gracious! Read your leaves. Good heavens above, you're a funny one, you are."

Funny? She can't be surprised by my question, based on our surroundings and what she's told me about herself. But I smile and nod, playing along. It's helped to break the ice anyway. I blow across the top of my cup, sending the rust-colored liquid rippling away from me. Instead of tasting it, though, I put it back on the saucer and take a deep breath.

Better to just dive in.

"I've been thinking about what you said yesterday," I venture, then pause. How do I admit that I was wrong and that I do need her help?

There's no judgement in her eyes. No gloating, no, "Yes, I knew you'd be in touch, you skeptical young lady," and for that I'm relieved, but it doesn't make it any easier to get the words out.

"When you said that something dark was following me," I say in a rush, "what exactly did you mean? Can you explain?"

She sighs, stirring her tea and taking a sip before responding.

"As I've told you before, I'm intuitive. I sense things that others cannot see. Things that, maybe, humans aren't meant to see. Do you know what an aura is?"

"Like, those lights in the sky? The ones over Alaska?"

She chuckles, her laugh lines deepening.

"That's the aurora borealis. No, an *aura* is a kind of energy field that each one of us radiates, invisible to the naked eye. It's your own personal, spiritual thumbprint."

"Oh." I mull this over. "And you can see this?"

She leans forward. "I can."

"So . . . you can see mine. Like, right now?"

She nods, never breaking her gaze.

"Yours is murky, dear. There's something latched on to you, something that only you can shake off."

Does she mean Monster?

She continues.

"But it isn't so much your aura I wanted to speak to you about than that place you're staying in . . ."

"Why? What about it?"

"You've been experiencing strange things, yes?"

I shift in my seat, the upholstery whispering against my jeans.

"I might've."

She sighs again.

"I've known the Marshalls a while but had never set foot on their property until yesterday. When I did, a force hit me, unexpected. Initially, when I first met you, I saw things. Things that didn't make sense. Heartbreaking things."

Despite my better judgement, I urge her to continue.

"I sensed . . . fear. Pain. And sorrow, loneliness. A desire to hide. No, that's not quite right. More of a *need* to hide."

I sip my tea to cover my surprise. She picked up all that just from looking at me?

"And that inn . . ." She shudders, eyes closing as if to shut out the memory of what she sensed.

"What?" I ask. "What about it?"

She shakes her head. "The Marshalls are your employers. I shouldn't say."

"Please tell me. I'm staying there; I have to know if something isn't right."

She looks at my neck, and I wonder if the choking left a mark. In my haste, it didn't occur to me to check.

"Horrific things," she whispers. "Twisted, unnatural, per-verse. I wish – I never would have imagined what I felt when I walked through that door."

Curiosity unfolds inside me, like a cat waking up from a nap – uncurling, stretching, and tasting the air with a yawn.

"They're likely not aware of the atmosphere inside their home. They mustn't be, because if they knew, I doubt they'd stay. Although, never underestimate the power of roots. It's been Raina's family home and business for generations. Not many people have that claim these days. And Raina's a tough cookie, not easily rattled. Not to mention – and I hope you won't think ill of me for saying this – they aren't exactly the most open-minded couple I've ever known."

"So what's causing the, uh, 'bad feeling'?"

"As I said before, there are restless, angry spirits roaming that property." She shrugs. "I'd have to spend some time in there to learn the details, and I don't think Raina would appreciate such a thing. Quite conservative, that woman, bless her."

I hesitate, then reach in my pocket for the bottle of nail polish. She tilts her head curiously when I hand it to her. The instant the glass touches her skin, her face falls, mouth turning down into a deep frown. Her eyes droop with sadness. "Oh," she breathes. "Oh my."

"Does this mean anything, do you think? It's kind of been . . . bothering me."

She nods, rolling the bottle with her thumb. It clinks against her rings.

"I can see that."

"Really?"

"Yes. I think I can see exactly how this object has been upsetting you. Phantom smell, correct? Displacement?"

"Yeah, and markings on the wall too. I don't know how it's happening."

She puts the bottle on the table and doesn't look at it again. "If you wish, I will dispose of it properly so it doesn't bother you again."

"Can you do that?"

"Yes. But I would need the Marshall's permission, seeing as it came from their property."

"Oh."

The door squeaks open, signaling a customer.

We look up as a tall, slim woman walks into the store. Everything about her is long and straight, from the chestnut-colored hair on her head to the rigidness of her spine, the perfectly angled crow's feet around her eyes to the clean lines of her khaki pants. She zeroes in on a shelf as if she knows exactly what she came in here for and where to find it.

Isabella pats my knee.

"Would you excuse me just a moment? Abigail! How are you?"

She walks over to the woman and gives her one of those hugs that I imagine feels like safe harbor in a storm, made of tight squeezes and gentle rocking the way a mother sways with her child.

The woman, Abigail, returns the hug, but doesn't smile.

"We're out of sage," Abigail says matter-of-factly, turning back to the shelf. Just as she reaches for something, Isabella gently stays her hand.

"We have a new blend," she tells her, letting go of Abigail's hand. "It's still your favorite sage from New Mexico, only it's bundled with lavender to promote positivity. I think you'll like it."

"I think I'll stick with what works. But thanks."

"Sure, fine. How's Jake doing?"

Abigail perks up.

"Really great. Doing really well."

"That's wonderful!"

Abigail's lips shift into what must be her version of a smile. It's more like a grimace.

I'm eavesdropping so hard that I stop concentrating on my tea. The cup rattles again, sloshing tea over the handle and drawing their attention.

"Sorry," I say, feeling sheepish.

Isabella waves a hand.

"Don't be silly. Napkins are on the tray. Have you met Abigail yet? I bet not, you haven't been here long enough. This is Abigail Osbourne, she was a fellow teacher at Fox Valley Elementary. Abi, meet Hazel. I'm sorry, dear, I don't believe I ever learned your last name."

"J-Jacobs."

Shit. I didn't mean to blurt out my real surname.

"Hi." Abigail nods curtly before turning back to the shelf. She grabs four bundles of what must be sage and then addresses Isabella.

"These will do for now."

"Sure, honey."

Isabella rings her up, giving me sidelong glances. She places the sage in a bag, but before handing it over to Abigail, she says, "Would you mind holding on for just one moment?"

Isabella lowers her voice to just above a whisper, and I strain to hear their conversation.

"I think Hazel could benefit from Jake's services. You know how he's always looking for a new case? Well, here's a potential for him, right now."

Abigail's small brown eyes remind me of a teddy bear's – dark, glossy, and all-seeing. She pins her gaze on me, and we consider each other in silence.

"I don't know," she finally says, twisting a yellow wedding band around her finger. "He's been so busy lately, I don't see how he'd find the time to do it, frankly. Daytime is impossible, and I like him to be at home, with me, in the evenings."

Isabella gives her a reproachful look.

"Now, Abi. We've talked about this. If you love someone, let them explore their passion. He will come back to you."

She comes around the counter and grasps both of her arms.

"Look at me. This girl needs help. Jake can do that. We both know he has the skills. He's forward-thinking, logical. Keeps a cool head under pressure and that's exactly what she needs. Right, Hazel?"

I look back and forth at them.

"Honestly, I have no idea what you're talking about," I say.

"Oh, right." Isabella laughs. "Is it alright if I tell her?"

If the woman doesn't want her husband helping me, that's fine. I stand up and bring the teacup to Isabella, placing it in her hands.

"Sorry, I don't think so. I've been gone long enough already. Thanks for the drink, though. I've gotta go."

"But Jake can help you!"

Abigail says, "Leave her be. He shouldn't do this anyway. It's been a while, and he might be rusty."

"Now you know that's not true. Please, Hazel. Stay."

Abigail presses her lips together, and that annoys me. Here we go again – someone telling me what I can and can't do.

I make fists at my sides.

Why does that get the best of me? Why do I feel the need to prove that I can make my own choices, regardless of consequence?

"Okay," I say, standing firm in my decision. I will at least hear what Isabella suggests. Besides, who knows what weirdness is waiting for me back at Keystone?

Isabella claps her hands together and grins.

"Good. Good! I honestly believe Jake can help. He's a paranormal investigator – hey now, let me finish – he takes a very scientific and thorough approach. Braver than a beast in a blizzard too. You won't find him running screaming from the premises just because of a few dangly cobwebs."

I suck the inside of my cheek.

"A ghost hunter?"

"Paranormal investigator," Abigail snaps. "My Jake is very good at what he does. Professional."

"Does he have a website?"

"A private blog." She tilts her head. "But we don't just hand out the password all willy-nilly."

"This," Isabella says, "is a girl in trouble. The place where she's staying is showing signs of activity."

Abigail huffs. "And where is that?"

"Keystone Mill Inn."

Her eyebrows lift, crinkling her freckled forehead. "You're serious? That bed and breakfast up the hill?"

She considers while Isabella squeezes my shoulder.

"Okay," Abigail says. "Here's the deal. You'll come to our house for a meeting first. We'll see if he even wants to do it."

Isabella snorts.

"He'll want to, you can be sure of that."

"But no guarantees."

"Fine," I say.

She gives me her address and tells me to come by the next afternoon. I guess I'm really doing this. My body shivers as I remember the phantom hands around my neck, the panic, the fear.

As if sensing my distress, Isabella comes forward and places a warm hand on my shoulder. "Hold on one moment." She disappears behind the beaded curtain and returns with something cupped in her palm. "Black tourmaline," she says. "For protection. Please wear it."

I reach out for her hand and grasp a smooth, slithery chain. Pulling it up, silver catching the light, reveals an ink black stone dangling from the end. It's the size of my pinkie finger and shaped to a point at the tip.

"Need help?" Isabella moves forward, ready to assist.

"No, no, I got it." I put the chain around my neck and clasp it securely. It hangs heavy against my sternum, so very different from my initial pendant. Whether it does any good or not remains to be seen.

"Okay, um." I turn to Abigail. "I guess I'll see you tomorrow."

If I make it 'til then.

Seventeen

It was a long night waiting for creepy stuff to go down. Every creak had me on edge, expecting the pressure on my neck to return. But it never did. Around two in the morning, I thought I heard footsteps on the stairs, but I'm not certain. It wasn't until four I was finally able to get some rest.

Maybe Isabella's crystal actually worked.

I wake past noon.

In the bathroom, I examine my neck in the mirror, wincing at the pinkish-purple mark that spreads beneath my chin. It's shaped like a handprint. If I'm staying – for Skippy, and *only* for him – I need to get to the bottom of what's going on.

* * *

I'm on my way for the consultation with Jake Osbourne.

I pull the truck into a nice-looking neighborhood, cute but not too fancy, with lots of ranch style homes. Sprawling yards are occasionally dotted with a child's trike or football abandoned in the crunchy grass, just waiting for the warm season to be played with again. It's one of those older neighborhoods, where each house has its own distinct character, not like all the cookie-cutter boxes erupting in modern suburban unity.

I pull onto the cement driveway of address 212. It's a weathered blue clapboard house with Christmas lights still lining the gutter. Children's toys litter the lawn, and I wonder just how many kids Abigail and Jake have.

I walk up the stepping stone path to the front door, feeling nervous.

The doorbell trills when I press it.

The curtain in the window moves. Abigail's face appears briefly behind the glass, brown hair pulled back in a giant claw, a pinched expression on her pale face. She invites me inside, unsmiling.

"Have a seat." She gestures to a couch pushed up underneath the window with a ruffled valance. "He'll be home soon," she says, picking up toys and things from the living room floor. "You want a drink? A snack?"

Her words are friendly, but her tone is not. We're off to a great start.

"No thanks," I say politely. I'd like this to be as painless as possible.

I sit down and look around the room. There's an empty fireplace topped with framed photographs on the mantle. Abigail in a white wedding dress beams for the camera, arm clasped to a handsome man in a suit. That must be Jake. Other photos reveal a little boy, progressing from a chubby-cheeked baby to the stiffly posed school photos of elementary school. His blond hair, cut severely, frames a freckled face. His mischievous grin reveals a couple of missing teeth.

"That your son?" I ask.

Abigail nods, barely glancing at the photos, resuming her task of tidying.

I cross my legs. Awkward tension fills the air, thick and oppressive. My foot jiggles. I assume Jake gets home from work around four thirty, since that's the time Abigail told me to arrive. I open my mouth to ask what line of work he's in when a massive school bus roars up the street, stopping just in view of the window. It brakes, practically splitting my eardrums with its screech. I watch as kids file out of the bus, one by one, and scatter throughout the neighborhood like cockroaches.

The little boy from the photos comes dashing through the yard, stopping to kick a few dead leaves into the air. He mouths "hi-ya!" like a ninja, and another burst of leaves explodes into the air. He runs to the front door, schoolbag bouncing on his back, and noisily enters the room, stomping his feet, kicking off his shoes. They thud against the wall, and Abigail shouts "Hey! Neatly!" in an exasperated tone that suggests they have this conversation every day. He drops his backpack on the ground and starts pulling out binders and notebooks and loose papers that have been crumpled up inside without any care.

Abigail clears her throat. "We have a visitor," she says to him, hands on hips.

"It's okay," I tell her. "I don't mind."

He seems to have found what he was looking for – a composition notebook, the cover marbled in red and black. With one hand, he pushes his hair out of his eyes, and I notice a larger smattering of freckles across his nose that didn't come through in the pictures.

"Hi," he says. "I'm Jake."

I stare, dumbfounded. "Jake . . . junior?"

Raucous laughter. "That's funny."

I swivel my head to stare at Abigail. She crosses her arms over her chest, daring me to argue. But I have to question this. A kid? I was expecting her husband. From the way she and Isabella made him sound, I thought Jake was a fully grown, experienced man. Not a child kicking his shoes around. "What the hell?"

"Careful," Abigail warns. "Language. We don't swear in our house. Please respect that."

"Sorry, but . . . is this a joke?"

Jake plops down next to me on the couch, opening his notebook. "I hear you've got a spirit problem. Isabella told me some, but I need more details."

I am totally confused. "I'm sorry, I'm just a little . . . Mrs. Rhodes didn't say . . ."

"Oh, Isabella comes too 'cause she's a medium. She told you that, right?"

I shrug.

"The reason she's not here right now is because she doesn't like knowing too much in advance. Says it 'muddies her mind,'" he curls his fingers into air quotes, "and 'sways her senses.' But she likes to stay with me on investigations. For safety. And she told me you'd need hard evidence. So that's what I'm here for!"

I scratch my chin, picking at another stress pimple that's pressing through my skin. "Are you really a ghost hunter?"

"Paranormal investigator." He levels me with a gaze as piercing as his mother's, and there is no question that he is Abigail's son.

"Sorry," I concede. "Paranormal investigator."

"That's okay!" And he's back to flipping through his note-book. "People get it mixed up all the time."

"Um, don't mind me asking, but exactly how old are you?"

"Ten. My birthday was last week. We had a Batman theme party at the Sport House. It was so awesome!"

"Cool."

His smile melts as he skims his notebook. I peer over his shoulder and realize it's a list of questions. "I wrote them down in case I forget any," he explains, tapping the page with a Captain America pencil.

"Oh. That's very, um, thorough of you."

"I know. So can you tell me when the activity started?"

"Uh, well, I don't really know how long it's been happening. I noticed it about a week ago. But it seems to be happening more and more frequently now."

"Okay. That's normal. Things get ignored for so long that when hauntees finally realize they're dealing with the supernat-ural, they forgot exactly when it all began. Is there a particular time of day when the spirit is more active? Have you seen it? Heard it? What other kind of unexplained phenomena have you experienced? Don't worry, it's my first priority to rule out the paranormal. We'll need to go over each event in as much detail as possible to help find the root cause. Is there a particular location on the property where activity happens the most?"

He sounds like a little adult. I'm reluctant to admit that I'm impressed by his professionalism.

"The attic," I say. "Definitely."

"It's always the attic, right?" He laughs.

"Can I ask? How many of these investigations have you done?"

"This is my sixth. I started a little over a year ago. The first time almost doesn't count. It was kinda silly, and no one believed I could actually be serious. It was an old farmhouse. Mom didn't know what I was doing, I was with my friends. It was spooky. But my friends thought it was cool how super calm I was while they all freaked and ran away. I saw something, a flicker of a lady, but didn't have equipment to capture proof, unfortunately. So I asked Mom to let me go back, just me and her, with a camera. She thought I was crazy at first, huh, Mom?"

Abigail presses her lips together.

He flips about halfway through his notebook and shows me a page marked "EVIDENCE." Taped to it are photos, with dates and times written underneath. He points to the first one. "See this here?"

I lean forward. The image is of a darkened room, some kind of residence based on the furniture in the background. A heavy white mist blurs one side of the photo.

"That's the woman. I know it is. She came back to me for a picture."

"It's unexplained," Abigail interjects. "We had it analyzed at the photo lab."

"Yup." Jake grins. "You can see there are more pictures, orbs and mist and, ooh. This one's my favorite, see how it actually looks like a face peering around the doorframe? We didn't see it at the time. So cool, right? I have some audio too, but it's hard to hear."

"Wow." I have no other words. The images are weird and unsettling, especially the figure peeking out. It's not an obvious human, but there's clearly an outline of a face and eyes turned toward the camera. How is that possible? Will there be photographic evidence of what I've been going through? Audio? Video? I shudder to think what we'll see.

"Okay, so." He turns the pages back and consults his notebook again. "Ruling out structural causes, we'll take some pictures and leave recording devices in the attic. What else can you tell me?"

I talk about the sounds and the smells, the faucet and the shadows.

"Great. This is all really good stuff. Now, context. When was the house built?"

Hmm. Raina mentioned it that first day, didn't she? But for the life of me, I can't remember.

"A while ago. I don't know."

"No problem. How about the surrounding property? Anything historical, cemeteries that you know of?"

God, I hope not.

He looks at me curiously.

"What about running water? You're up the hill, right? That's where the river is, right, Mom?" He looks to Abigail for confirmation. "It feeds that waterfall my class visited last year. That's gotta be contributing. About how far is the river from your place?"

"Not too far, I think."

"But distance-wise, how far would you say it is?"

"Um . . . it's walkable."

He asks more questions along this vein before throwing his hands in the air, exasperated. "What do you mean you don't know? How can you not know? You explored the place, right?"

"Yeah, some."

"Well, I don't believe you."

We stare. Dust tickles my eyes and I blink.

"Look," I say. "Sorry I don't know the lay of the land, okay? I'm just house-sitting. Or technically, I guess, inn-sitting. Looking after the place while the owners are out of town. I'm supposed to be there for another week, but I can't if it's gonna continue like this."

He huffs. "Well, did you at least get permission from the owner?"

I squirm. "Yes?"

"I'll need to verify with them because I can't do a session without the owner's permission."

I'm sure Raina really wouldn't go for this. If I asked, she'd think I'm crazy and find someone else to take my place. I'd have to kiss my bonus goodbye. Not risking it. I sort through my wild thoughts, hatching a plan.

"I'll have her call you," I say. Only it will be me, pretending to be her. If I practice, I'm sure I can nail her voice.

We lie to kids all the time – at Christmas, during Easter. What's one more?

"Okay," he says. "Assuming you get permission, let me tell you how this works. I'm only allowed Saturdays, so we have to wait 'til then. I got homework and tae kwon do and stuff during the week."

Saturday is too far away. "I don't think I can wait that long. Things have gotten . . . serious."

"Oh, well, I don't know." He looks to Abigail, who sighs.

"Okay," she says. "Tomorrow, right after school, providing you get all your homework done. Anything to get this over with."

"Okay!" Jake lights up. "Here's how it works. We go through the house, and Isabella feels the energy when I track it with my devices. Mom'll wait in the car."

He rolls his eyes, probably annoyed having Abigail tag along. I don't blame him – she's kind of a killjoy. But we're safer in numbers, right? Especially with an extra getaway car.

"Then I go through our findings and give you the results. But I have to ask you something first."

He turns somber.

"You have to be very brave during the investigation. No screaming, no running away, no interfering with the evidence. Do you think you can do that? Can you be brave?"

This, from a ten-year-old.

"Yes," I say. "I think I'll survive."

"Good. Do you have any questions for me?"

"What do you charge for your, uh, services?"

He shakes his head. "No pay. Mom won't let me take money for it. It's considered practical experience. I should be paying you for the opportunity to flex my investigative skills."

If only.

We wrap up our meeting, me promising to have Raina call. We shake on it, his tiny fingers soft and warm in mine.

* * *

The fuel light blinks on, nearing empty. A few miles outside of Jake's neighborhood there's a little gas station, so I pull into a spot.

Walking into the shabby convenience store to pay with cash, I wonder if Raina will reimburse me for it. I'll have to be more careful about driving around in the future, just in case. I fuel up the truck, the heady fumes of petrochemicals making me dizzy.

A pickup truck turns into the lot, lining up along the other side of my pump. My heart flips at the sight of the familiar painted letters of Foley's Plumbing.

I glance at the driver's side window.

An old man I haven't seen before, with gray hair mostly covered by a greasy looking ballcap, taps his gnarled fingers on the steering wheel as someone steps out of the passenger side.

Oh, God. It's Brian.

He hasn't noticed me yet. He goes about setting up the pump, whistling through his teeth as I stand there watching. My hand cramps on the fuel trigger, squeezing hard.

He glances up and does a double take.

Waves.

I duck my head, pretending not to notice.

He props up the nozzle to fill his truck automatically and – oh Lord – comes around the tank.

"Hey," he says.

I nod in greeting, smiling thinly. "Hi."

"How are you?"

"Doing good." Awkward pause. "You?"

"Can't complain. That's my dad."

He jabs his thumb back toward the truck.

The old man waves, and I raise my hand.

"Seems nice," I say.

"He's the best." He rubs the back of his neck. "I'm surprised to see you. Thought you weren't ever coming down the hill again, from the way you spoke."

I shrug and look off in the distance. "Things change."

"I see."

I keep my gaze over his shoulder, trying to look indifferent, when something across the street stiffens me.

Standing on the side of the road is a figure next to a stopped car. He's backlit, so the details of his face are lost on me from this angle, but the height, shape, and the, well, *aura* scream familiarity.

On impulse, I step closer to Brian and angle my body so his acts like a shield. My shoulder brushes his chest, and I can physically feel his voice rumble when he asks, "Everything alright?"

I avoid looking up into his face. I can only imagine the confusion that must be written all over it.

"Mm-hmm."

I desperately want to peek and see if the figure is still watching me, but I dare not risk it. Instead, I lean into Brian's warmth and hope that the moment will pass without incident. *Please don't let him see me. Please, God.*

Brian raises his arms as if to encircle me but thinks better of it. He clears his throat.

"I was hoping maybe you would call me if you did come down. I enjoyed lunch with you and would like to take you for dinner, if you'd let me."

I lean around him just a smidge, checking for the person.

A long-haul truck growls past, blocking my view, and I chicken out, quickly hiding behind Brian again.

Dinner? Who can think about dinner at a time like this?

I sigh, finally meeting his eyes. Up close, in the cold, they sparkle as if dusted with sugar crystals. "Look, you're really nice, but I got things to deal with right now, and the timing couldn't be worse. Sorry. But thanks for asking."

"Well, if you change your mind, you know where to reach me. You seem real interesting, Miss Hazel. And you're pretty to boot."

My cheeks warm with a blush. "Well, thanks. But I . . ."

I can't deal with this right now.

I turn away, yank the nozzle from the truck, and sloppily shove it back in its holder, spilling gasoline all over my feet. I don't have time to go back inside for the change – in this case, the loss is worth the hurry.

"Whoa," he says. "Everything okay?"

"Sorry, Brian – I can't."

"Wait, hang on just a second."

"I really can't."

There's no time to hear his response.

I hop in the truck and turn the key so hard I fear it might snap. The engine growls in protest before puttering out.

Damn it.

My fingers trembling, I force myself to turn it more slowly, wishing I had the power of super speed.

I glance out the window toward the figure – but he's gone, car and all. Even still, I put my weight on the gas pedal. The tires take a second to gain traction, squealing, clearly not used to such demand. I'm aware I might be drawing more attention to myself – attention from Brian, attention from *him* – but I'm not taking any chances.

Eighteen

Pretending to be Raina is easier than I thought.

I block the number of the inn so it won't be identified by pressing star, six, and nine, just like I saw on TV once. When Abigail answers, I lower my voice to match the guttural tone of Raina's. Briefly explaining the situation, I tell her that Hazel has permission to do "whatever needs doin'" to feel safe and comfortable. It does the trick. These people must not know about signing contracts or anything if all it takes is someone's word to gain their trust. Lucky for me, though, it works.

* * *

The next afternoon, I find myself scrubbing at an unsightly mess on the living room rug.

"Skippy, you jerk," I grumble. "You couldn't just hold it in? Couldn't wait 'til we go outside?"

I sound mad but I don't really mean it. We've formed an attachment now that we hang out all the time. I lean back on my heels and examine my progress. I bet he's pawing at the shed door where I put him, whimpering his apologies from across the garden. I need him out of the way for what we have planned today. "Sorry, Skip. We got company coming."

Company. Do an aging medium and a ghost hunting child really count as company? And what if they actually find something? Part of me hopes they do, just to validate my experiences. But another, more logical, part of me dreads the idea. What possessed me to invite them over for a séance or whatever it is they do?

The ceiling creaks overhead, as if in response to my thoughts. Never mind. I remember now.

* * *

I open the door wide. "Hi, guys."

Isabella indicates Jake should go in before her, but he shakes his head. "Ladies first," he insists, hoisting his backpack over his shoulder.

"Why, thank you, young man," Isabella says with a smile, entering the room.

Her cheerfulness fades, and I wonder if she senses something.

She turns to me. "We need to prepare. You're welcome to join us, or you can wait outside in the car with Abigail."

I notice Jake's mother sitting primly in the front seat of a minivan, a book already propped open on the steering wheel. White clouds rising from the back of the van indicate the engine running, presumably for heat but maybe also for a quick getaway.

I close the door. "Should I lock it?" I ask, unsure of ghost hunting protocol.

"I want to say yes," Jake says, "because if the door were to, like, swing open or something, and we know it was locked, there's little question that's paranormal. But Mom wants 'easy access' if something goes wrong. She's a worrier."

"I would too, if I were a mom."

Jake tilts his face up to look at me. "You don't have any kids?"

"Nope."

"Are you married?"

A bark of laughter escapes from deep in my chest. "That would be a negative, kiddo."

"But you're old enough, aren't you? Do you have a boyfriend at least?"

The humor of the conversation evaporates as I remember why I'm here. "No," I say, after a moment's silence. "Not any-more."

"Oh. Well, I think dating is dumb anyway."

"Couldn't agree more."

Desperate for a change of topic, I ask him the first thing that comes to mind. "Does it bug you that your mom tags along?"

He shrugs. "Kind of. But when she's out there, she's part of 'control.' If she sees someone trying to mess with us, playing a prank or something, she can beep the horn and let us know."

"Has that happened before?"

He flushes and scratches his cheek. "Well, no, but it's good to be prepared. I take my findings, like, very seriously. Can't have any doubt. 'Cause then who will ever believe what I do is real?"

Fair point.

Isabella, who'd been walking the perimeter of the entrance with a grim expression, turns to us and softly clears her throat. "We should begin," she says, her tone grave.

I show them to the living room where Jake dumps his backpack on the couch and starts digging through it, much like the other day. But it's not full of school supplies like last time. He pulls out his composition book with the notes of my case and a neon yellow binder, followed by a couple of cell phones ("for picture evidence"), a couple of flashlights and extra batteries, candles and matches ("as backup for the flashlight batteries"), a compass, and two contraptions he raises over his head.

"Boom!" he shouts, laughing. "My pride," he waves one in the air, "and my joy," he waves the other. "My EMF and EVP meters. I've been wanting them *so bad*, and finally, I got them for Christmas! They were all I got, but so worth it."

They're both rectangular, one with a dark screen across the top half of it, and the other with what looks like a little microphone sticking out at the end.

I ask, "Are they useful?"

"Useful? They're, like, the best! Every serious paranormal investigator uses them. This one measures electromagnetic frequencies. See?" He switches it on, and a red, digital zero fills the screen. "The numbers go up or down when it detects a change in the energy around us. Isabella can usually sense it first, but this gives us a measurable reading that we can track. Experts agree it's a sure sign of spirit activity. And this one records electronic voice phenomena. Spirit voices that we can't always hear."

Spirit voices? I think of the growl and shudder.

"So what's that thing?" I point to another item that looks like a mini projector.

"Laser grid."

"Like *Star Wars* or something?"

He laughs like I said something funny. "No, duh. You know those laser pens you can tease cats with? Well, it's like that, except it's a whole bunch of lasers at once. It projects, like, a sheet of red dots across a large area in a room." He spreads his arms wide. "And if any of the dots blur or distort, it can mean the presence of something paranormal. If we get it on camera, then that's evidence."

"Really? Sounds impressive."

"I got this one on the internet. I saved my allowance." He sounds so proud I can't help but smile at his enthusiasm.

I'll say one thing: this kid came prepared.

Isabella starts pulling things out of her own arsenal.

"What's that?" I can't help but ask.

She holds up what looks like a halved clamshell, except it's enormous, almost bigger than her hand. "It's an abalone shell," she explains, setting it on the coffee table and taking out a bundle of sage that I recognize from her store. "Sacred. We burn sage on it when we're finished to detach any energy that might linger with us beyond the session."

Jake straightens from his dizzying array of equipment and puts his hands on his hips. "I need to walk around and explore your claims before we start." He waves the list he wrote during my interview. "Will you come with and show me exactly where these happened? Let's start at the top."

"Sure."

Up in the attic, he nods sagely. "We'll take pictures," he says. "Audio too. We'll do some connection work here with Isabella."

Next, the bathroom.

"This is the faucet that turned on by itself?" He leans over the basin, examining it closely. He taps the handles and the spouts, reminding me of a miniature plumber. "It looks pretty old, could be the original setup. Which means . . ." He flushes the toilet.

"What are you doing?" I ask.

He holds up a finger. "Just wait," he says. He turns on the faucet for a minute, then turns it off. The toilet bowl refills with water and stops. A moment later, I watch the handle move forward as the faucet squeaks back on, full force.

"What the hell?" I jump back. "What just happened?"

He giggles. "Older plumbing sometimes does this, but people don't take it into account when listing paranormal experiences they have. The water turning on? It's a build-up of pressure from the toilet. Did you, uh, *go* and then wash your hands after? While the toilet ran?"

I think back. "Yeah, I did."

"Welp." He shrugs, his gangly arms swinging by his sides. "That explains it. No ghost."

"Wow, I'm surprised you knew that."

"You'll be surprised what else I know." He grins.

Cheeky kid.

I watch in fascination as he puts everything in place, checking to make sure the devices work and setting up the laser grid so it blankets the wall beneath the attic hatch. The dots are faint but visible, and sort of creepy. I'm glad he explained it to me before turning it on. He props a phone up against the device, presumably so it can record any disturbances in the grid.

Isabella comes up to me. "Would you mind going around and closing all of the blinds, please, Hazel? We don't want it too dark, but bright sunlight can hide more than you'd realize."

"Sure, but uh, shouldn't we be doing this, you know, in the middle of the night?"

Jake blows a raspberry. "Myth. Ghosts are active all the time. Isabella's right about the sun. That's why most people don't notice weird stuff until it's dark and quiet."

Upstairs, I make sure all the shades are pulled in the guest rooms, including my own. Pulling the cord, the twine rough between my fingers, the blind drops with a clatter.

"*Hey.*"

I whip around. I didn't hear anyone come up with me. "Yes?"

There's no one there, but it sounded right next to me.

Goosebumps prickle down my arms, and I back out of the room, checking the hallway. Empty. Isabella and Jake's voices softly murmur downstairs, having a conversation. Are they playing a trick on me? Getting me good and scared so I'm more susceptible to so-called "evidence"?

"Ha ha, you guys," I call down the stairs. "Very funny."

Isabella appears at the bottom of the stairs, brows knit in concern. "What was that, dear?"

"I said, ha ha. You startled me."

Her frown deepens. "Sorry, darlin', I don't know what you're talking about. We haven't done anything upstairs."

Ice trickles down the back of my neck.

"Why don't you come down now. From what you say, the activity has already begun."

Glancing over my shoulder at the empty space behind me, I hurry down the stairs, my boots pounding heavily on the wood.

I join them in the living room and finish closing the blinds, the cords slipping through my trembling fingers.

"Oh, I forgot to tell you!" Jake slaps his forehead. "This is a perfect example. I only have one rule, okay? It's super important. Never go anywhere on your own. If you have an experience, you need someone else to back you up, otherwise, it could've been anything, and it can weaken the credibility of our findings."

"Duly noted."

Their right hands stretch out between them, fingers touching. Jake motions for me to do the same. "Join in!"

I step closer and place my hand on top of theirs.

"Be brave, on three," he says.

"We do this at the start of every investigation," Isabella explains. "Tradition. Brings good luck." She winks.

I've only been brave once, when I ran. Following through with the deal despite my pounding heart, escaping with a monster's prize, feeling nervous but also somehow glorious and powerful. Was that bravery? Or foolishness?

Jake counts to three, and we all shout, "Be brave!"

So it begins.

Nineteen

At first, nothing happens. I almost expected a clap of thunder or an eerie howl in the distance. But no. The sun keeps shining, warming the blinds, and the birds still chirp outside. It's actually pretty boring. No white sheets with blackened eye holes, no sudden freak thunderstorms, and no boogeymen popping out shouting "boo!"

Isabella closes her eyes and inhales slowly through her nose. Jake says, "We can't talk to her now. At least, not more than a few words here and there. It disrupts her connection to the other side."

"Okay. So . . . how do we do this?"

He reaches for the flashlights and hands me one. "Keep this on you at all times. Just in case."

"But it's not dark."

He tilts his head and silently chastises me with his eyes.

"Fine, whatever."

"Here. You hold this too." He shoves the EVP recorder in my hands. "Don't rub your fingers over this part, it's the microphone. And here, this paper has a list of questions we can use to coax activity. Keep it in your pocket."

Isabella speaks, her voice soft like velvet. "This particular room is clear, but I'm feeling drawn toward the hall."

"Then let's go," Jake says.

Isabella seems to drift into the hallway, her steps light and unhurried, leading us like baby ducks. We stand still, facing the staircase, waiting for something. But, of course, nothing happens. Nothing ever happens when you want it to.

"How long do you usually wait in each room?" I whisper.

"Try not to whisper," Jake says at normal volume. "It can interfere with the audio results. We give it at least five minutes, sometimes more. It depends. When I'm older, Mom says I can stay out longer, which means I'll spend six or eight hours on an investigation, like a real job. I can't wait."

"The pull is still here," Isabella drones. "It's not moving."

And neither are we. I'm not sure what I expected, but it certainly wasn't standing around in silence.

Five minutes or so pass, but it feels like five hours. I stretch my neck; it makes little popping sounds as I roll my head from side to side.

"What's in that room?" Isabella asks, pointing toward the office.

"The office, but we're not really supposed to go in there. It's private."

"There's something inside." She gazes at the door. "Jake, didn't Raina give you permission to explore the entire property?"

"Yeah, she did."

Isabella looks at me expectantly. "Get the key, then, please."

How did she know it was locked?

I fetch the key and open the door.

Isabella starts walking in but rebounds in the doorway as if she's hit an invisible wall. "Oh my word," she sighs, breathless, winded. "Heaviness. Oppressive. Weight on my shoulders, pushing down." Her tone is neutral, as if it doesn't really bother her, which can't be the case based on what she's saying.

Jake looks meaningfully at the audio recorder in my hand, and I quickly thrust it toward her to capture her voice. "EMF averages zero point two in here," Jake adds. "It just spiked to a one."

"What does that mean?" I ask, trying not to whisper. Their clinical tone is starting to freak me out.

"The energy changed," he explains. "Something happened to it. It's commonly believed that spirit entities can manipulate the natural energy in a room."

"So what do we do now?"

"Ask questions. Have your list?"

I put the flashlight in my mouth and dig in my pocket, scratching my fingers on the keys I'd shoved in there. I unfold the paper. It's marked up with handwritten questions.

Jake indicates with a jerk of his chin that I should begin.

I clear my throat, putting the flashlight in my back pocket, its cylindrical base pressing into my backside. Boldness courses through my veins.

"Is someone here with us right now?" My voice carries and fills the office space. I wait a few minutes like Jake previously instructed me to do, to give the spirits time to gather energy to respond.

"Even though you might not hear an answer," he says, "it could be picked up on the devices in some way. So whatever you do, don't rush. And keep asking questions. Go through the whole list. You never know what will prompt a response."

So I do just that.

"What is your name?"

Pause.

"Is this where you lived?"

Pause.

"How did you die?"

Based on my watch, we stand quiet for about five more minutes before Isabella says, "It's so warm in here. The heat is rising."

"We turned the heat off," Jake says. "Remember?"

That's right, no mechanical interference. No air conditioning, no lights, nothing that doesn't run on batteries. I can't feel any heat – if anything, the temp is dropping.

"It's pressing, squeezing. I have to get out of this room. Something wants me out, and I'm going to respect that."

She goes into the hallway, leaving the office door open. She points to the ceiling. "I'm being called this way."

She's off, her footsteps light on the stairs.

"Come on," Jake says.

We go after her.

She stands right below the attic door, staring up at it. "We need to pull this down. I'd rather not, but we must, must, must!"

She keeps repeating the word "must" like a toddler throwing a tantrum. Her eyes shut so tightly her lids blend into her wrinkles – one long crease beneath her eyebrows.

Disturbed by her reaction, I dash into my room for the chair I used before. Its frame is cold as ice, but I chalk that up to the heater being shut off. I drag it into the hall, place it beneath the hatch, and step up. I avoid the memories of what happened the last time I opened this and pull the ring.

"Jake, grab the chair," I say.

He pulls it out of the way and places it against the wall.

The ladder stretches to the floor with a weighty squeak. It groans heavily beneath my feet. I pull out the flashlight as it is ten times darker up here than down below. "It's a tight space, you guys," I call over my shoulder.

"You go, Isabella," Jake says. "You're feeling it, and we can't waste that. I'll take readings down here."

Isabella carefully climbs up behind me, and I scoot further into the crawlspace to make room, kicking up dust that tickles my skin and fills my lungs. I swallow a sneeze before gliding my flashlight around, looking for anything weird or out of place. Nothing unusual that I can see, but Isabella audibly sucks in a breath.

"So much pain," she says. "Awful, brutal. Female. It's a woman reaching out. But it's not me she wants. I believe this message is for you."

I look around at the boxes covered in shadow.

"I'm sensing desperation. Fighting, a struggle to get out, out, out. Pounding. Scratching."

I shine my light in all four corners of the crawlspace and in the cracks between the boxes. There's nothing up here. Nothing living, that is. Oh God. "I hear all those things, Isabella. When there's no one else around. Banging and thumps. I've heard all that."

"Do your questions!" Jake calls. "I'm going to take some pictures."

My hands shake as I consult the sheet of paper once more.

I begin asking the questions. "Is someone here with us?"

Click. The camera shutter from Jake's phone startles me, and I have to catch my breath. I hold out the recording device further into the darkness. "What's your name?"

Click.

"Is this your house?"

Click.

"How did you die?"

Click.

"What do you want?"

Click.

"Am I safe here?"

Click.

"Hey, guys?" Jake calls. "Did you just hear that?"

I lean over the opening and see him standing just below, phone in hand, but he's not examining his photos – he's looking down the stairwell.

"Hear what?"

"A door."

"Which one?"

"Just a door downstairs."

"No, we didn't hear anything."

"Well, we need to make sure no one's messing with us. Mom might be too into her book and missed something."

"Maybe Skippy got out?" I suggest. But that's stupid, he's in the shed, isn't he? And dogs can't open doors.

"Come investigate with me."

"Okay, I'll be right there." I turn to Isabella. "I'll be right back, okay?"

She's trembling, eyelids drooped. "I need to get down," she says. "So much suffering in this space. Oppressive."

"Okay, you go down first, then."

Isabella grips the ladder so hard her knuckles turn white, and she moves at a snail's pace. When she is safely on the floor, she sinks into the chair, holding her head in her hands. "It's following," she says quietly. "It's coming down like a tidal wave, I need to catch my breath. Oh, it's so painful."

My chest feels hollow. I am so out of my element. "Are you going to be okay? Do you need to stop? How about some of that sage? I can get it for you . . ."

"No, we must go with Jake. We have to make sure the investigation isn't compromised. Who knows? The door could have been another spirit wanting attention. It will only take a minute."

"Okay." We head downstairs, and I ask Jake which direction he thought the sound had come from.

He shrugs. "Not sure. Let's check it all. This is why I had you secure all the doors before we started. No chance of a stray breeze accidentally shutting one and us mistaking it as paranormal."

"Hello?" he calls out.

A beat passes with no reply.

"If there really was someone messing with us," I venture, "they wouldn't necessarily respond. Right? That would defeat the purpose."

His lips pucker. "I guess you're right, but I have to say I tried." All of the doors are still closed. Jake peeks out the front window. "Mom's still there, reading. Oh, she's looking up now. She sees me." He waves before dropping the curtain again. "Okay, let's –"

Isabella cries out behind us.

Jake's eyes widen. We turn to find her sprawled on the floor as though she's been knocked flat on her back.

"Isabella!" Jake screams, his shrill voice cracking on the last syllable.

"What happened?" I drop to my knees beside her. "Can you sit up? Here, let me help. Are you hurt?"

She groans and waves my hand away. She sits herself up, but her head seems too heavy for her neck by the way it droops. She presses a hand to her forehead. "I'm overwhelmed," she says. "I need to leave, for my own health. I need to clear the energy from my body before we can continue. I'm sorry."

"No, no, it's okay. Do what you need to do. Can I help with anything? You want that sage stuff now?"

I have no idea what else to offer her.

She shakes her head. "Not yet. I need to go outside. I can't take the pressure in here."

Jake agrees. He looks pale and frightened. "I've never seen her like this before," he whispers to me as we go downstairs. "Drained, yeah. But this?"

I reassure him the best I can, but I feel useless, not really understanding what's happening.

We follow her outside to the porch. Abigail sees us and straightens in her seat. Jake goes over to the van to explain that we're just taking a break.

I hover nervously around Isabella as she sits on the porch step, the cold probably seeping right through her skirt. But she seems calmer now – I'm surprised by the near-immediate difference. Fresh air seems to make a big difference for her. Her breathing has returned to normal. Maybe a few deep breaths will help calm my own nerves. The air smells like faint wood smoke and damp earth.

I'll never admit it out loud, but she really scared me in there. "Are you feeling better now?"

She takes a minute to answer, watching Jake explain our progress to Abigail through the open driver's side window.

"He's such a good kid," Isabella says, ignoring my question. "We should all be so impassioned by our hobbies." She hangs her head again.

Tentatively, I touch her arm. "You don't like it?"

"I didn't get to choose this." She sighs and lifts her gaze. "I always thought, when I was a small child, it was normal to feel things that weren't there. To hear voices from the grave. I believed everyone could, so I never questioned it. My parents called me imaginative. A storyteller. It never occurred to me that they didn't believe what I was telling them. By third grade, though, it became clear there was more to it, and I was ridiculed. My own friends called me a fruit loop, said I belonged on a funny farm. And all that time, the gift never left. I willed it away, but it became painful to ignore. I started getting migraines. The doctors couldn't explain it. It took a very long time for me to accept it for what it is – a true gift that I could utilize to help people. In college, I helped a friend find closure when her brother died. It was physically uncomfortable and sad, and I couldn't get out of bed for days afterwards, but she was so grateful, and I could see the value of what I do. She's the one that encouraged me to open the shop. It hasn't been easy, but it has been worthwhile."

"How did you start working with Jake?"

She smiles. "He loves that show, *Spirit Seekers*, doesn't he? He pestered Abigail for ages to find a dousing rod. That's what brought them to my store. I didn't have one, but I saw potential in him and we became friends."

"Abigail doesn't seem too keen."

"She just worries. She's a good mother who's concerned for him, is all. That's why she asks me to join him. She feels that having an adult is important, and even better that the adult understands what he's getting into and can serve as a protector and a guide. He has come so far from that first case. He'll go places with this, help the public understand that spirits do exist and are not always to be feared. He will be the catalyst for the understanding of the paranormal. I expect great things from him when he reaches adulthood."

"Huh." I let all of that sink in. "Spirits aren't *always* to be feared?"

"Well, there are exceptions, aren't there?"

We look up as the van door slams. Jake approaches. "Uh, guys?"

"Yeah?" I stand up and offer Isabella a hand, which she takes, grunting a little as she gets to her feet. Her knees crack with the movement.

He stops walking. His head tilts back as he stares up at the second floor. "Come here." We stand next to him and look up to where he points. "What's that?"

Twenty

I shield my eyes from the afternoon sun and squint in the light. What does he see? The breeze blows a few strands of hair in my face, and I push them aside, frustrated. That's when I see it.

One of the guest bedrooms upstairs. A curtain in the window, pulled to the side. A shadowy figure behind the glass appears to be watching us, and my mouth fills with the bitter taste of metal. The curtain drops, swishing back and forth.

Isabella gasps. Jake's eyes are so wide I'm afraid they'll bust out of his head.

"Holy crap," I say. "That was a person. Right?"

"It had to be," Isabella confirms.

"We have to trap them to be sure," Jake says, walking backwards to the van. "Mom. Mom!"

Abigail immediately gets out of the vehicle. "What is it, honey?"

"We need your help. Can you go with Hazel around the back of the building and check for an intruder? And hurry!"

"An intruder?" Abigail raises her eyebrow. "We should call the police, then."

"No, Mom. It's only to help verify what we saw. Please. We need two teams of two on both sides of the inn to prove that a person really wasn't there, that it was something else. If it's a person, they could be slipping out the back and running away *right now*. We have to hurry!" His voice rises in pitch. "Come on!"

His excitement is contagious. I can kind of see why he loves doing this. It's a thrill for sure. He takes off for the porch.

Isabella sets her lips in a grim line. "He's right, you know," she says, nodding at us before trailing after him.

Abigail sighs heavily and shakes her head.

"Well?" I say, frustrated at her lack of urgency. "Let's go."

I walk around the house, not even checking to see if she's following, and approach the back door off the kitchen. Rattling the handle, I find that it's locked as it always has been, which means no prankster came out this way at least. I take the keys from my pocket and release the lock. It's a little stiff, so I concentrate my weight on it as I push the door open.

It rubs against the linoleum floor with a long, ear-splitting squeak. Cautiously I step inside, on the alert for a dangerous intruder or freaky ghost. I'm met with nothing inside the kitchen.

I sense Abigail peeking over my shoulder and check to be sure it really is her. Can't take any chances here.

We skulk through the kitchen, and I peer around the doorframe into the dining room. We cross into the living room and look around.

All clear.

We check behind furniture and in closets, and there is no one hiding in here. The back door was locked – no one could've escaped that way.

"If you'll keep watch here, I'll check the office and the bathroom," I say.

She agrees.

I quietly peek in the downstairs bathroom. I creep into the office and check every potential hiding place. Nothing. I meet back up with Abigail, and we sit on the couch, not saying a word. We hear Isabella and Jake walking around above and wait for them to come down. When they do, Jake looks elated.

"There's no one here!" he cries, giddiness evident in his expression. "But we saw that! We all saw that, didn't we? That was awesome!"

"I think it's time to wrap up, buddy," Abigail says. "It'll be dark soon, and you have homework."

"Awww."

"It's been an eventful hunt," Isabella adds. "I'm sure you'll want to go through the recordings and see if anything pops up."

Jake nods so fast I'm surprised I don't feel a breeze. "But we have to come back," he says. "Please, Mom? This place is a hot spot, I can tell. We've only just got started."

Abigail stands up. "We'll discuss it later. Get your things and don't forget your coat."

Clearly frustrated, Jake stomps his feet as he goes around collecting his equipment.

"Warning," Abigail says. He sighs dramatically, but lightens his step.

Carefully putting away his equipment, he looks up at me with hopeful eyes. "You will let me come back, won't you? This was too awesome. We have to keep it going. We tapped into something, didn't we, Isabella?"

"Just do as your mother says," she tells him.

We pack up and head outside, where I watch fascinated as Isabella fills the abalone shell with dried, silvery leaves. They're almost as gray as the sky, and I get a whiff of fragrance, fresh and herbaceous. Isabella strikes a match and holds it to a leaf. A tendril of smoke drifts upward, seemingly hesitant. She encourages the smoke with a gentle blow, and suddenly it's billowing into the air around us in fragrant, roiling clouds.

"First, we cleanse ourselves of anything that might do harm," she says.

Holding the shell in one hand, she uses the other to direct the smoke around herself in rhythmic, circular motions. She inhales and holds it in her lungs for a moment. She then waves the smoke around us individually, swirling it from head to toe. It's hypnotic and I do feel more relaxed when she's done.

We say our goodbyes, and Abigail and Jake head for the van. Isabella falls back and meets my eyes. She speaks in a low tone, and I have to strain to hear her above the breeze rustling the trees. "There are a whole host of restless entities residing here. I would feel better if you slept somewhere else tonight. Sage is only a mild cleanser – it won't protect you from malevolent spirits."

"It won't?" I touch the heavy crystal around my neck. "But what about this? You said it would help."

"It should, at least a little bit. I don't know if it's strong enough to stand up against what's brewing here." She presses her lips together. "I need to rest. Don't tell Jake, but this afternoon was particularly draining. And for that reason, I don't feel comfortable leaving you alone here."

But I have nowhere else to go. And I'm counting on that cold, hard cash in my hand in a few days' time.

"I must insist you make other arrangements."

"Okay, I will." She's obviously distraught, so I will say whatever I need to make her feel better. I can't say that I'm thrilled about sleeping here any more than she is, but what other choice do I have?

I should have known better than to lie to a psychic.

"You aren't leaving here. And you should. Come stay with me, at least for the night."

What if Raina calls and I'm not here? What if she questions my trustworthiness? She might pull my bonuses. She might not pay me at all. Then all of this would be worthless. "That's really nice of you," I say. "But it feels unethical to leave when I'm getting paid to watch the place."

"Well, just phone Raina and explain the situation. I'm sure she'll want a progress report anyway."

How, with her ability, does she not realize I lied about Raina's involvement? I rub my forehead, mussing my eyebrows. "What about Skippy?"

She hesitates. "I'm allergic to dogs. He could stay outside, though."

I look up at the sky. Thick clouds like white gravy smear across the sky. "There might be ice tonight. Skippy would freeze."

She thinks for a minute, looking very tired. Her pale skin has a gray cast to it, and she doesn't seem as vibrant as the last couple of times I saw her. She holds up a finger. "If you can't come to me, then I'll bring someone to you. Let's call Brian and have him stay. If things get worse tonight, he can take you to his home for safety."

"Oh, I'm not sure that's such a great idea."

"Why not? He's your friend, isn't he? That's what friends do – help each other out in times of need. I'm sure he'd be happy to watch your back."

I'm sure he would, in more ways than one. "We're not exactly what I'd call friends, though, Isabella."

She raises her eyebrows. I blush at the unspoken insinuation.

"Too bad," she says. "I couldn't live with myself if something happened because I left you alone. Either you come stay with me or Brian stays with you. I'm positive he'll take the couch for the night if that's what you're concerned about."

"I'm not concerned about anything." Let's just get this over with. I straighten my posture to show I mean business. "Give him a call."

Twenty-One

Darkness falls by the time the doorbell rings. Skippy's nails clatter in his haste to greet our visitor, and I have to nudge him aside to open the door.

"Hey," Brian says when I let him in. His cheeks are flushed and his hair is damp.

"Is it raining?" I ask, feeling stupid the moment the words leave my mouth. Of course it is. That's why his jacket is peppered with raindrops.

He smiles, though, unbothered by my idiotic question. He leans down to scratch behind Skippy's ears. "Yep. Cold as ice too. Think we're in for another freeze, hopefully the last of the season. I can't wait for spring. The warmer months are a lot more agreeable, don't you think?"

"Sure. Summer is my favorite." I want to smack myself. Why is it whenever he's around, everything I say comes out as pathetic and dumb?

"Sorry I couldn't get here sooner, had a couple clients to get to."

"That's okay."

"I'm glad you called, but I gotta be honest. I'm a little confused about why I'm here."

"How much did Isabella tell you?"

"That she did one of her readings in here and felt you're in some kind of danger. Of the, uh, 'immaterial' kind? She didn't really elaborate, so . . ."

I sigh. "Right. Well, you know her better than I do. Is she the kind of person to exaggerate? Melodramatic much?"

He chuckles, dimples appearing beneath his five o'clock shadow. He rubs the short bristles on his chin, thinking of an answer. "She worries. She's like a mother hen in that respect."

"Yeah, I totally get that vibe from her. She did a reading, I guess, if that's what you call it."

"Release any ghoulies?" He wiggles his fingers as if he's trying to spook a five-year-old.

"Ha." I think of the figure in the window and avoid his eyes. "Not quite. But Isabella seems to think something of the sort. Here, give me your jacket."

The smooth nylon is still warm from his body and smells like woodsy deodorant. I hang it up and walk into the living room, where I've already prepared the couch with sheets and a pillow from a guest room. I shivered the whole time I was upstairs, imagining a figure hiding behind the curtain, and made quick work of grabbing the items and running back down.

"Thanks for doing this," I say now. "She was getting really pushy there for a minute."

"No problem. I am at your service." He plops on the sofa, crossing his legs dude-style and draping his arms over the back.

"Just . . . make yourself at home, I guess."

"Thanks."

I rub my thighs, the fabric of my jeans rough against my skin, my palms suddenly damp with sweat. I gingerly perch on the edge of the coffee table.

"Are you hungry?" I ask. "I haven't had dinner yet. Wasn't sure if you'd want to eat with me. I can make us something."

"Sure. I can always eat."

"Okay." In the kitchen, I take stock of the ingredients as if I don't already know what's in here. Spaghetti. Plenty for two. Carb-heavy, so it will make me drowsy and help me sleep better.

"Let me help."

I jump and put my hand to my chest. I feel the rapid thumping of my heartbeat beneath my trembling fingers. "Don't creep up on me like that. You scared me."

"Sorry." He looks around the kitchen. "I just wanted to help."

"Fine, put a pot on the stove to boil."

"Aye-aye." He salutes me and I shake my head. He's so corny. When that's done, he asks what else he can do.

"Um." I check the fridge. "There aren't any fresh veggies for a salad, but we can make garlic bread."

"Sounds delicious. I hate vegetables anyway." We get to work boiling the pasta, toasting the bread, and warming the sauce. "Hey, lookie what we've got here," Brian says, his head in the pantry. He comes out holding up a dusty bottle of wine. "Care for some zinfandel, m'lady?"

"Where did you get that? Put it back. Raina said no alcohol."

"Ah, but she isn't here, and this bottle looks like it was forgotten a while ago. It's just begging to be drunk. You know, before it turns."

"Turns into what?"

"Uh . . ." He squints at the label, pretending to read it. "Vinegar. Yeah, that's it. Red wine vinegar."

"Right." I scoff. Although, if this was some leftover bottle forgotten in the pantry, maybe Raina really doesn't remember it. And she did say only the liquor cabinet was off-limits. A small glass wouldn't hurt. In fact, it might help me fall asleep faster, which I desperately need what with ghosts *and* a cute guy beneath the same roof tonight. He uncorks it with a mild pop, pouring some into the little mason jars the Marshalls use for glasses. "Cheers."

"Cheers." I tap my glass to his, the soft clink echoing the giddy feeling bubbling up inside me. I have to remind myself this is not a date. He's here as a favor to Isabella. I can't let my guard down, especially with this glass in my hand. Sweet and tangy, the first sip immediately relaxes my shoulders. I've never had more than a few sips of beer, and that tasted like foamy gym socks, so I was never interested in pursuing alcohol.

Monster was the one with the vices.

When everything is finished cooking, we plate up and sit across from each other in the dining room. The air is warmed with the aroma of garlic and butter, and the wine leaves a bittersweet film on my tongue.

This is much needed after the antics of the day. The first forkful of twirled spaghetti is bliss, and I sink into the bite with an unexpected moan.

"That good, huh?" Brian asks, noting my reaction.

I nod, humming in the back of my throat. Who knew that something I'd been eating every night could be this satisfying? Maybe it's the company that makes a difference.

I gesture with my fork that he should dig in. He's inelegant, sucking up the noodles at an alarming pace. His chin gets stained orange from the tomato sauce. He gives a thumbs-up.

"That is good," he says around his mouthful of food, cramming a bite of garlic bread in there as if he has all the space in the world. I snort into my glass, trying not to laugh, but it doesn't work. The wine has loosened me up, my muscles feeling soft for the first time in weeks. Let's face it, I've finally relaxed and it feels so, so good.

We chat a little bit. At first it's awkward, but having already shared a meal together at the diner, it's more comfortable now. This time, I don't have to worry about strangers being introduced, of being seen or remembered in detail. This time, it's just me and him and a cozy room in a – let's face it – romantic inn all to ourselves. I kind of wonder if Isabella didn't just invent the whole ghost thing in some elaborate scheme to hook us up. I wonder if he's involved in it somehow. Did he maybe ask her to set up the whole thing? For all I know, he did. The thought should make me furious, so why does it make me tingle instead?

We eat second helpings. We pour more wine, filling the glasses to the very top, careful not to let it run over. He tells me about his childhood growing up here, playing in creeks and streams and fishing with his grandpa. He tells me about hunting with his dad and how his mom makes the best homemade pumpernickel bread in the world. Apparently, it's won a few ribbons at the county fair. Eventually, he falls silent, leaning back in his chair and sipping his wine. He eyes me curiously over the rim of his glass.

He sets it down and wipes his lips. "Here I am going on and on about myself and I haven't let you get a word in edgewise. Sorry about that. Once I get going, it's kind of hard for me to stop. Mom says it's one of my lesser traits, but I make up for it in other ways. Anyway. Tell me about yourself. Where, exactly, did you say you're from again?"

"I didn't."

He puts a hand over his heart. "My fault entirely. I'm such a rambler."

"You're fine. I like hearing you talk. I wish you would talk some more."

"Now that I know is a lie." He laughs, his eyes twinkling. "But really. How did you find yourself babysitting an empty old building in known-for-nothing Fox Valley? Are you a relative of the Marshalls?"

Here come the questions. With a stone sinking in my stomach, I remember why I didn't want him around me in the first place. Too many questions. I shake my head, my thoughts sloshing around inside my skull.

"You don't want to hear all that," I say, standing. I'm unsteady on my feet, and for a second, I shuffle to remain upright. I regain my balance and start noisily clearing the plates. "It's so boring. It'll put you right to sleep."

He stands and carries the glasses, following me into the kitchen. I put the plates in the sink and run the water, hoping he'll take the hint and drop the subject.

He doesn't. "I don't believe that," he says, setting the glasses on the counter.

I'm not sure if it's the wine or his nearness that makes my knees buckle.

"Easy there," he murmurs, his hand on the small of my back. His touch sends electricity up my spine.

"I-I might be a little tipsy," I admit. Which is embarrassing. I'm supposed to be twenty-one. Doesn't that mean I should be capable of holding a little vino?

"That's okay. Here." He gently moves me aside. "I'll clean up. Why don't you go sit down and relax a bit?"

"You sure?"

"Positive."

"Well, okay. I might take you up on that."

"You better." He flashes that grin once more.

I stretch out on the sofa, luxuriating in the carefree mood that's taken over me, and close my eyes. I might be more than a little tipsy. I'm such a lightweight. It feels as though the couch is tilting beneath me, rocking back and forth. Long, languid movements. I've never been on a boat, but I bet this is what it feels like. Soothing. Like how a baby must feel being rocked in a cradle.

This makes me think of Mom, and now the sadness leaks from my heart like the sand in an hourglass, filling my body up with grief. I press my lips together and concentrate on holding back the tears. It doesn't work. The warm drops trail slowly down my face. I really miss her. I didn't have enough time to prepare, to say goodbye properly. I press my hands to my face, breathing deep.

"You alright?" Brian's presence beside me causes the hairs on my arms to prickle and stand up, reaching out for him even when I will not. I sniffle, and instantly his arms are around me, warm and strong and comforting. He lifts me into a better position for a hug, and with an unrestrained sob, I wrap my arms around his neck, holding him so tight I'll be humiliated when I think of it later. He shushes me, sounding like the wind through tree branches. "It's okay," he says. "Whatever it is, it's okay."

THUMP.

We both jump at the sound against the window. The curtains are drawn, so we can't see what's outside in the dark. I'm disappointed that he releases me from the hug. It was nice.

"What was that?" he asks, getting up to check. Moving the curtain aside, he peers out into the dark but shrugs. "Maybe it was your ghoulie," he laughs.

"Maybe." I don't feel as flippant. After everything that's been happening, I'm almost not even surprised. The landline phone chirrups, and that startles me even more than the mysterious thumping sound.

I answer it. "Hello?"

"Hazel?" Jake's voice meets my ear. "Hi! This is Jake again."

"Hey. What's up?" I'm surprised he's calling.

Brian peruses the bookshelf, occasionally reaching out to touch a weathered spine.

"I'm going through our results, and you'll never, ever guess what I just heard on audio."

Jake sounds so excited I can't help but smile. "What did you hear?"

Brian pulls a book off the shelf and sits down on the couch, the sheet and blanket bunching up around him as he cracks it open for a read.

"We got a voice!" Jake cries. "It wasn't any of us. I can hear us talking clearly. I had to listen really, really hard but I heard it. Like, underneath our voices. Does that make sense? But it's there. I wanted to tell you."

"Um, cool. What did the voice say?"

"It's just one word, and it goes so quick I almost missed it."

"What's the word, Jake?"

He takes a deep breath for dramatic flair. "Temper."

I forget to breathe.

"It sounds like 'temper.' Like, angry? Do you think the entity is mad at us for looking around?"

There's no way. No way he could know. But then, how? Or maybe it really is temper as in angry.

Brian notices me watching and holds up the book so I can see. It's the romance novel. He grins and wiggles his eyebrows.

"And that's not all," Jake continues. "We got a visual too. I wanted to ask if it's okay to come back tomorrow. If it's okay with you, I'll ask my mom and Isabella. This is way. Too. Awesome. Please say yes. Please!"

My inhale is strained, shaky, and my chest feels tight.

"Um, Jake, I have to think about it."

"But we only just started! What's that thing old people are always saying about hitting the hot iron?"

"Strike while the iron is hot?"

"Yeah, that. Come on. Who knows what else we could get? Please, let's have a second round. Just say yes and then I'm sure Mom'll let me."

I pinch the bridge of my nose, a headache forming behind my eyes. What am I doing? Indulging the fantasies of a child, even a disciplined one, can't be a good thing. But to pretend nothing strange is happening is to be blind. I can no longer lie to myself. I squeeze the phone.

Jake's voice begs in my ear, please-pretty-please. I might kick myself later for it, but I say yes. His scream of delight is so piercing I have to pull the phone away from my ear.

Twenty-Two

Hanging up, I sit next to Brian, burying my face in my hands. I can hear the paper slap of the novel being shut.

"Mind me asking what that's all about?" he asks.

I raise my head and give him a woeful look. "Jake wants to come back tomorrow for another round."

"You're kidding."

"He claims to have picked up an otherworldly voice on tape."

"Really? What'd it say?"

I hesitate. "Temper."

"Huh." He mulls this over. "That is strange."

If he only knew.

"So you having him back around?"

"I . . . guess so. Yes. If his mom's okay with it and if Isabella's free. She seemed a little worn out after today. She might not be up for it."

"Don't underestimate Mrs. Rhodes. She'll be here in a heartbeat if you guys ask her to."

"But should we? If it makes her sick?" I shift my weight, tucking my foot up beneath me. "Can I ask you a question?"

"Fire away."

"Do you believe in ghosts?"

He leans back, stretching his arms up into the air before resting his palms on the back of his head.

I watch him with anticipation.

"Truthfully?" he asks. "Not really, no. Never had a reason to. Mostly, I think it's just a made-up thing people tell themselves. Like, when a loved one dies, it makes them feel better. You know?"

I shrug. Yeah, I know.

"What about you?" He tilts his head, looking at me curiously.

"I don't know. I didn't think so, but now all this funky stuff is happening that I can't explain. I don't know what to think or do or how to feel about it."

"It's okay to be confused." He reaches for my hand. I stare down at our entwined fingers. His palm is warm and dry, a sturdy comfort, an anchor in the midst of chaotic sensations roiling inside of me.

"Hey," he says. "You got a tattoo?"

He takes my arm where the sleeve has shifted and the edge of the heart is visible. I pull it back, but not fast enough – he sees the heart, the initials. If he's surprised, he hides it well. He looks at me questioningly. I shake my head and tug the sleeve down as far as it will go, over my knuckles, stretching the fabric so hard it becomes almost sheer. "It's nothing," I say. "An embarrassing mistake. A . . . misguided declaration of sorts."

"One hell of a declaration if you ask me."

"It wasn't – never mind."

He touches my sleeve, gently, hesitant, as if I might flee the room at any second. "It's okay. These things happen." He pulls back and lifts the hem of his shirt to reveal his own ink on his ribcage. A very large, very colorful image of Big Bird holding a sign that reads "MOM."

I burst into laughter. "What is that?" I ask. "How did you – why did you . . .?" I can't get the words out for my laughter.

He drops the hem, covering up the image, and grimaces. "Lost a bet senior year. Stupidest thing, really. Let's just say it involved asking out the head cheerleader. Epic fail on my part."

"What, the dare or the tattoo?"

"Both, really."

"So, she wasn't interested?"

"I never worked up the nerve." The air shifts into something electric as he meets my eyes. "Told myself I wouldn't chicken out again if I ever got another chance."

I want to keep touching him, and it's that very reason why I pull away. This is going too fast. "We don't even know each other," I offer as explanation when his face falls.

"It's okay," he says. "I understand."

"Do you, though? I mean, really. Strange girl comes to town, and your first thought is to ask her out? Hold her hand?"

"Let me stop you right there." He pins me with a fervent glare. "You're not a stranger, not anymore. And yes, my first thought was damn this here girl is pretty, and I wanted to get to know you better. And if my forwardness offends, then I apologize. I never meant to pressure you. I won't ask you out, even though I still want to. But if you ever have a change of heart, let me know. Because, Hazel, I like you."

When he's done talking, I'm left speechless. You could roast marshmallows over my flaming face, and I can only imagine how red it must be. My heart wants to leap out of my throat, and I swallow hard. Despite everything, I want so badly to kiss him. The apology, respect for my decision, and simple honesty about his feelings has flayed me, left me wide open and vulnerable in a way I don't want to be. I lick my lips, wondering if I should change my stance on the whole dating thing.

He looks as if he's about to speak again.

THUMP.

We turn to the window.

"Coincidence?" Brian suggests.

THUMP-THUMP-THUMP. A series of rapid thumping rains down on the glass, like someone banging on the window.

"That's it." Brian gets up and marches to the front door.

The blast of cold air when he opens it curls my toes.

When he returns, he looks simultaneously angry and perplexed. "Nothing out there," he says, shutting the door against the cold. He shivers a little, rubbing warmth back into his arms.

"Here." I hand him the blanket. With thanks, he swings it around his shoulders like a shawl, and I stifle a giggle.

"Get a little fashion inspiration from your new favorite book?" I tease, holding up the romance novel.

"Oh, give it here," he says, sitting down.

The moment is lightened, but I can't pretend I'm not shaken.

Is it my imagination, or are strange things happening more frequently now? It started ramping up long before I brought it to anyone's attention, so what could've possibly triggered it? Is it me? Am I the one agitating the ghost just by being here? Raina and Bob couldn't possibly be experiencing this stuff; they would have at least mentioned it, wouldn't they? Just a heads-up, girl, you might hear some strange sounds in the night and get petted by an unseen force. It's all good though, see you in a few weeks! Right.

Did I bring it with me? Could something have attracted it to me before I even left, you know, like my bad aura that Isabella was talking about? It was all such a whirlwind. But whose ghost could it be? It's not like I killed anyone. The only person I knew that died was Mom, but I can't imagine she'd want to frighten me like this. But how else would the spirit get the idea to say "Temper?" Or maybe it really does mean the word like "angry" like Jake thinks, and not what I think it was trying to say?

Chills slither down my spine. If Jake catches the word again – perhaps in its entirety, as my full name – I'll have to come clean. About everything. It would be good to know if it – whatever it is – is going to follow me when I leave.

"Penny for your thoughts?"

I look up. "Do people really say that?"

"Sure." His smile crinkles the skin around his eyes. "I just did."

My only reply is to push him on the arm. He laughs. I find myself wishing he would hold my hand again, and I remember our conversation before we got interrupted. My stomach flutters as I recall how close I was to leaning forward and kissing him. Does he even realize?

Skippy pads into the room, a rubber chew toy shaped like a squirrel hanging from his lips. He drops it in my lap and takes a few steps back, panting. "What?" His ears perk up. "What do you want?"

"I think he wants you to throw it," Brian says. He snatches it from my lap and dangles it in the air, eliciting a jubilant response from Skippy. He throws it into the entry room, and Skippy darts after it, scrabbling for purchase on the wood floor. He returns with his prize and drops it at Brian's feet, no longer caring to play with me. Brian indulges the mild game of fetch for a while before Skippy loses interest and lies down on his bed. He yawns, his pink tongue curling around a mouthful of air. Brian yawns, and then like a chain reaction, I'm struck with the need to suck in some oxygen as well. We have a laugh about it and then decide it's time to call it a night.

I don't know if it's stubborn bravery or foolishness that makes me go upstairs to sleep. Maybe I'm embarrassed to let Brian know I've been sleeping in the Marshall's truck. He doesn't believe in ghosts, after all.

I pause beneath the attic door, flooded with thoughts of the day. But it doesn't matter. The truth is that I am a solid living person, flesh and bone and blood, and an invisible wisp of nothingness can't do anything about that.

I push the memory of being choked to the back of my mind. I'd been sleeping on my back, so I must have just swallowed down the wrong pipe or something. Naturally, that would wake me up. Anyone would. It doesn't mean a vengeful spirit is out to get me. And Jake even disproved some of the crazy stuff. So I can relax. I'm wearing tourmaline from a bonafide psychic, for Christ's sake, so I must be good. I raise my middle finger to the attic. Take that, Casper.

In my room, I change into pajamas and climb under the quilt, the fabric cold at first but warming up with my body heat. I pause before turning off the lamp by the bed. It's not that I'm scared per se, it's just that I like knowing what's around me.

I've even pulled the closet doors wide open. Nothing's going to hide in there to jump out and say "boo." I think of Jake and his courage. I'm braver than a few bumps in the night. I turn off the lamp, instantly drowning the room in darkness. I blink, and in a few moments my eyes adjust, softening the edges. I can make out the outline of the dresser, the desk, and the radiator. Everything is as it should be. I relax, letting the alcohol help me drift off to sleep.

* * *

I'm awoken by the sound of my door opening, the night-light in the hall illuminating the room. I squint. Didn't I close it so it latched? In my sleepy state, I can't remember. I hear Skippy patter into the room. He must have nosed it open. Probably needs to go out. Sighing, I roll over. "What do you want, Skippy?" I wait for his usual "I need to go outside" whimper. When it doesn't come, I open my eyes.

Nothing.

I look over the edge of the bed and around the room.

Nothing.

But I definitely heard his doggie footsteps coming in here. I never heard them go back out. Chilled, I pull the blanket up to my neck. My eyes are frozen wide, ready to catch sight of anything unusual or out of place. I force myself to blink. The natural tears from doing so stings my dried-out pupils.

I recall Jake and his natural-born bravery. He wouldn't freak out at a moment like this, and he's just a kid. He'd stay calm and find a rational excuse. "Skippy?" I call out, just to be sure he's not under the bed. I hope beyond hope that he'll scamper out from the ruffles, playing a doggie version of hide-and-seek. He doesn't.

A breeze must have opened the door. It might not have latched securely, an oversight on my part. The footsteps? A by-product of my sleepy state. That's all. Even still, part of me wants nothing more than to go downstairs with Brian. I wonder if he heard anything? Maybe I'll ask. Verify that a second person shared the experience. It's what Jake would do.

Downstairs, the only source of light is the night-light plugged into the hallway, casting eerie shadows that stretch up along the walls at disconcerting angles.

I tiptoe into the living room, letting my eyes adjust. I can just make out Brian's sleeping form on the couch, bundled up beneath the blankets. He's snoring lightly.

Skippy is also fast asleep in his bed, twitching his leg.

And yet, I get the distinct feeling I'm being watched. I look behind me. Something slithers in the dark, fast, out of sight.

I practically leap on the couch, shaking Brian. "Brian. Brian!"

He stirs, groggy. "What? What is it?"

"There's something in here," I whisper. I point in the direction of the shadow.

Alert, Brian sits up and throws the blanket completely off the couch. He stands and I snuggle into the warmth of the cushions where he slept, watching him. "Where did you say?" he asks.

I point again. "Over there. It disappeared."

"Turn on a light."

I pull the cord on the lamp next to me and stand up, intending to hit the wall switch next, when he stumbles backward, cursing. "We got a crawler."

Bitterness seeps into my mouth. "A what?" I barely get the words out around the thickening of my throat. "Brian?"

"It's gone now. I don't know what that was, but it was something. Like, something crawling along the ground."

"An animal?"

"Dunno."

I hurry to turn on the overhead light, and we are momentarily blinded, blinking away the spots.

We look around but can't find anything out of the ordinary, which is both disconcerting and a relief.

"What did you mean by 'crawler'?" I ask. "Like a snake? It was too big to be a snake. Is there a wild animal in here?"

"I don't know. It was too dark."

Well, dang. I'm not sleeping upstairs by myself at this point. "Will you stay in the bedroom with me?"

He tilts his head; the pillowcase left creases on his face. And it's only then I realize what he's wearing – or rather, not wearing. Shirtless and in boxers covered with smiley faces, he stands before me in his underwear, and I blush from feet to face.

"I – uh – I mean, would it be too much to ask for you to sleep on the floor? I can't take anymore surprises tonight."

"No worries. I've got you covered." He carries the blankets and pillows up the stairs, and I follow behind, grazing the rail with my hand. He creates a makeshift sleeping space on the floor next to my bed. "I feel bad asking you to do this," I say. "First the couch. Now the floor."

"Next, you'll be putting me outside with the dog."

I don't say anything.

"Hey, it's okay to be afraid. When things aren't normal, it's natural to feel uncomfortable."

"But I should be able to tough it out."

He shakes his head. "Not necessarily. Everyone is different. So are the circumstances. One person's cake is someone else's Brussels sprout. So don't beat yourself up just 'cause you want a little company in the middle of the night." His cheeks redden. "That came out wrong."

We're such a pair. "I get what you mean. Thanks."

"No prob. Now, rest up. From the looks of things around here, you're gonna need your energy for part two."

Twenty-Three

"It's not as sunny today, so that's good." Jake immediately gets to work setting up his equipment. "A gray day is optimal for taking pictures. But it's getting windy, so we have to take that into account during the investigation. The sound it makes, like, whistling and stuff. And branches tapping on windows. It'll automatically have to pass as environmental." He sighs as though disappointed.

Brian and I share a look. Is he thinking about last night too? When I woke up this morning, he was already downstairs, making pancakes. He'd even put on Raina's apron with the horses galloping across the skirt. I couldn't help but snort when I saw it. He did a little twirl with the spatula in hand and said, "You like?"

"You better get that thing off before you stretch it out and Raina holds me accountable."

"I just wanted to make us some breakfast. Thought you'd appreciate the look."

I chuckled, daring to glance at the skillet. The pancakes were perfectly round and golden brown.

"My mom believes all men should be able to cook the basics," he said. "She taught me and my brothers how to make pancakes, obviously, and omelets, macaroni and cheese, baked chicken, and tuna casserole. I must say my casseroles are to die for."

"You don't say."

"I do say."

And I must say those pancakes, drenched in rivers of pure maple syrup, really were delicious. It was almost enough to make me forget about the crawling shadow from the night before.

Almost.

But now we're focused on the task at hand. At first, Jake wasn't too cool about letting Brian stay.

"I don't know him," he whined when I pulled him aside to talk about it. "And too many people can trip us up. Can he be silent? Can he be brave? How do I know he won't wuss out and go running screaming at the teeniest, tiniest creak? He might, you know. People always think they're tough until they're tested. Especially the big guys. That's when they go crying home to mommy."

"Come on, Jake. Add one more person to the team. Just this once?"

And that's how Brian comes to be standing next to me as Jake eagerly pulls out the phone to show me something on the screen. "Watch this," he says with glee. He sets the video to play. I'm looking at the laser grid splayed out beneath the attic, the tiny red dots projected against the wall. "What am I supposed to be seeing?"

"Just keep focusing on the lower left corner."

I stare. One of the dots blurs slightly, only for a second. I blink. It's back to normal.

"Pretty cool, huh?" Jake beams at me.

"Can I see that again?" Sure enough, that blur was not a trick of my eyes – it really happened. "What was that? A camera glitch?"

"Glitches don't look like that. Something was moving up there while we were downstairs. Crossed right in front of the grid. According to the time stamp, it was right before we officially started. How awesome was that?"

"Pretty awesome."

"And you have got to hear this voice," he says, holding the recorder up to my ear and pushing play. "It's so cool."

A burst of static threatens to pop my eardrum. I cringe and pull back.

"Whoa, sorry!" Jake turns it down but only marginally. "It has to be loud so you can hear it. Hang on."

He rewinds it and plays it again. This time I listen closely.

"Did you hear it?" he asks.

I don't want to disappoint him. "Sorry. I didn't quite catch it."

He sighs, rewinding. "Listen harder." He plays it again. And again.

And this time, I catch it. A low, breathy "*tem . . . per*" hovering just below our conversation. We never heard it at the time. But something spoke the word. At least, I hope it's just the word it meant to say, and not what I fear it *tried* to speak.

Jake methodically sets up his equipment once more.

"I really wish I had some night vision technology," he says wistfully, testing the battery in his EMF meter. "For when I start investigating at night. Whenever that is. I'm gonna ask for some camera attachments and even some goggles for Christmas. It might take a couple Christmases, though. They're like a million bucks, and Santa has a budget."

I can imagine Abigail saying such a thing, and it's amusing how he imitates her, even pinching his features into an expression of disapproval. I'm surprised she even let him come back so soon. She seemed pretty intent on limiting his investigations. I wonder what he told her to sway her decision.

"What do you need night vision for?" Brian asks.

"They have them on *Spirit Seekers*. It's why the screen is mostly green and black, so they can see things in the dark. Hard to get, though. At least for kids."

Isabella sits in the armchair, sipping a mug of tea she requested I make for her. She still looks pale and not up to task if you ask me.

"Are you okay?" I whisper, kneeling beside her.

"I'm fine," she says. She gives me a faint smile. "I just didn't sleep well."

I don't know how she's going to do it. She looks like she might pass out at any moment.

Jake hands out the goods, making sure we're all geared up. I tuck the flashlight in the waistband of my jeans. The voice recorder is mine again. "Since you had so much luck with it yesterday," Jake explains. I don't argue. This is his circus, and we are his animals, poised to jump through rings of fire at his command.

He clicks record. "Saturday, March nineteenth. Twelve oh two pm. The Keystone Mill Inn. Those present are me, Isabella,

Hazel and her, uh, friend Brian." He leaves it running and passes it to me, looking at us expectantly. "Let's split. Me and Isabella upstairs, you two down here. Hazel, you know what to do now?"

I nod.

"You have your list?"

"I'm becoming old hat at this, young sir." I salute.

He makes a face. "Whatever that means. Okay. Meet you back down here in twenty minutes. Sync your watches. No phones allowed, other than mine for picture taking. Make them silent. Not even vibrate, 'cause that could mess up audio. We had an interesting day yesterday. Let's see what else we can get."

* * *

I'm beginning to wonder if we set our expectations too high. We've been at it for an hour and, unlike yesterday, have nothing to show for it. Brian is showing incredible patience, doing as he's told, holding things, staying quiet. Every now and then I glance over to see how he's doing, hoping he's not too bored. Maybe all the action yesterday was a fluke. The kind of thing every ghost hunter probably dreams of but rarely gets.

Jake doesn't seem deterred, though.

"It's normal," he says when we touch base in the living room. "Sometimes there's action, sometimes not. Mostly not. You just have to wait. We had a lot yesterday, so the entity could be tired. It takes a lot of energy for them to make themselves known. That's why we have to be patient." He glances at Brian, though I'm not sure why. Brian's been a model guest. Maybe Jake's still annoyed I asked him to stay.

"We had some, uh, personal experiences last night after you left," I say. "Maybe that's why it's extra tired."

Jake perks up. "You didn't tell me. You should have told me! What happened?" He reaches for his notebook and sits on the couch, rapt. "We'll write it down for your file."

"A 'please' wouldn't go amiss, young man," Isabella says.

He sighs loudly. "Would you *please* tell me what happened."

"Okay." I pause. "Well, I heard what sounded like Skippy coming into my room last night. In fact, the door opened on its own."

"And it wasn't Skippy?"

"No, I checked. He was sleeping downstairs. So was Brian." I look at Brian with raised eyebrows. Does he want me to keep going? Maybe he's a private person and doesn't want to share the weirdness he saw.

He takes a deep breath as if steeling himself for the firing squad. "We both heard banging outside last night, but from what you suggest, it was probably a tree branch hitting the house in the wind."

"Sound logic," Jake says with grudging acceptance.

"But then after that, there was this weird shadow," I pitch in, checking Brian's face to make sure he's okay with it. He stares at the table, hands clasped in front of him. "It was angled funny and kept moving around, low to the ground. We called it 'the crawler.'"

"That. Is. So. Awesome!" Jake's face lights up. "Man! I wish I'd seen it. The crawler. That is so cool. We should have left video running all night. Why didn't we think of that?"

"Because you didn't know you were coming back today for it, remember?"

"Oh yeah." He chews on a hangnail, brow furrowed as if deep in thought. "Maybe we should change partners. Sometimes mixing things up can shake the energy loose. Right, Isabella?"

She nods. It's weird that she's hardly speaking, and I vow to ask her again later how she's doing. I might not know her that well, but I'd feel bad if she got sick doing this because of me.

"Alright," Jake injects authority into his voice. "Let's do this."

* * *

Isabella and I take the upstairs. The phone rests in the corner of the hallway, pointing up at the attic just like yesterday. Maybe the camera caught something while we were downstairs talking. She and I walk into the first bedroom on the right. Now that we're away from the others, I venture to ask what's on my mind. "You're not really fine, are you?"

She looks toward the window where the curtains are drawn tight.

"Don't take this the wrong way, but you don't look so good."

Still no reply. Why won't she look at me? She hasn't looked me in the eye since she got here, which I wouldn't have noticed if she hadn't been so direct with me from the start. "Are you mad at me? Did I do something wrong?"

"No, dear." She shakes her head and turns to me, finally raising her eyes to my own. "You've done nothing wrong."

"Then what's the matter? 'Cause you seem a little off. Is it the investigation? Or something else? If it's personal, I'll stop asking. I just don't want you to get sick because of me."

She holds up a hand. "You're troubling yourself for nothing. I didn't mean to frighten you. It's just – how do I put this?" She sighs. "This house. Something didn't feel right, and now I know for sure that it isn't."

"What do you mean?"

She drops her voice to a whisper. "The spirits are finally showing me the truth. I have seen it. I never would have known, and now I don't know what to do."

"Truth about what?"

"This place . . . is flooded with entities. They just keep coming, drowning me in images, words, sensations." Her eyes are wide but unfocused, and my stomach turns over at the hazy gaze. She keeps talking. "They're relentless, filled with hate, seeking vengeance. That's why they reach out to you, to stop it from happening. To make them pay."

"Make who pay? Stop what?"

"I have to sit down." She sits heavily on the bed as though invisible weights press her down. The mattress groans beneath her.

I kneel down next to the bed. "Do you need something? Water? An aspirin? Raina probably has some in the medicine cabinet. I'll get it for you." I turn to go, but she grabs my arm, keeping me in place.

"No," she says, forceful. "You can't be here. You must leave. It isn't safe. The spirits have shown me so." She interlaces her fingers with mine. "It's not safe."

A soft cracking sound meets my ears. Isabella's eyes, round like saucers, trail from my necklace down to the floor where black shards scatter at my feet in a pile of gray dust. The crystal around my neck has broken in half. I touch the remnants of the pendant, the jagged edge catching on the fabric of my shirt.

Does this mean it blocked a psychic attack?

I open my mouth to speak but get cut off by Abigail's horn. Short beeps from the van – loud, quick, and demanding attention. My legs fill with sand. Everything's in slow motion. Isabella jumps up from the bed and rushes to the window, but it seems as if she's gliding, taking her time. Just as she pulls back the curtain, the intermittent beeping turns into one long, drawn out blast. Isabella gasps and leaves the room, urging me to do the same. I follow, wishing I could hurry, but it feels like I'm wading through mud. The horn threatens to rip my head apart, the buzz filling my brain until it drowns out my thoughts.

Brian stands at the front door. "Stay inside," he orders, his voice authoritative, and for once I comply. He swings the door open and strides out to investigate while Isabella leans against the wall, her eyes drifting closed. I stand close to her in case she faints. I hate not seeing what's happening outside. The horn stops without warning, and the quick silence is almost as painful. The seconds tick by like hours until he comes back inside, alone, closing the door behind him. He locks it, which alarms me. His right hand is littered with cuts. Some of them look deep; bright red blood dribbles down his arm.

His face is stony.

"Oh my God, what happened?" I step closer to him, reaching for his hand to examine the wounds. "What's up out there?"

"It's Abigail." His throat catches and he coughs. "She's dead."

Twenty-Four

"What?" My ears didn't hear him right. He can't have said what I think he did.

"Shot. In the head. Right through the glass. I had to break the rest of the window to unlock the door. She must've seen them coming." His eyes harden. "There's someone out there, and they're armed."

"Oh my word," Isabella whispers.

Instantly, I know this is my fault. He found me. I brought him here. Swallowing bile, I force myself to go to the window and pull back the curtain. The driver's side door of the van is open, the window busted, jagged shards of glass lining the frame like teeth. Bloody drool gathers at the sharpest points, dangling but refusing to drip. Abigail's on the ground where Brian must have laid her, her head a bloody mess. I see it like a film strip in my mind – the gun, silenced, only needed one clean shot through the glass, making her slump over the horn.

"Oh God, oh God," I chant. "I'm so sorry."

"Get away from there!" Brian yanks me away from the window. "Don't move, okay? Get further back inside the house, away from the glass." I huddle closer to Isabella against the wall.

"Hey," Brian says. "Where's Jake?"

It's at that moment I realize we're missing someone. "Oh my God, Jake. He was with you."

"He was. But then the horn went off and everything was a blur. Jake? Jake, buddy, where are you?"

"Jake!" I call. "Come here right now!" Panic engulfs me, hot and quick, and I press my knuckles hard against my teeth. Has he seen Abigail yet? My instinct is to protect him, not only from imminent danger but also from that horrible, terrible sight, to keep from staining his memory with this gruesome image. No child should ever have to see their mother that way. How did this happen?

"C-Could it be an accident?" I say, more to myself than anything. "A hunter maybe? People hunt here, right? Maybe it's someone who lost control of their gun?"

Brian gives me a withering look, and I feel like an idiot. No, of course that's not what this is. It's time to confess. Because I know who's out there. I can't lie to myself or anyone else anymore. Not while we're holed up like fish in a bucket, waiting for the bullets to rain down on us.

"Listen, guys, I have to tell you something." Never did I dream it would come to this. "The person out there, he's –"

"Shh!" Brian crouches. Isabella and I follow suit. He raises a finger to the air, and we listen. Footsteps outside, heavy and slow. Stalking the house. Brian beckons and together we crawl to the living room, stopping behind the couch. Staying low,

Brian takes a cell phone out of his pocket. "Signal's shit," he whispers. "Have yours?"

I shake my head. I mouth the word, "Landline." He nods. We pause, listening, but can't hear any footsteps from this part of the building. I start for the kitchen, but he puts a hand out to stop me.

"I'll get it," he says. I watch him, his slow, jerky movements like an animal on high alert. I'm reminded of the crawler we saw last night. His head darts to the windows as he passes by, probably listening for footsteps or checking for shadowy movements beyond the curtains. When he gets to the dining room, he stands and quickly shuffles into the kitchen, out of my sight.

My breathing seems too loud, too labored. Each breath makes my chest hurt. Isabella's completely checked out. Next to me, her eyes close, and she leans against the back of the couch. I grab her hand, no hesitation this time, and squeeze her fingers. She doesn't react.

"Isabella?" She's breathing, at least, her chest rising and falling. Her mouth hangs slightly open. Oh God, is she okay? I shake her shoulder, and she groans softly. It must be too much for her. The energy sucking ghosts and all-too-human monster prowling outside, killing on a whim.

Someone wake me from this nightmare.

Brian hasn't returned from the kitchen yet. The grandfather clock ticks every other second, a sharp tap to my eardrums, the only sound loud enough to hear over my breathing. I crane my neck, peering past the dining room to the open kitchen door. I can't see further than that.

What is he doing? Has he called the police? Is he talking to them right now? Help could be on the way, but who knows how long it will be before they get here – Keystone is miles and miles away from civilization.

Checking Isabella one more time, I move forward on my hands and knees toward the kitchen.

Just as I reach the dining room, Brian walks out of the kitchen, both hands on top of his head.

My stomach plummets when I catch sight of the figure pressing a handgun into his back. Brian may be larger in weight and height, but his captor has a commanding presence, and not just because of the weapon. His wiry body thrums with dangerous unpredictability – that's what makes him a threat. Brian's eyes widen when I stand up. He shakes his head a little, his subtle way of telling me not to approach.

But I have to. The man that's terrorizing us is familiar to me. I know every strand of hair on his arm, the V-shaped wrinkle that always forms between his eyes when he's sizing someone up. I know those full, pink lips intimately. I could even tell you the stories behind the tattoos running up his neck. Because I know him.

And the time for running has passed.

"Where's the hippie?" Monster growls, looking past my shoulder. His pupils, wide and glassy, flick around, unfocused. With his free hand, he keeps slapping his skin the way you do when mosquitos buzz around – but it's too early in the year for the pesky insects. He's definitely on something, which makes him even more frightening. "She hiding too?"

"She fainted. Please don't hurt us."

"And the kid?"

Oh thank God, he hasn't found Jake. I can't tell him he's missing. I can't send him hunting after a child. Maybe I can distract him. "How did you find me?"

Brian's eyes widen.

I shake my head, ashamed to have brought him into this. It was my problem and my problem alone.

Monster laughs, his whole head thrown back. "Your phone."

"But I threw it away."

"You didn't think I could still recover your email, your phone history? And by the way," he says. "Hazel Hopewell? Really? You use your mom's name and expect me not to find you? It would've happened sooner or later."

My face burns because it's true. It was a stupid move, and I should never have talked to anyone, let alone give them a name. I should have been more creative, at least. But I wasn't, and now we're here and one of us is dead, a child is missing, Isabella's lost it, and the guy I was maybe starting to crush on is held at gunpoint. All because I didn't clear my history and give myself a better alias.

Like I said, stupid.

"You always were too sentimental," he says. "With a name like Temperly, you'd think you'd be more of a hothead."

"At least I don't have a stupid nickname," I retort. "Who names himself after an energy drink and expects to be taken seriously?"

I can't believe I have the balls to stand up to him like this. I should know better. He strides forward and smacks me across the face, still aiming the gun at Brian.

Brian takes the moment to reach for it, but Monster's too quick.

Using the momentum of the slap, he turns and clasps Brian's hand, twisting hard enough to make him grunt. "What, you're trying to be a hero? Save the girl? Newsflash, she ain't worth the bullet I'm gonna put in your head."

He twists harder, and Brian's face contorts with pain.

"Stop it!" I shriek. "You're hurting him!"

Monster chuckles but releases him, directing him to sit at the dining table with a wave of his gun. Brian sits at one of the high-backed seats, rubbing his wrist. His expression is unreadable.

"So it really was you I saw at the gas station," I say. "You were watching me." Things rapidly click into place. "Have you been messing with me this whole time? Banging on the windows, jumping on the roof and whatnot?"

His grin, once sexy to me, has turned slimy. "I haven't jumped any roofs but I might'a played around last night for some fun."

"Come on. The attic? You did that."

He tilts his head, twists his lips, looking genuinely confused. "Nah, I ain't been inside the house."

So, some things are still unexplained. That doesn't make me feel better. In fact, nothing about this situation feels good at all. "Please put the gun down. You've got me. You win. Let them go, they're nothing to you."

"Shut up, bitch, you're even dumber than I thought. Now sit." He nods toward the dining room table, so I slip into the seat next to Brian, slow, so he doesn't think I have any ideas.

"You shot Abigail," I say quietly.

"She was pressing on that horn like I-95 traffic. Saw me creepin'. I wasn't ready for my grand entrance yet, so I had to shut her up."

Tears spill onto my cheekbones unchecked, rolling down my face and dripping off my chin onto the table. I quietly swallow a glob of snot so it won't run down my nose. I try not to sniffle. I don't want to alert him to my emotions. He always knew how to twist my feelings into something ugly.

"Why didn't you just show yourself last night?" I ask. I know I'm taking a big risk being assertive this way, but I need him talking. If he's not talking, he's bored, and if he's bored, he's dangerous.

He chuckles. "Why didn't I show myself the day before? Or last week?"

The urge to vomit ripples through me. He's been here this whole time? I felt so shielded by this hick town in the middle of nowhere. But all along he's been sneaking around, aware of my every move. I thought I was so slick. Turns out I'm nothing but a fool.

"I been watching you, girl. You won't believe the rig they got out in the shed."

"The shed?" That cramped little box outside? He's got to be joking. I've been in it, and that is definitely no place for a hide-out. "What do you mean, rig? Is that a tool?"

He laughs. "Shit, you don't even know. Setup. TVs. There's more to that shed than you seen. More layers. I was there when you got the ladder, but you didn't see me, did you? They got cameras all over this house, Tea."

Ice fills my veins, slowing my heart. Cameras? What is he talking about? Why would the Marshalls have cameras? I highly doubt they have a theft problem out here. But then again, what do I know? If it's true, they must be hidden good. I shiver, thinking how close he's been this whole time.

"Security cameras," I say, false bravery hardening my tone. "To catch sickos like you. You'll be caught. You won't get away with this."

"Won't I? I'll disable them and destroy the footage." He claps his hands together, the gun handle between his palms, and I jump. "Poof, disappear. And you'll disappear with them. You like disappearing acts, right? That brings me to why I'm here."

He turns the gun on me. There are similarities to the last time. He was high out of his mind then, and he's high now. The difference, however, is the scariest part of all. Back then, he was laughing, making a joke of it, though I didn't think it was funny at all. Now, he's cold, serious. He means it. The black tunnel threatens to swallow me whole. His hand trembles.

"I want my money."

"I don't have it."

He swings the gun upward and pulls the trigger, sending debris and dust from the ceiling fluttering onto the table like fallen snow. I flinch. I have never seen a gun in action before. The sound is enormous, and my ears ring as a result. Brian leans closer to me as if to shield me as best as possible. Monster aims at me once more. "Let's try this again. I want my money, yes, that's right, the bundle you stole from me. It's simple. You took a package to Mike, *my* package, and he gave you cash. I waited for that cash, but you never showed. You disappeared. Now, you better believe I checked with him, and he got the goods. But I'm still sitting here, empty-handed. So, the way I see it, you betrayed me. You're a thief. Untrustworthy. What a blow. I was devastated when I learned this. I love you, Tea. But this?" He waves the gun back and forth between us. "Cannot be. We are officially done. Finished. I can't stand to look at you. You're breaking my heart, you know that?" His face scrunches up as though he might cry. "I love you so much, so why did you have to do this? Why did you have to be so fucking cold?"

"You love her, so you threaten to hurt her?" Brian says. "That sounds a little backward if you ask me."

Dear God, he's trying to keep Monster's attention on him. I wish he wouldn't. He doesn't deserve to be caught up in this.

"No one asked you!" Monster turns to him. "Quit nosing in business that's not yours, or you'll get this bullet in your face."

Brian raises his hands in deference, but glances at me. I can't look at him right now. Monster's completely upended our lives. How could I have ever fallen for this guy?

And where's Jake? I'm afraid to ask. It seems Monster has gotten caught up in his issues, as he usually does, and possibly forgot about him. I hope that's the case, because if he remembers Jake, he'll respond one of two ways. Go in search of him, or admit the body's in the kitchen, limp and lifeless. That would break me. If he murdered a child, I'll kill him, if it's the last thing I do. Either way, Jake wouldn't get out of this alive. I hope to all that's holy that he found a good hiding spot.

Isabella stirs in the living room, drawing Monster's attention.

"You," he barks. He beckons with a sharp jerk of his chin. "Join us at the table, grandma. Get in here, nice and slow."

She approaches with her hands in the air, never once breaking her firm eye contact with him. She settles in at the head of the table and rests her hands flat on the wood.

"Now," he says. "This can be done the easy way or the hard way. I'd prefer the easy way, 'cause it's quicker and I'd like to be heading home. It's kind of a drive, you know? But the hard way could be lots of fun." His smile is menacing. It would be fun for him – definitely not for us.

"The money wasn't real," I tell him. "It was only a couple hundred, the core was Monopoly."

"If that were true, you would've come back."

"Didn't you see it on the cameras?"

He jerks his head from side to side; his neck makes a cracking sound. "You weren't flashing any cash by the time I got settled."

"You were played. Mike ripped you off."

"Can you prove it?"

I hesitate. "Well, no. I threw it out."

Another smack. Of course he won't believe me. The first time in weeks I tell the truth and no one believes me. He thinks I'll say anything to keep the cash. A couple of hours ago, maybe I would have. But now? With multiple lives at stake?

Isabella looks surprisingly serene as if she knows something we don't. "You won't get away with this," she says. She sounds absolutely certain.

A deafening bang ricochets around the room, and I instinctively cover my ears, pressing against the painful vibrations. My eyes clench shut, but then I realize I have no idea who, or what, he shot. I open them.

The bullet caught a lamp, ceramic dust raining down among the shattered pieces. His aim is off when he's under the influence. For a split second, I revel in that fact. If his aim is off, that means he's less likely to actually hit us. Except that makes him angry, so he tries again, making me cry out . . . and again . . . until Isabella slumps forward on the table as blood seeps from her head. It wets her wild, curly hair, turning the orange color a true red. I scream. I scream so hard my throat tears apart, but what is soreness compared to death?

"Quit that screaming right now, Tea, if you don't wanna eat lead too." My screams quiet into sobs, my face slick with tears and mucus, my chin trembling. My heart aches. She was a good woman – it didn't take long to know that – and she didn't deserve this. If I hadn't come to Fox Valley, she would still be alive. So would Abigail. Who's next on the list?

Monster resumes his questioning as if nothing has happened, as if he hasn't just taken an innocent life. He digs in his back pocket and tosses a thin coil of plastic to Brian. "Secure her wrists and make it tight. I'm watching you, so if you try anything funny . . ." He mimics firing the gun, mouthing the word, "pow." He grins, flecks of brown sludge wedged between his teeth as if he's been eating beef jerky and hasn't brushed in a while.

Brian circles the thin, milky-white zip tie around my wrists in front of me, pulling it tight. When he raises his eyes to mine, I see a swirling mixture of emotions: apology for having to restrain me, confusion about the situation, heartbreaking grief for Isabella and Abigail, and anger. Pure, red hot, anger. Toward me? Probably. Toward Monster? Definitely. I hope he won't try anything stupid and get himself killed too. In this inconvenient moment, I'm forced to acknowledge that, yes, I have feelings for this sweet country boy, and I couldn't bear it if I lost him too. We were just starting to get to know each other, and I'd like to keep doing so. I don't know if there's a heaven or a higher power, but I pray silently and desperately to whatever god there is that we – me, Brian, *and* Jake – will make it out of here alive.

Monster rounds the table to check I'm secure, feeling the bands and yanking my wrists, testing its strength. Holstering the gun beneath his arm, he turns to Brian, tying his own cord so tight Brian winces. Monster smirks. He looks at Isabella for a moment and checks for a pulse before nonchalantly pushing her over. Her body indelicately thumps to the floor, and I bite my tongue so hard I taste blood. He takes aim again. My stomach roils; without meaning to, I lean forward as the pancakes from breakfast make a nasty reappearance on the table. In any other circumstance, I would be mortified, but terror and grief drown out the feeling of embarrassment.

"Damn it, Tea. You couldn't just swallow it?" Monster covers his nose with the back of his free hand. "Argh, that's disgusting. You're so gross, you know that?" He sighs. "Get up."

Standing proves a little awkward when your hands aren't free. I'm light-headed from crying and a little off-balance. I lean on Brian for support. Words cannot describe how much I hate myself right now.

Monster jabs the gun in my back, bruising my spine as he pushes me forward into the living room. I hoped to go in the kitchen to see if Jake is there, dead or alive. But instead, I look frantically around the living room for him. He's not in here. Please, please, let Monster have forgotten him. He orders us to sit on the couch, and we drop onto the cushions, awaiting his next move.

Footsteps upstairs rattle the ceiling above us. *No, Jake*, I think. Stay still. Stay hidden.

Monster instantly looks up and scowls. "Forgot about that little bastard you got in here running the show. Don't either of you move, hear me? If I find out you even lifted an ass cheek for a fart, you're both done. And don't you dare puke again."

He stomps up the stairs, leaving us alone.

I intend to do what he says, I mean, that's what you're supposed to do, right? Give the mugger the purse and you won't get hurt, that's what they tell us. I mean, what can we do anyway? We're trapped in this new world, and Monster's the one in charge. So I get a little antsy when Brian heaves himself up to a standing position. "Are you insane?" I hiss desperately. "Sit down. Please!"

"No, I'm not doing this. That guy is psycho." He raises his bound wrists high above his head and brings them down with a grunt.

"What are you doing? Please, stop. Sit down before he comes back." I have one ear tuned to any sound upstairs, just waiting for that dreadful gunshot, that moment when Monster crosses even further over the line and takes a child.

Brian doesn't answer me. He lifts his hands above his head again and brings them down faster, his face turning red with the effort, and I realize he's trying to break his ties. I can't seem to catch enough air – each open-mouthed breath is shallow and unsatisfactory. My chest begins to hurt.

The third time Brian brings his hands down, his elbows point out like chicken wings and a mild snapping sound can be heard. He did it. He's free.

"How'd you do that?" I ask, incredulous. He drops to his knees in front of me and examines the locking mechanism on my restraints.

"Survival tactics," he says. "It's mostly a matter of physics. My brother's in the Army, taught me a few things. Of course, it was supposed to be hypothetical . . ." Using a fingernail, he slips the lock from the plastic teeth and releases me.

"Oh my God," I whisper, feeling numb. "Are we escaping? Is this even possible?"

"Go," he says. "I'm calling the police, but you need to run. Now."

I can barely stand, my legs are so shaky.

"Go!" He pushes me toward the dining room, and it's as if a firecracker has been lit beneath me. My mind shuts down, and my body moves of its own accord, through the dining room, into the kitchen, hand on the door to the outside and my freedom.

I risk a quick glance back at Brian and see he already has the phone pressed to his ear.

"Go," he mouths, and I don't need telling twice.

Twenty-Five

The cold wind bites my unprotected skin the instant I open the door. But despite the chilly temperature, adrenaline warms my veins. I piston my arms, pumping them at my sides as I head for the trail in the woods.

I'm passing through the garden when the thought of cameras stops me. Security I understand, but if that's the case, why not keep the screens in the office? Why outside in the shed?

I approach the shed with caution. Skippy's barking his head off – the gunshots must have agitated him. But clearly having some stranger in the cluttered box with him means nothing.

Some watchdog.

I let him out, and he runs toward the house. I hope he'll be of some use to Brian and not just another target for Monster's wrath.

I step deeper into the shed, careful not to trip on a rake.

Monster's been in here, hanging out. Watching. But where? I start moving things, careful not to make a sound, not to draw attention. I'm also careful not to cut myself on any of the rusty tools. Tetanus would just be icing on the cake, wouldn't it? I get to the back wall where various tools hang from a pegboard. I look around. There are no TVs in here. There's no space for a grown man to kick back and spy on his girlfriend. He could've been making it up. He could've been staying in the bedroom next to mine for all I know. I've wasted time doing this – time that could've been used getting away.

That's when I notice it. A faint crack in the wall, just to the side of the pegboard. It runs vertically from the floor to just above my head.

An outline of a door.

If I hadn't been looking for something out of the ordinary, I'd never have noticed it. There's no handle, no distinct features identifying it as a door. What's back there? I push against the plank, and it gives way to a dark, narrow room. I feel along the wall for a light switch, but there isn't one. I reach out in front of me, blind, hoping there aren't any spiderwebs. A thin, knobby pull chain meets my fingers, and I give it an experimental pull.

A single, yellow lightbulb buzzes to life.

Wooden stairs lead deep into the earth.

What's down there? A storm cellar, maybe? I look over my shoulder. There isn't time for this, but I have to know. The steps creak as I make my way down.

Again, no light switch, but a pull chain.

I gasp.

It's not a storm cellar.

It's a full-on bunker.

When Monster said there was a setup, I didn't imagine this. Concrete walls and packed dirt earth give the place a musty smell. Small televisions line the wall, the lightbulb reflected in their dark glass screens. A couple of folding chairs lean against the wall across from them – as well as a cot. The end of the room is lined with shelves filled with row after row of canned foods and bottled water. A bucket with a lid reads in thick Sharpie "unpotable."

Lightheaded, I look around the TVs, feeling their sides, searching for a plug. I find one and push it into the socket. The screens come to life. This doesn't seem like a professional security system. There's something unsettling about the do-it-yourself vibe. I look at the screens and my mouth falls open.

Security? Really? Is that the guise this is under? Because what I'm seeing shows beyond what a typical system should see.

Tiny squares fill the screens with grayscale images of the house. The entryway and living room, the main rooms, the hallways. But in addition to those are the guest bedrooms and the bathrooms, and what look to be the inside of the closets. The Marshalls have eyes on every square inch of the place, in every place you're supposed to feel secure and private. I've been naked in plain sight. I think of the showers I've taken, the changes of clothes. There's no way of hiding – the cameras are angled in such a way to take in every single thing that happens under that roof.

I move closer to the glass, the warm static fuzzy on my skin, and wildly examine the rooms for Monster or Brian. I can't see anyone. Maybe this isn't a live feed? I push some buttons experimentally and the machine whirs to life, ejecting a book-shaped plastic object. A video. It matches a stack of old VHS tapes resting neatly on a shelf, their matte black spines unlabeled. I put one in the rectangular slot, and the machine swallows it whole. The tape whirs for a moment as the video loads. The screens then flicker to show the same rooms, most of them empty, only now there's someone in the kitchen – a girl, making a sandwich from the looks of it. She's young, probably in college, with pale hair and a carefree bounce to her step. Why is she the only one there? Is she the Marshall's daughter or something? A guest, even? There's no sound, but she holds up a butter knife and appears to be singing into it like a microphone. She probably wouldn't do that if she knew she was being watched. I fast-forward a bit and watch her scurry around the building – cleaning up after her sandwich, doing a load of laundry, working on a laptop – and in all of that time, she's alone. When she heads for the bathroom and strips down for the shower, I look away.

That's when I notice the bottle of lubricant on the floor next to the chairs, along with a folded up, crusty towel. Holy hell.

They're perverts, plain and simple.

I whip around at Skippy's barking outside. It's muffled down here, but I don't have time to process this new development. Brian took a risk for me, and I can't blow this chance.

I bolt from the shed and shoot off into the woods, blinded by terror, a cold gray fog obscuring my vision from within. I push aside branches that puncture my skin, twigs cracking beneath my boots.

I'm not sure how far I've gone before I hear footsteps running up behind me. Friend or foe? Brian or Jake or Monster? It's definitely not Skippy; it has the distinctive two-step sound of a human being.

I look over my shoulder and my stomach drops.

Monster's on my tail.

What happened to Brian? I hope he got out. I pick up speed but I'm not accustomed to running, favoring milkshakes and fries over the gym. I'm seriously regretting that choice now, but how was I to know I'd end up running for my life? I'm not psychic.

That makes me think of Isabella and I cringe.

Run, Temperly. Faster. Think bullet train.

No, crap, don't think *bullet*.

I force myself to keep going, despite the sharp, agonizing cramp that pierces my side. Somehow I blot it out. My legs, however, want to give out, and I can't have that. I have to go even faster.

Monster shouts and I toss a quick glance back in his direction. He's on the ground, having tripped on something.

I don't dare stop. It gives me just enough time to veer off in another direction, into thicker wooded territory. Because of the sheer density of trees and undergrowth, I'm forced to go slower but I don't stop. I keep going. He may have picked himself back up already. He may have seen me come this way, but maybe not. I'm hoping he keeps going straight, but, as my luck would have it, I can hear him following me. I lose myself in the running, darting around trees, hoping to throw him off balance. It doesn't work.

It feels like I've been running for hours. Eventually, I hear the river rushing in the distance. Maybe I can lose him there. I aim for the sound. Some of this area looks familiar. This is where I walked Skippy, isn't it? Enormous rocks border the water's edge, haphazardly stacked up on each other like blocks. They're damp and cold but I climb them anyway, scrambling up as fast as I can go, hoping to slither down the other side and get to the water. It'll be freezing, but I think I can lay low in the current just long enough for him to look past me and move on. I'm desperate enough to try it.

What felt like minutes must have been mere seconds because he is right behind me with longer strides, now climbing the rocks, inches within reach.

He grabs my foot, and I stumble off balance, falling flat on my stomach. I hiss as a jagged stone scrapes just beneath my ribcage. Without a jacket, there's no buffer against the environment. I scrabble for purchase on the rock, but he yanks me down, sliding me back toward him.

My jaw sets. I can't go out like this.

My muscles tighten in preparation. I rock violently onto my side and, with a guttural roar, bring the heel of my boot down on his hand, his wrist, whatever I can stomp. I smash down again and again, occasionally getting my other leg in the process, but I can barely feel it with the desperate energy coursing through me.

His grip loosens – he's let go. Only now he's tangled up with me, our arms and legs knotted together somehow. I'm way off balance and tilting awkwardly. Our combined weight pulls us down the rock, and we tumble, hitting all the sharp parts on the way. I will definitely have bruises after this – *if* I come out of this.

Hitting the water knocks the wind out of me and I gasp, sucking in a mouthful of slimy liquid despite the massive ache beneath my ribs. The water is shallow but icy; it cuts through my nerve endings like hundreds of frozen scalpels.

But that's nothing compared to the flame of fear lit in my belly.

We wrestle, gripping each other's arms in a battle for dominance, splashing in the water. He pushes my face beneath the surface, and I'm blinded by an explosion of bubbles in the murkiness. I wriggle, but his grip is like iron. I kick back with my foot, but the weight of the water slows me down. My lungs burn for oxygen. Thankfully, the same water makes him unsteady, and he drops a bit, struggling for balance. I use his moment of weakness to break the surface with a gasp, and by some miracle, I slip out of his grip and crawl to land. My clothes are sopping wet, and the frigid air bites right through them. My bones hurt from the chill. But still he's right behind me before I can even get to my feet. On the muddy, pebbled bank he quickly pins me, straddling my body. He puts his hands on my throat, and the sensation is familiar. I have a flashback of invisible hands on my neck, pressing down on my fragile esophagus, squeezing the life out of me. The only difference this time is that I can actually see my attacker, and I know he won't stop until I am dead.

I could have prevented this. The very instant I felt uneasy, I should've bailed on the Marshalls, taken what they gave and left the rest. Would it have made a difference? Since he was watching, Monster would've followed wherever I went. At least my conscious would be free; there would be no innocent blood on my hands. Every fiber in my being aches for Jake, now motherless. It's a unique pain I wouldn't wish for anyone, and it's my fault he has to experience it.

Nausea sets in as the pressure in my lungs increases, desperate for precious, life-giving air. I close my eyes. I don't want the last thing I see to be Monster's face. I've had enough of him for one lifetime.

The pressure releases.

I gasp and cough, struggling to replace the air my lungs desperately missed.

I open my eyes.

I can feel Monster's weight on top of me, but he's no longer snarling down in my face. Instead, he's slumped over my torso, motionless. Slowly, I bring up my hands to touch his head, the lightest of pats. His hair, once silky, now feels oily and smells faintly like peanuts. A ripe, onion-like odor wafts around him. He needs a good wash. Apparently, there was no shower in the bunker.

His chest moves against me – he's breathing. His eyes are open, staring blankly into the distance. What new kind of game is he playing?

I push him off.

He stirs and I scoot back. Every part of me aches, but it's not as painful as the fear that he'll come to his senses and strangle me again. I look for something I can use as a weapon, a stick or something, and I look up to see a dark figure in the trees. Before I can process what I'm seeing, it disappears. I stare at the spot where I'm certain a person stood.

Despite everything that's happened, all that I've seen, I still can't bring myself to believe it's anything other than a trick of my mind. It must be from lack of oxygen. I press myself up to stand on wobbly feet, returning my gaze to Monster. What's wrong with him?

He stirs again, and an almighty rage blurs my senses. Blood pounds in my ears, and a sensation of renewed strength electrifies my muscles. How dare he torment me like this? Playing games like it's Halloween? How dare he ever put hands on me, threaten my life? How could he do that to Abigail, to Isabella? I think of the violence he's inflicted on those he deemed enemies. How many others has he left in his wake?

How could I let myself get involved with a killer?

A guttural cry escapes my lips, and I bring my face within inches of his. I scream over and over at my tormentor, the release my body and soul have been craving all this time. Drool stretches down my chin, unchecked.

I grab the largest stone within reach. I barely register its hefty weight between my hands, adrenaline filling me with the strength of ten bodybuilders. Its jagged surface feels rough and prickly against my palm.

The clouds part, sunlight hitting the mineral, and it sparkles like a diamond.

I bring it down on his face, hard.

From there, the movement is automatic, my arms swinging up and down, up and down. The violence brings, to my surprise, immense relief. I barely register the tears wetting my cheeks, mixing with the spray of warm blood, or the sickening whack of flesh and bone beneath the rock.

When my arms tire, my senses return with a heavy sense of dread.

What have I done? My fingers still clutch the rock, now painted a glistening shade of cherry, and I force myself to drop it. It falls to the ground in slow motion, tumbling, trailing tiny droplets of blood. I shiver, the cold finally making its presence known. My teeth clatter, my breath forming clouds in the air.

Monster's face is a mess of blood and cartilage.

I did that?

Time slows to a crawl. Is he alive? His chest isn't moving like before. My chest constricts as my soul battles itself over what I've done. Obviously, I want him out of my life, and killing him, in that moment, seemed like the only option. But thinking about murder and actually following through are two different things. It was self-defense. He wouldn't have stopped. It was him or me, and there was no way I could let him walk out of here with more of my blood on his hands.

My shaking hand feels for his pulse.

I've never been good at first aid. When we had CPR lessons in health, I struggled to find the pulse of my partner, pressing all over her wrist for ages until I thought I felt the lightest beat in her veins. I could've imagined it, but I passed the course anyway.

Now, it matters more than ever whether I find the pulse. I have to know if it's over.

I lay my fingers on the inside of his wrist, cringing at the blood splattered across my skin. I hold my breath, tuning into the life force that could still be coursing through his body.

Nothing.

I move my fingers around, pausing every now and then, waiting.

Still nothing.

The instructor said the artery in the neck makes a stronger pulse than what you'd find in a wrist. Grimacing, I reach for the skin beneath his jawline.

I can't feel anything. The skin lays smooth, quiet, no tell of a heartbeat.

I've taken a life. Have I been swayed, possessed even, by that weird figure I saw? Or have I simply snapped?

My heart hasn't received the message yet, still jackhammering away, threatening to crack a rib. Can I even claim self-defense since he was passed out on the ground? What do I do now? I can't keep running in the woods; I need to get the truck. I need to get to town.

But first, I have to check on Brian and Jake.

I push myself upright and freeze. Across the river, a huge black mass lumbers toward the water.

A bear.

It stops at the edge and watches me, probably wondering if I'm friend or food. We eye each other for a moment. Just as I'm wondering how quickly bears can swim, it turns away. The sight of such a formidable beast renews my strength.

I leave Monster on the riverbank and run back toward the inn. My lungs burn with each inhale and my legs feel like jelly, but I make it, bursting through the kitchen door.

"Brian?" I call. "Brian, answer me!"

He's not in the kitchen. I snag the truck keys off the hook as I pass into the dining room. Isabella's still there, the congealed blood that's pooled around her head darkening with each passing minute. I look away as I pass her. My breathing is ragged as I cross into the living room.

There's another body, one that wasn't there before.

Skippy lies motionless behind the couch, and I fight the compulsion to sink to my knees. A smattering of bullet wounds marks his haunch, blood trickling down his leg. He must've tried to attack Monster. I want to touch his fur, run my fingers over his silky ears. He was a good boy. I sent him back here to his end. Guilt eats away at my heart – I should have left him in the shed, out of sight. It's my stupid choices that have brought so much death to this place.

"Hazel?"

I look up at the timid voice near the hallway. "Oh, Jake." I stumble forward, fall on my knees, and wrap him in a tight hug. I'm not sure my arms will ever let him go. "Are you okay? Are you hurt? Did he hurt you?"

"No." He sniffles, pressing his face into my shoulder. His twiggy arms threaten to crack my ribs, he squeezes so hard. "I didn't see him. I hid in the towel closet."

Down here? I think about the sound that drew Monster upstairs. That wasn't any of us. I shiver and his shoulders hunch as he begins to cry.

"Shh, shh, it's alright." I think about Abigail. "Did you – you didn't look outside, did you?"

I can feel him shaking his head, his nose grinding into my shoulder at a painful angle. It hurts, but I don't let go. I can't let go.

"Mom's horn scared me. Not at first, the short beeps, but the long one. Brian looked. Then he pushed me down to the ground and told me to stay down. And when it stopped, I just didn't feel right. So I hid in there and made myself quiet. I don't know why I did. I just did."

"That was very brave, and very good that you did, Jake." I look around. I have to trust that Brian got out, that he was able to handle himself. We have to get out of here. But I can't have Jake see his mom in that state. Not like that.

"Okay, Jake? Listen." I pull back so I can see his face but keep my arms around his waist. The front of his shirt has a wet mark now, and his eyes are magnified by glittery tears.

"You're all wet," he says blandly.

"I fell in the river. It's going to be okay, but we have to get out of here. We have to go get help. I want you to keep your eyes on me, okay? It's very important. Can you do that?"

He nods, sniffling.

"Be brave, on three. One, two, three."

"Be brave," we say, though his voice is softer and more watery than mine.

Hand in hand, we walk to the front door when I'm alerted to a scuffling sound outside. It's heading right for the door. My heart leaps in my throat. It could be Brian. Or something else – a bear, a ghost, one of Monster's soldiers?

"Wait," I whisper, stopping. We can leave through the kitchen – but we'll have to pass by Skippy and Isabella. My heart sinks. There's no other option. "Cover your eyes."

He does what I say, and I lightly grip his shoulders from behind, gently guiding him to the kitchen.

More scuffling, outside the kitchen door.

"Wait," I whisper again, listening. The door handle jiggles, and a sharp dart of panic pierces my gut. I turn Jake around and quickly steer him back to the front door but pause when long shadows waver outside the window.

I shake my head and try for the kitchen again, but the door handle is still rattling with vigor.

Are we . . . surrounded?

Fuck.

Twenty-Six

"Upstairs." The last place we should be, but what other options do we have? With trepidation, we backtrack, tiptoeing up the stairs. On the landing, I point to my bedroom, and Jake goes in there, closing the door. I stay pressed against the wall at the top of the stairs, listening.

Footsteps echo below, pausing at times. Someone's checking out the house. Is it Brian? Didn't he call the police? Where are the sirens? The squad cars? Shouldn't someone be here by now? I hold my breath and slink backwards as the footsteps get closer to the landing.

Is it Monster, back from the dead?

I crane my neck, hoping to catch a glimpse. I stumble on the top step and grab the rail to keep from falling, cringing at my stupidity.

Then I see him. "Brian." His name comes out on a relieved breath.

"Hazel?" Brian tilts his head. "That you?" His eyes lose some of their softness. "Or should I say Temperly?"

My stomach flips inside out with guilt. Not the sensation I would hope for when he uses my real name. Is he mad? I wouldn't blame him. If the situation were reversed, I'd be pissed off too. My voice is subdued. "I was looking for you."

"I saw you run in here. Are you okay?"

"I'm fine. Jake's with me. He hasn't seen a thing."

He exhales heavily. "Small mercies."

He comes up the stairs, and I get a better look at him. Monster must have punched him at some point – his left eye is red and swollen shut, and he has a split lip. A drop of blood squeezes its way through the cut and dribbles onto his chin. It's nothing compared the bloody state of his hands. I wince, thinking how painful his cuts must be.

"What happened?" I ask.

"I can't get a signal up here, and he's cut the landline." Each word is laced with despair. "I couldn't reach the cops. I'm sorry."

I close my eyes. It doesn't matter now. He reaches for my neck, touching the handprints that Monster must have left behind. Despite everything, my skin erupts in goosebumps from his touch.

"I'm gonna kill that guy," he mutters.

How do I tell him that I've beat him to it? It doesn't even seem real to me yet.

"No," I say. "It's okay. Trust me. But we should get out of here, like, now." I step back, and his hand drops. I feel the absence of his touch as acutely as the sting of ice-cold river water. "Jake," I call. "Jake, come out. It's only Brian. We gotta leave now."

But he doesn't come. I call again, and when he still doesn't come, I worry.

"Hold on just a sec," I tell Brian, and head for the room, calling Jake's name. He sits on the floor at the foot of the bed, cross-legged, staring into space, arms limp at his sides. On the floor in front of him is the EMF meter. He must have had it in his pocket this whole time. "Jake? What are you doing, kid? Come on, Brian's waiting for us. We're leaving."

Why won't he listen? He stays rooted to the spot, blinking slowly, as if contemplating something I can't see.

"What are you looking at?" I ask, frustration growing inside me. I drum my fingers against my thigh.

"There are people in this house," he says, deadpan.

"Yes, people that are trying to leave and won't go without you. Now come on, we don't have much time."

He shakes his head, unhurried, eyes wide. That's when I notice the atmosphere in the room – thick and oppressive, as if the air has weight to it. A headache builds at the top of my skull.

"They wanted to leave too, but they couldn't. That's what Isabella says."

Thumping, fading down the stairs. Where's Brian going?

I turn my attention back to Jake. Isabella? I made sure he couldn't see her body. I shielded him from that. He can't know that she's dead unless he peeked. I crouch down next to him. "How do you know this?"

"Because she's telling me."

It feels as if a bucket of cold water splashes over my head. He can't mean what I think he means. "She told you? Like, before?"

He shakes his head, still not meeting my eyes. "Telling."

"Right now?"

"Uh-huh."

A crash below us shatters my attention. Something's going on with Brian downstairs. Oh God, has Monster's crew arrived as promised? Have they found his body and come seeking revenge? Or could it be the murderous ghost? Does Brian need my help? I want to call out to him but shrivel up instead. I need to protect Jake at all costs. I need to keep him in my sight. I keep him talking even as I work out an exit plan in my mind.

"Is that –" I swallow and start again. "Is that who you're looking at? Can you see her? Like, right now?"

He nods. "Yep."

"H-how?"

His eyebrows scrunch, and he tilts his head as if listening harder. "It's her gift. She can reach out from the other side, but it's not as easy for us to hear her."

Sounds of a scuffle directly below us, muffled by the floor. I clench my fists, fingernails pressing sharp into my palms. What is happening?

Jake finally drags his eyes away from the empty space and looks at me. "She says she's sorry she couldn't stop it, but wants you to know what she said was true."

The woman said a lot of things. "Can you clarify?" I ask as I move to the windows, sliding the curtains aside and checking outside for any weirdness. It all looks normal.

"That he won't get away with this. The others will make sure of that."

"Others?" I drop the curtain and listen for more sounds downstairs. It's fallen quiet. It's time to move. "Come on, Jake. Let's get going."

"The others living in this house. They all died here, not that they wanted to. They fell for the trap, just like you."

Trap? What is he talking about? The cameras in the shed? That's just a nasty perversion. An illegal one, yes, but hardly fatal. We don't have time for this. I figure the only way to get him moving is to dive right into the madness. "Hey, Jake? How many people are in the room right now?"

"A lot. Girls. Just like you."

That's when my attention is drawn to the EMF meter again. Where it used to say zero, there are now a bunch of numbers jumping all over the place. I touch Jake's hand, feather light, not wanting to startle him.

"That's . . . really neat, Jake. But we really, really have to go."

Another voice, deep and raspy, replies.

"Do you? Really?"

I jump as Monster fills the doorway, looming. Why isn't he dead? He had no pulse – right? It must've been super faint, or I pressed on the wrong spot. I groan as I realize I messed up again, just like in health class. His destroyed face – pockets of flesh completely torn away, revealing the fibrous muscle underneath – still bleeds. His wet clothes cling to his frame, showing off every sickening line of his body. Blood and river water drip pink puddles onto the floor.

"You have somewhere to be?"

I can imagine how painful moving his jaw must be. The drugs and adrenaline must be numbing him to it.

He takes a step into the room, and I put a protective arm around Jake.

Monster clucks. "Uh-uh. I don't think so. You're not going anywhere until I get what I came for."

"I told you, the cash was fake."

"And I told you, lying will get you nowhere. I'm getting my money, and if you're short, you're gonna owe. You know what happens when people owe."

He wheezes and coughs, spitting blood onto the floor. I wonder how easy it would be to shove him over and run. Do I risk it? Or does the fact he's still alive mean he's even stronger than I thought? I have Jake to think about. If I fail again, then I'm jeopardizing his life as well as my own.

"No."

He presses his ear. "Excuse me? Did you say you *don't* know?"

"No," I whisper. "I know what happens."

"Then tell me, Sweet Tea, what happens?"

Jake shivers in my arms, and I hold him tighter. "We don't have to talk about it. I'll come willingly if you promise to leave the others alone."

"What, like your new boyfriend downstairs?"

My spine prickles. If Monster's up here, then something must have happened to Brian. He probably heard Monster stumbling in downstairs and went to check it out. I can't bear the thought of what Monster must have done to him, and his next words confirm my dreaded suspicion.

"Took care of him already. But I'll leave his body alone if that's what you want. Can't make the same promise about the kid, though. I might keep him. Like a pet. Would you like that?" He addresses Jake directly. "Huh? You wanna come stay with me and learn how to be a real man? Chasing fairies. Fuckin' bullshit."

I move in front of Jake, shielding him from view. "Leave him alone and I'll get you your money."

"How?" His nostrils flare. "How do you plan on doing that? Useless. You've always been a fucking tease. I'd *love* to hear your plan to pay me back, but after all that time in that cramped shed, I've lost my patience."

He grabs my hair, yanking up so hard I'm sure I'll have a bald spot. I release Jake, and he scampers into the far corner away from the door, cowering. I need him to do the opposite. "Run, Jake!" I cry. "Run!"

"Nah-uh." Monster claps a hand over my mouth, and I struggle against him. He grips my arms, restraining me. "You do that, little buddy, and you'll go straight to heaven with your mommy. Is that what you want?"

Jake sobs openly, his anguish cracking my heart into pieces.

I try biting Monster's hand, but it's too flat and smooth against my lips. I remember being a kid and roughhousing with my friends; sometimes we'd cover each other's mouths just to be silly. We'd lick the hand that was silencing us and, nine times out of ten, they'd immediately let go. Somehow I don't think a lick would be very effective against Monster. If only I had a weapon. If only . . . I think of the gun safe. I need to get in the office. But how?

"Maybe we should show him what happens to people who don't obey me. Yeah?"

Fear, white-hot, pierces my stomach. That can't happen. I won't let him make an example out of me, especially not in front of Jake. The child has been traumatized enough as it is. I have to make this right. But how?

There is a scuffling sound by the open door, like scratching on wood. If I didn't know better, I'd think it was Skippy. I can almost hear his "I need to go outside" whine. But it's not Skippy, is it? Jake is still in the corner, crying into his hands.

Monster spins toward the door. His grip doesn't loosen, and I'm now awkwardly facing the bed.

"What was that?" He twitches violently. "Who else is in here? I thought there were only you two left." He twirls around again, looking behind him. The jerky motions make me dizzy, but that's the least of my problems.

He drops his hand from my mouth and crushes it on my neck, so even the slightest struggle takes my breath away. "What are you talking about?" I ask.

"Something touched me," he says. His throat vibrates on the back of my head every time he speaks. "From behind."

"There is no one else."

"You lie once, you'll lie again. Who's in here?"

I whimper as he slides his bony forearm against my tender neck. He won't be satisfied with any response, so why bother?

"Hey!" He whirls around again, and then again. "Kid! You did that."

Jake's face drains of color, and he shakes his head. He's still hunched in the corner – there's no way he would've approached him.

A clattering sound like plastic cups hitting the floor comes from behind us, which is strange because I haven't seen any here – the Marshall's prefer using glass mason jars. It doesn't matter what the sound is – all that matters is the silver lining it provides. Monster's startled enough to loosen his grip. I don't pause to question this good fortune. With a grunt, I jab my elbow into his stomach. I was aiming for the balls, but I'll take what I can get. He doubles over, and I slip free.

Grabbing Jake, we run downstairs, tripping over ourselves in our rush to safety. At the door, I pause.

Monster's pretty quick, and he'd caught up with me outside even after I had a head start. We need a different strategy. We need to arm ourselves.

"Hold tight," I whisper. "Eyes closed, just like before." He obeys without question, and we tiptoe our way to the kitchen. I'm careful to maneuver him around the bodies so he doesn't trip, and in doing so, I realize Monster lied about Brian. He's not down here, dead or alive. He must've gotten away somehow. Where'd he go? Jake clutches my arm so hard my fingers go numb.

My nerves are so tight you could strum them like guitar strings. My body practically hums with tension. All's quiet – what's he doing up there?

In the kitchen, a new sort of panic takes hold. "Oh no." The key hook is bare, the ring of keys missing.

"No, no, no." We shuffle as quietly as we can to the office, but still the rustling of our clothes, our shallow breathing feels too loud. I try the handle.

It's unlocked.

I steer us inside and gently close the door, turning the lock. The click of the locking mechanism is like a bomb going off, and I hope Monster didn't hear it. Hopefully, he assumes we went outside, like originally planned.

After coaxing Jake off my arm, I lurch toward the gun safe but stop short by what I see – or rather, what I *don't* see. It's empty. The safe is empty, not a single weapon in sight.

"No, this can't be happening." Despair tinges my voice as I run my hands over the cold steel shelves, knowing that even as I do so, it's useless. What happened to all the guns? The rifles? There were three of them, for Christ's sake! A feeling lodges in the pit of my belly, heavy and thick like mud. Did he come in here and take them?

No weapons. No safety for us. This is it. If we get caught before we reach the truck, we're finished. Jake sobs beside me, wetting my sleeve with his tears. It's official, I'm going to hell.

When Monster comes for me, there's nothing more I can do to stop him.

Wait, what's that sound? Rapping on the door, soft but insistent. My heart freezes. That couldn't be Monster. It's too gentle. He would just break the door and barge right in. Could it be the spirits Jake and Isabella claimed to be roaming this place? I'm not opening the door for anyone, not even ghosts.

"Hey, let me in."

A shaky breath rushes out of me.

"Brian?" I open the door, relieved to see that he's alive and well – and well-strapped.

He has weapons on every inch of his body, looking every bit a bloody soldier. The rifle's slung across his back, the handguns nestled in black holsters beneath his arms. He scoots into the room, and I quickly lock the door again.

"He said you were dead," I say, reaching out for him.

"He lied," is all he says before scooping me into his arms. He's solid and warm. His heartbeat thumps against mine and it feels reassuring.

Then I pull back. "You took all the guns!"

"I just wanted to be prepared for anything."

"How did you know they were even in here?"

He tilts his head. "Most of us 'round these parts have guns. I took a chance. Lucky the Marshalls don't seem too concerned with password privacy."

I chuckle, but it's without humor. "Are we really doing this?"

He presses a handgun into my hand. It's cold and heavy. He releases the safety. "Yes," he says. "We are protecting ourselves from a madman."

"You guys go, find help. He'll track me wherever I go, but he won't follow you if I'm still here. This is my mess, after all."

"Not an option," he growls. "We leave no one behind."

"But I did steal from him. I deserve it. You guys go."

"Don't ever say that." His tone is fierce. "No one deserves this. Did Isabella and Abigail deserve to have their lives taken? Innocent bystanders? No. Don't ever say this was meant to happen. Only one thing is meant to happen – we get out of here alive."

Jake huddles close to Brian.

"I'm glad you're here," he says quietly, sounding even younger than his ten years.

"Well, let's just get through this first before you say that." Brian sets his lips in a grim line. "Let's go. Head straight for my pickup."

Brian peeks into the hallway, checking and listening for any sign of Monster. The front door opens and he stiffens, holding one arm to keep us back. He raises a gun with the other arm.

This is it.

"What the cotton-pickin' hell is happening in my house?" Raina's thunderous voice rains down on us with a boom.

Twenty-Seven

I gasp. What are they doing here?

We exit the office and stand face-to-face with the innkeep-ers.

She points a finger at me, her expression murderous. "Young lady, you have a lot to answer for."

Bob doesn't say a word. He just stands slightly behind her, nodding his head.

"I can explain," I say, moving around Brian to stand in front of him. He lowers the gun. "But it's not safe. We have to go outside."

I try moving past her, but she reaches out to stop me. Con-fused, I look at her, my eyebrows twisting my forehead into a knot. "What are you doing? Didn't you hear me? Our lives are in danger."

"Of getting gunned down by some scrawny city boy all hopped up on chemicals?" She sniffs once, hard. "Pshh. You urban folk don't know nothin' about real fear. He's just a gnat."

"What?" How can she be so calm? Have I fallen asleep and walked into a dream? "But he's killed people!"

"Yes," she nods. "And your point? We've all killed something or other 'round these parts. Ain't that right, Foley's boy?"

Brian narrows his eyes, glancing at me. He seems to be communicating something in his gaze, but for the life of me, I can't interpret what he's trying to say.

And that's when Monster appears. Footsteps pound like thunder down the stairs, and he stands before us, eyes wild. His gun is nowhere in sight. I push Jake behind me, just in case.

Raina stares him down, hard.

"Piece of shit," she says. "You took my baby. You took my precious Skip."

She just got here, how does she know that? She couldn't possibly have seen Skippy yet. What is going on?

"What?" He turns around in circles, slapping his shoulder as if something's touching him.

"You took the one good thing in my life, boy. There's no replacin' my peanut butter. You ever know the love of an animal? It's pure. They're pure light. Pure good. An' you put a bullet in 'im."

She wipes her nose. I think she may be crying.

"How did you rig up this goddamned house?" he cries, his voice shrill. "How are you DOING THAT?"

"Doin' what?" Raina huffs, clearly annoyed. "Bob, he's clearly done for. Fix him."

Bob pulls a gun from seemingly nowhere and pulls the trigger, the blast splitting my eardrums.

I stare, wide-eyed, as Monster drops like a rag doll to the floor, twitching. Jake sobs into my back, his cries running up my spine.

They just saved my life, so why don't I feel relieved? Something about the look in Raina's eye – cold and hard, like marble – makes my stomach wobble. My thoughts, all over the place, wrestle to make sense of how this went down, breaking my head apart in the process. How could the Marshalls do something like this – just like him? Yes, I believed I took him out first. He was dangerous, scary, and tried to kill me. But now he's really gone, just like that? I only wanted safety – not a body count. They were so casual about it too, like it was nothing. That's what fills me with unease.

My stomach sinks. No one lives close enough to have heard the shots, let alone panic and report it. If by chance someone did hear, they'd just assume someone's after a deer or whatever kind of animals they enjoy murdering out here.

Oh God. What is happening?

Raina rolls her eyes. "Well, now that's another mess I gotta clean up." She sighs.

How can she be so calm, like nothing's happened? How did she know about Monster at all?

The truth smacks me like a truck.

There's only one way they would have known about him – and it's the same way he was keeping tabs on me.

My legs start to give out, but I will them to keep me upright. "You – you've been watching."

"Yes." She nods. "We been watchin'."

Quick as a cat, she strikes me with her open palm. My cheek burns from the slap, but it's nothing compared to what we're facing. "That," she says, "is for killing my plants. You didn't even *try* to care for 'em. And now I gotta start all over. Yeah, we watched everything. Even him, watching you. Got these new apps – my lovely grandnieces showed me how – connects security right to your cellular phone. When he came sniffing around, well, I just wanted to see what would happen. So we chatted a bit, and oh you've been a naughty girl, haven't you? Lying to your elders? Thought we'd let him have a little fun 'fore we came back. We went to a motel down the hill and let him stay in the shed for a bit."

"Why didn't you help me?" A lump forms in my throat. "Why didn't you stop him?" Then, the real question I'm almost too afraid to ask. "*Why* were you watching? You were supposed to be in Raleigh."

"Shush now. No need for questions. The whys and hows of things ain't gonna matter much to you in a minute." She nods toward Monster's body. "Need you to do some heavy lifting for us first. Take his body out back. Isabella too. You wasted all our good compost by neglectin' my plants, so we gotta rebuild. You know human bodies make for excellent fertilizer? We feed the soil the way the soil grows food to nourish us. Give and take. Quite biblical if you ask me."

She knows lives were taken in her home and she doesn't even bat an eye. Her cold, down-to-business response makes my skin crawl, like insects wriggling beneath the surface. I imagine maggots worming their way in and out of decomposing flesh buried in the garden and fight another wave of nausea.

"Ah, hell. And the chit in the van out front. Have the boy drag her 'round, put those muscles to good use. Bob, you watch him." She walks right up to Brian and holds out her hand. "Come on now, hand 'em over. They ain't yours to begin with."

Indecision clouds his hardened eyes. I can tell he's reading the situation. Gauging how much of a threat they really are before proceeding. He slowly raises the firearm. Could he actually bring himself to shoot a person – an unarmed, elderly woman, no less – even after what they did?

She snaps her fingers. "Come now, ain't got all day."

He still doesn't give in, and she clucks her tongue.

"You ain't really gonna hurt me with my own weapons, now, are ya? 'Cause I don't think you got it in you. Oh, you're a hunter alright, that I can tell. You got the balance right, comfortable with a firearm. But to take a human? That's a whole other kettle of fish. You ain't ever practiced. Got in your head that it's wrong 'cause that's what they teach you. But what they don't tell you is how much more satisfying it is than downing any buck. That's somethin' my daddy taught me young. Known my whole life how great it can be." She considers him for a minute. "Maybe you can get to know the feeling." She gives me a sidelong glance and a sly smile. "Why don't you take care of her?"

He visibly recoils.

"Just try it. She's gonna die either way, this could be your ticket out of here. Do it and we'll let you go. Right, Bob? We know you won't say nothin' 'cause we got the cameras all over this place. A little editing on the film – my grandnieces'll show me how – a snip here, a splice there, and you're free. We'll wash our hands of you. Or, forfeit your golden ticket and die with her. Think how sad your papa will be to hear the news that a crazed guest went on a shooting spree. Hell, we might even make national news!" She giggles. "Think how good *that* would be for business, eh? Free advertisin'. You hear that, Bob?"

Bob only nods. Raina sighs and frowns again. "It's up to you, son. Take her out and we'll let you live."

Brian hesitates.

"Ugh, fine. Bob?"

"No, no wait!" Brian cries, holding up his hands in surrender. "I'll do it."

What? He turns to me with anguish in his eyes. He's visibly upset, but his jaw is set, signaling his determination.

My heart plummets with dread.

I haven't known him long, but I didn't get the feeling he'd succumb to such an atrocious act. I never imagined Brian – sweet, kind, thoughtful Brian – could ever turn out like Monster, and that's why I was falling for him.

Tears roll down my cheeks, but I can't feel them – my skin is numb with anticipation.

It won't take much for him to do it. He has way more experience with a firearm than I'll ever have. Maybe not toward people, but any target practice would've prepared him.

"Jake," he says. "Come here."

Jake fervently shakes his head against my back.

"Jake," Brian calls again. "Come away from her. Now."

"It's okay, Jake," I whisper, pulling him out from behind me. "You need to go with Brian now. Just go with him and close your eyes." I look at Brian. "Promise you won't hurt him. Promise you'll look after him. *Please.*"

He nods.

Jake sobs openly, face tomato red. He gives me one last glance before shuffling behind Brian on unsteady feet.

So this is really happening. I think I knew, deep down, my days were numbered the second I chose to run. I close my eyes and take one last, shaky breath, bracing myself for the pain and the darkness. I guess now I'll find out what's on the other side. Maybe I'll see my mother again. The thought fills me with an unexpected sense of peace.

My last breath turns into another one. And another. The darkness never comes. I open my eyes. He's aiming at Raina, face hard as stone, while Bob has his own sight turned on him.

Raina chuckles. "Right," she says. "The hero type. Shoulda known."

The tension's thick as glue. I don't dare breathe. If a single strand of hair blows in the breeze, I'm positive they'll fire without hesitation.

Brian speaks through gritted teeth. "Make a move, Bob, and she'll go down with me. That's a promise."

Time slows. Every blink takes three hours. I can't hear anything over the frantic beating of my heart.

Coldness seeps past my legs like ice water, my toes tingling from the sudden drop in temperature.

Raina squints and flexes her fingers – does she feel the cold too? Maybe I can get her talking again, try to delay the inevitable. Only problem is, my chilled lips don't cooperate. I stutter. "Wha-what are you –"

Raina tsks. "Darlin', we don't have to tell you anything more–"

My feet are like cement, hardened to the spot. The air ripples behind Raina, wavering like the view I get whenever I'm about to cry. I blink, expecting warm, fat tears to dampen my face. And that's when I realize my eyes aren't watering. I'm not tearing up.

Everything behind Raina is blurry, wavy, but she's clear as day. If I were crying, wouldn't she get blurry too? She seems unaware of the weirdness happening around her. The air thickens with a fog-like substance. It rises from the floor like a grayish quilt – a backdrop.

There's movement inside the mist, and my brain cannot compute what my eyes are seeing. I've gone numb from my head to my toes, and my heartbeat slows.

Raina seems frozen, her eyes trained on me, her mouth pursed mid-word. Has time stopped entirely? At this point, it seems anything is possible.

Raina's right. She doesn't have to tell us anything because, behind her, rising in the mist are wispy images – translucent, ill-formed shapes wavering in the air, separating into five individual columns, becoming more distinct. Darkening into shadow figures, like the one I saw by the river.

Five girls.

Deep down, I know they're the ghosts of her victims. Call it intuition, gut instinct. Whatever it is, I have no doubt about what I'm seeing.

My eyes widen; I can't look away, can't unsee the horror playing out in slow-motion before me. Time has stopped completely, the grandfather clock no longer ticks. We're in a space in which up is down, right is wrong, and nothing as arbitrary as time matters.

The girls move. Arms wave, legs flail – is this a reenactment? For my sake?

The air crackles with electricity. I suck in a sharp breath as the crawler appears, silent, jerky motions signaling a kind of distress one should never experience. Then my mind fills with the pictures they're trying to convey.

The Marshalls are pure evil.

Visuals come to me, washed of color and sound. It's like a silent film. The room transforms, and I relive their experiences with them.

One's a fighter – she's not going down easy. She swings her fists at Raina right here in the living room, barely connecting, and a charm bracelet on her wrist catches the light. It's the same one that's in their office. She suddenly freezes, mouth gaping open. Eyes full of horror, she slowly looks down. An arrow tip juts from her abdomen while blood, dark as ink, blossoms around it like a flower. She slumps to her knees. Above her head, I see the crossbow in Bob's hands.

The scene swirls, erasing like an Etch A Sketch. It settles around me like falling snow, arranging itself into something new. Trees sprout up from the ground, surely piercing the ceiling, though I can no longer see it. It looks like the woods outside, trees and undergrowth stretching as far as I can see. A figure darts past my right side, blurry. She stumbles, her face contorted in pain, crying. She looks up and freezes. She's wearing a University of Denver T-shirt, and I remember the pen I played with in the office. Her panting turns rapid. She pushes herself to her feet and hobbles away. Just before she's out of sight, her shoulder jerks and she stops. I hold my breath. Something about her posture seems familiar, like Isabella, like Monster. It's the freeze frame of someone who's been shot. I think I know what happens next. She tilts forward and lands on one knee, but she can't hold the position long. She collapses fully onto the ground and doesn't move again. Is anyone else seeing this or is it just me?

I smell nail polish, the familiar nip curling the hairs inside my nose. The trees vanish, and I'm standing in the bathroom behind a girl facing the sink. She appears to be giving herself a manicure. She looks up, face reflected in the mirror, as though startled. Out of all of them, she looks the most like me, down to the freckles spattered across her nose. Guilt races across her features and is quickly replaced by fear.

I'm standing still, but her face zooms into a close-up. Hands, from out of nowhere, grip her neck. She bats at them, staring at someone I can't see, but I know without a doubt it has to be one of the Marshalls. She mouths the word "don't" and I'm reminded of my first day here, the breathy word I was certain that Raina said. But I was wrong. And the message in varnish wasn't telling me to stay – it was saying "don't" and "go" as two separate statements. Maybe she knew what was going to happen, maybe she tried to emulate the choking sensation to get me to leave. Her struggle goes on for ages, and I duck my head, unwilling to watch, unable to change the outcome.

I think I understand. Of course. This is why I'm here. I was to be the next victim. How could I not see? Isabella tried warning me. They lured girls here under the pretense of needing an inn-sitter and fulfilled their most heinous desires. Raina did most of the killing, I figure, while Bob enjoyed the sneaky homemade movies out in the shed.

I'm back in the present, directly across from the crawler. My gut reaction is to shrink back, away from the monstrosity, but I can't move – my limbs weighed down by dread.

She slithers toward me and rises up so she's only inches away from my face. I can't look away. She's not fully formed, just a translucent, swirling mist, but what's supposed to be her face is only inches from my own. My breath catches. Somehow, she doesn't have to show me. Somehow, I already know. It's like she's pushed the memory into my head. I wish I didn't have to know this. I wish I could wipe my mind clean of the gruesome truth.

They took a hammer to her knees so she couldn't escape and kept her in the attic as some sort of pet. She banged on the wall, the floor, anything she could reach to alert visitors to her plight until the Marshalls broke her wrists as well. It wouldn't have worked anyway. It was the off-season. She lingered there, in pain, until she died of infection. They were simply curious how long it would take. It took longer than this poor girl would've liked.

I press my teeth into my knuckles and close my eyes. Hot tears seep from beneath my lids, wetting my face. I've seen enough. I don't know how much time has passed – time seems irrelevant now – but it can't have been long. Things pick up speed again as if nothing happened.

Raina's eyes widen. Her lips part to let out a wheeze, drawing Bob's attention.

"Raina?" he asks, still aiming steady. His voice is higher and softer than I remember. "You alright?"

She tries to answer but can't seem to get out more than a faint cough.

"Raina?" Clearly alarmed, Bob lowers his gun and steps closer to her. "What is it, hon?"

And then she's down on the ground, writhing and gurgling, struggling to breathe. Bob rushes to her aid but can't seem to figure out how to help. He flutters his hands above her body uselessly.

The spirits gather behind her, watching me, waiting. My gut tells me they're behind this, they've subdued her for a reason.

I know what I have to do.

I walk up to Brian and reach for one of the holsters. He puts his hand out to stop me, covering mine with his own. He shakes his head. I gently peel his fingers off my hand and bring them to my lips. I kiss the dark, flaky blood covering his knuckles and taste the dirt and iron on my lips. I wrap my hand around the handle of a pistol and pull it out of its snug, leather home. I check the safety, make sure it's off.

Brian doesn't wait to see how this ends. He grabs Jake and propels him toward the front door, skirting around the hysterics on the floor. I wonder if they'll wait for me, or if they're already halfway down the drive.

I've never felt such purpose in my life. Each step closer to Raina is deliberate, calculated. I'm surprisingly calm. It's like an out-of-body experience – I'm watching this whole thing play out from above. Maybe I'm dead too, and this is just my scene to share with the next victim.

Raina writhes on the floor, twisting this way and that, groaning all the while. I stand over her, watching. The gun feels heavy in my hand, dangling by my side.

"Hey," I say.

She doesn't acknowledge me. Her head whips back and forth, sweat beading her skin and dampening her hairline.

"Hey!" I try again.

This time she turns her head to look at me, even as her body flails the other way.

"How could you?" I ask. "How could you trick us like that? You never needed help watching the inn. You lured us here under false pretenses. You hurt them. You *killed* them. And you were going to kill me. Or were you going to do some sick experiment first? Like the girl in the attic?"

My grip on the gun is slick with sweat, but I don't feel nervous. This feels right. Like maybe I found this place for a reason, a higher purpose. The girls want revenge, and I can give it to them.

"What would you have done with Jake, huh? A little kid? You murdered someone right in front of him and were prepared to do it again. Were you planning on taking his life too? Did you think it wouldn't matter since his Mom's already gone?" My voice cracks. I take a deep breath, composing myself before I lose my strength.

"You're not going to hurt anybody anymore," I whisper, tasting wet salt as tears slide down my face and seep between my lips. "Either of you."

Bob watches me, his features drooped with sadness. He doesn't move by her side to stop me. Why? Does he feel guilty about what he's done? It's clear Raina's the boss of this situation, and without her, he seems lost.

I crouch next to Raina and, using the barrel of the gun, push a few stray hairs out of her face. She doesn't flinch. I can't tell if she's seeing me clearly or if whatever experience she's having clouds her vision. Who knows what she's being shown behind her eyes? I glance up and the spirits are gone. Where did they go? I look back and forth and over my shoulder, but they're nowhere to be seen. Are they satisfied? Did they just want me to scare her? Somehow, that doesn't seem likely. They wanted more. I want more.

"I wish you would apologize," I say. "I wish you would beg for your life. But there's no point in wishing. I can't change the past, but I can change the future. I can stop you from killing again."

I press the tip of the weapon to the center of her forehead.

I feel a presence behind me.

A warm hand on my shoulder.

"Don't," Brian says. "You'll regret it."

"But I have to."

"No, you don't."

A fresh wave of tears dampen the salty tracks on my face. "But she's hurt so many people."

"I know."

"She was gonna hurt you. And me."

"Yes. But you don't have to be like her. We can go get the police. We can end this correctly."

I shake my head and press the gun harder against her skull. Her skin wrinkles around the metal barrel.

"Temperly."

The way he says my name, softer than before, unravels me. Something coiled tight inside releases and comes undone. The gun suddenly weighs a hundred pounds. I lower it and shuffle back, away from Raina, away from the self I'd almost become.

"I almost did it," I mumble. "I almost did it.

"But you didn't. Now let's go, Temperly. Come on. Get up."
He helps me to my feet. "We gotta go."

We turn to leave.

Explosive pain in my shoulder. My legs buckle and I cry out. Looking back – Bob's standing, his own weapon trained on me. His face, screwed up in helpless fury, tells me he's not done, and without thinking I raise the gun, firing all the while. Each bullet carries my grief and rage. One shot for Abigail, one for Isabella. Another for Monster and one for each of the Marshalls and the atrocities they perpetuated. My aim is wild and has no clear target, but Bob shouts and drops to his knees beside Raina, who leaks blood from just beneath her left breast. His temple, grazed raw by a rogue bullet, drips over her wound as his face crumples. Raina doesn't make a sound. Her breathing intensifies, chest rising and falling like a frightened animal, then slowing.

"Come on," Brian says, tugging my hand. The movement ignites fresh waves of pain in my shoulder, but I wait, watching her chest, needing to be sure.

It stops moving.

Bob leans over her, crying.

I let Brian guide me to the door.

Outside, Jake waits in the running truck. We hop in, squishing Jake between us.

"Hurry," I say, looking toward the inn.

Bob stands on the porch, watching us. His expression is strange.

The engine rumbles as Brian steps on the gas. He turns the truck around, and we're off down the windy drive, headed back down the hill.

Twenty-Eight

Bob doesn't follow us. I know because I crane my neck to stare through the back window as the truck bounces along the winding road away from that horrific place.

Once we reach the main road, I force myself to turn forward. Over Jake's head, I see Brian in my peripheral vision but avoid looking at him directly.

"We need to go to the hospital," Brian says.

"No, police first. The hospital will take too long, and they need to know what's happened there."

He glances at me once before staring straight ahead. "You're injured." He sounds mechanical, like a robot or something.

I can't bring myself to look at the hole in my shoulder – it's throbbing, I know it's there. I clench my teeth and press my hands together in my lap, fighting the pain.

"I'm fine."

"You know they're going to take you to the hospital anyway, right? You could be bleeding to death for all we know. We're wasting time."

"Police," I spit, "first. Jake, how you holding up?"

Jake nods, quiet.

A few raindrops splatter on the windshield, and the wipers smear them away as if they didn't exist.

I wish we could wipe away this whole experience. Our body heat and foggy breath steams up the glass. I catch my hazy reflection in the side-view mirror. My face is covered in little red dots, like the laser grid, reminding me of when I had chicken pox as a kid. But this isn't a rash – it's blood, not entirely my own, and it itches for a totally different reason.

We head straight for the police station, a squat, nondescript building in a courtyard surrounded by more trees.

We're greeted by two sleepy officers named Johnson and Barry that come to life when they see us covered in blood. Upon seeing my wound, they immediately call for an ambulance, and when we mention homicide, send authorities to the inn. I demand to give my statement before the ambulance comes, before I lose my nerve.

They separate us, but the place is so small they only have one free room available. Jake, being a kid, gets the privacy while Brian and I sit on folding chairs on opposite sides of the main room. The place is cluttered with brown filing boxes and folders scattered haphazardly across a couple of desks. The mess is discouraging. Shouldn't the authorities be capable of simple organization?

I'm given a towel to press against my bleeding shoulder, though any sort of pressure makes my head go light. Instead, I half-heartedly dab at the mess, knowing full well it won't help.

Barry puffs out a breath that smells like stale coffee and clucks his tongue as he flips to a fresh page in his notebook. "Alright, now," he says, his coarse moustache wiggling with each word.

"We'll make this fast and we can stop if you need to. The ambulance will be here in a jiff. If you can tell me what happened, from the beginning."

Though we speak in hushed tones, I can still hear every word Brian says in the other corner. He speaks earnestly to Johnson, barely stopping for breath.

I inhale, tasting dust in the air, and start my version of the story. I get a swift, scornful glance when I explain about the ghost hunting and outright raised eyebrows at the mention of paranormal activity. I can't say I blame him. If our roles were reversed, I'd be skeptical too.

Afterwards, Barry nods his head and closes the notebook.

"That's quite a story," he says. I can tell by his tone that he doesn't believe most of it, and my heart sinks. What did I expect? I'm led back to the waiting area in the front as Barry and Johnson confer with each other and go in to speak with Jake. I sink into a hard, plastic folding chair facing the empty reception desk. Brian stays put on his side of the room, head in his hands.

The front door swings open, and a frazzled man enters, looking around nervously. He's not wearing a coat. Is he crazy? No. Concerned. He must have forgotten his coat in his haste.

"Hello?" he calls, leaning over the reception desk. He looks familiar. I've seen his photographs on a mantel. My tongue dries up as I suddenly realize who he is. "I'm here for my son, Jake? Hello?"

Barry comes out of the private office and immediately approaches Mr. Osbourne. They speak quietly, and then Barry fetches Jake from the office.

"Daddy?" The moment Jake sees him, his face crumples, and Mr. Osbourne scoops him into his arms. They hug each other tight, both of their shoulders shaking. I look away – it feels like they should have this moment without anyone watching, least of all me, the reason why they're even here.

I've done my part. I've told the officers everything, and now my brain's switching off and doesn't want to think about the horror we've endured anymore. My soul feels like it's been ripped to shreds, that everything I believed about the world, spiritual and otherwise, has been flipped upside down. I don't know what to think anymore, and I don't know how to process what I'm feeling, so I focus on the pain in my shoulder; it protects me from feeling too much else. I don't want to burst into tears because, if that first tear is allowed to fall, I'm sure I'll never stop.

The ambulance siren sings in the distance.

Sensing movement, I glance up just as Brian sits next to me on the hard, plastic chair.

"You alright?" he whispers.

I stare straight ahead, not answering. How am I supposed to answer that?

I'm not fine. I will probably never be fine again. But he needs that reassurance, the knowledge that I'll be okay. But will I? I know what's going to happen now. At best, I'll be fostered. If not, then group home it is. I give in to my fate. It was bound to happen anyway, I guess. I'll be eighteen by the summer and then I can make my own way in the world.

The world. I scoff. This place is the pits. Hell on earth is more than just an expression, it seems. We're all living in tragedy. Climate change, poverty, war. It's eating away at the human race, making us crazy, making us go after each other in horrifying ways. I can't be a part of that. I won't be.

It feels as if Brian is worlds away and not sitting just a few inches from me. His now-bandaged hand hovers tentatively above my shoulder, but it does nothing to draw me back from my cave of nothingness inside. I'm practically a corpse. If things had gone Monster's and Raina's way, I would be.

"Hazel?" His voice is low and earnest. "Temperly. I know you can hear me. Stop ignoring me, please. We're in this together. I'm not mad about the lies. Don't worry about that. It's nothing, done, forgotten."

I'm forgiven. Just like that?

"Please don't shut me out." He watches me intently. I feel his gaze on me like heat from the sun.

I will not waver. I have been violated in so many ways. Spied on. Harassed – by spirits, no less. Nearly murdered. What kind of life is this? Sound is muted in my head, like I'm swimming underwater. I finally break the surface and breathe. "I have to go home."

"Where's that?"

My nose prickles, a sure sign I'm about to start crying. I look up at the ceiling, willing my eyes to stay dry. "I don't know yet," I admit, ashamed. "Things have been a little . . . complicated lately."

"I wish you'd told me." He inhales, steeling himself. "I liked you. I still like you. I just . . . want you to know."

What good is that? I liked him too. But after this, I'll never see him again, so what's the point? I turn away. Maybe he'll read my body language and get the hint. It's time to move on. I'm going back to live with strangers, and from there? Then what?

Officer Barry approaches as the siren gets louder, a look of thinly veiled pity on his pockmarked face. "We got hold of your social worker," he says. "She's on her way. It'll be a wait, though, seeing as she's coming from up north." He says it with distaste, and I practically hear the capital letters, like "Up North" might as well be North Korea rather than a couple hours' drive. He checks his watch. "She'll likely come to you at the hospital."

If Mrs. Shapiro's on her way, then that's that.

"How 'bout you, son? They're nearly finished with you, so you can probably go soon."

Brian looks at me. "Would you like me to stay with you?"

I shake my head. "No, that's okay."

"You sure?"

"Yeah."

He exhales loudly. "I just feel like I should be here. For support."

"I don't need supporting."

He looks ready to argue that statement when the officer interrupts. "We have your contact information if we need to get in touch." He looks pointedly at Brian, who hangs his head, defeated.

"Yes, sir." Brian watches the officer walk away before standing. He rubs his hands on his jeans. "Well, then. Looks like I've worn out my welcome. Guess I'd better go."

He pauses and looks like he's considering his next words carefully. Whatever he wanted to say, he clearly thinks better of it because, with a long, pitying look, he lifts his hand in a defeated kind of goodbye and walks out the door as uniformed EMTs rush in.

Twenty-Nine

They arrested Bob that same afternoon. He didn't even put up a fight. Apparently, when they got there, he was out back in the garden, kneeling on the cold, hard soil. Weeping.

He confessed to everything. He and Raina had been placing ads for years, enticing people – girls in particular – to come stay alone in the inn so they could hunker down in the shed and watch them on secret cameras. It's sickening to think how they got away with it for so long.

Some guests were none the wiser, others, not so lucky. The ones that discovered their secret didn't live for long – Raina, a tough farm girl, had no problem seeing to that. But that's when it got worse because she started getting off on finishing their lives as opposed to just their naked bodies.

Bob confirmed everything that I'd been shown in that terrible house.

I don't feel sorry for him.

They're throwing the book at him, as they say on those old courtroom dramas. I know this because I've been keeping up with the story here at my foster home.

They're good people, my foster parents. A childless couple, all bright smiles and hushed tones. They mean well. At this point, that's something I don't take lightly. Knowing the kind of people that are out there makes me appreciate the good ones in here.

They wanted to send me back to school, but I can't manage it. Memories of the inn clutch at my ankles and crawl up my legs, slowly overtaking my body just like the way Raina was consumed by the hateful energy of vengeful spirits. Apparently, I have post-traumatic stress disorder, and I'm seeing a therapist for it. I don't know if it's helping, but I don't really have much say in the matter. Maybe in time, it will.

One thought keeps pecking away at me. Isabella thought the Marshalls were good people – with all of her gifts, how did she not sense what they were up to? I mean, really. Maybe all of this could have been avoided if only she'd realized everything sooner. She kept talking about how the *building* felt bad – how did she not see it was the people that owned the building that brought such an evil presence? Guilt eats away at me whenever I indulge these thoughts. She did the best she could. It's not fair for me to assume she could've stopped it. Even still, I can't help shifting the blame onto her, a deceased woman. What does that make me? Perhaps I'm the evil one.

The victims are never far from my mind. They're with me always, no matter where I go or what I do. Not literally, of course. Not like that night. But the memory of them is burned into my brain in such a way that I'll never be able to forget. If Bob had never confessed, the cops would still be searching for the names of the girls. But he handed the details over without a fight. Which means I will forever associate the names Jennifer,

Nikkita, Sarah-Beth, Emily, and Maria with those tortured souls in Keystone Mill. Are their spirits still lingering in that place? Or was their revenge enough to help them move on? These are the thoughts that keep me up at night, tossing and turning beneath the covers.

* * *

It's nearly dinner time, and I'm alone in the house. My foster parents have been at work all day, but they'll be back soon. I take advantage of having the place to myself by taking an extra-long shower, making the water hotter and hotter until it's nearly scalding, hoping it will melt away the feeling of guilt and fear that I wear like a bodysuit. But it doesn't work. Nothing does. My foster mom dedicated an entire shelf in the pantry to boxes of hot chocolate powder, just for me. I've been working through the packets methodically, not so much for comfort anymore but because it gives me something to do, to focus on. A mindless activity – rip sachet, pour contents into mug, heat it up, and stir – that keeps my hands busy and gives me a sense of purpose, however fleeting.

The doorbell rings. I pause, water blasting my raw shoulders. I listen, and it chimes again, that happy little suburban tune, so different from the jarring buzz at my old apartment. I turn the water off and reach for the towel, feeling incredibly exposed despite being alone in the house. I'm reminded of the chef's knife I'd kept in the Marshall's bathroom and quell the urge to look for one here. I quickly rub my skin dry and pull on my clothes, letting my wet hair drip rivulets down the back of my shirt. Who could possibly be at the door? An image of Monster flashes through my mind and I cringe. He's dead. He'll never stand on my doorstep again.

I creep on tiptoe through the living room toward the front door, wondering who's on the other side. Is it a neighbor needing something? UPS delivering a package? I peek through the frosted glass of the window decoration, pressing my nose against it so I can see clearly.

A dark, blurry figure walks back down the path, apparently giving up on anyone answering.

I should just leave it. Go back to the bathroom and dry my hair or something. But my hand drifts toward the handle.

Grips.

Pulls.

The spring air is warmer than at the beginning of the month, even though the sun's going down and inky darkness spreads across the sky like a watercolor stain. Streetlamps line the sidewalk, shining spotlights onto the cement. A breeze caresses my face, soft as cotton and smelling like cherry blossoms. I inhale and mentally chant my mantra: it's okay, I am safe.

The figure's back is to me, but I can see it's a man.

I step out onto the front porch.

"Hello?"

The man stops beneath a light and turns around.

I swallow a gasp.

It's Mr. Osbourne, and my heart stops. What is he doing here?

He approaches, in no apparent rush, hands in his trouser pockets. He doesn't stop until he reaches the porch, pausing just in front of the steps so that I'm standing a few inches taller than him. This is the closest I've ever been to him, I realize. His brown hair is thinning on top, and he has bags under his eyes as well as stubble on the lower half of his face, indicating he hasn't been sleeping much.

We stare at each other for a minute.

We don't speak.

Then he says, "You're Miss Jacobs?"

His voice isn't as deep as I expected.

"Yeah."

"Temperly Jacobs?"

I clutch the T charm dangling around my neck once more as if it's a protective amulet. "Yeah, that's me."

He nods, dropping his gaze to the ground. Another minute goes by without words. Not for lack of trying on his part. His mouth opens and closes, like a fish out of water. It's like he wants to say something but stops himself. The silence grows awkward, so I fill it with the question that's been weighing on my mind.

"How's Jake?"

He lifts his head so quickly I fear he might have whiplash. I expect to see a burning hatred in his eyes directed toward me – that's why he's here, isn't it? To see the girl that took his wife away from him, the mother of his son? The reason he's not sleeping, the reason he's a single parent. God, I don't blame him for hating me. I loathe myself. Except his blue eyes aren't burning with anger or repulsion. They're wide, so wide, but gentle. Sad. He nods again, slowly this time.

"Jake's . . . doing as well as he can for now. It's been . . . difficult . . . as I'm sure you can imagine."

Now I feel like an idiot for asking. I cross my arms. My shirt, soaked through by my hair, clings to my back. "Yeah. I can imagine."

"I'm actually here on behalf of Jake. He wanted to come, but I thought it best he stay with my sister for the night. You understand."

"Um, sure."

"He wanted – he wanted to know that you're well. He's been . . . concerned. For you."

"Really?" My heart warms at the sweetness of the kid. After everything I put him through, I don't deserve it. "He's so – that's really kind of him. I can't believe he wanted to know that. He's so different from other kids."

"Yes, he's pretty special. I was going to email you, then decided to call, but he was adamant I see you in person, face-to-face. He said that, scientifically, it's the only way to be sure you're truly fine. Body language, apparently. It's a thing."

"Right." I slowly uncross my arms. I gesture to the empty driveway. "Yes. Um, I'd invite you in, but . . ."

"Please, I understand. I parked on the street, I wasn't sure if I'd be blocking anyone."

My smile is weak.

"So," he says. "You're handling things . . . well?"

"Uh, sure, yeah. Well enough. You know."

"Yes. I can imagine." He suddenly jams his hand in his pocket and pulls out an envelope. "This is for you. It's from Jake. I haven't read it – he asked me not to."

I take it from him, my hands trembling. "Thanks."

Quiet. We're so quiet. But the awkwardness seeps away, little by little. We'll never see each other again, and though I feel a weird pang when I think about not seeing Jake, I totally get it. This was for closure. They both needed it – maybe I needed it too.

* * *

I sit on my bed to read the letter. He has pretty good hand-writing for a ten-year-old, not all chicken scratchy like mine used to be. I bet that was Abigail's doing – I can picture her leaning over his shoulder, coaching him as he practiced his letters.

I focus on the one in my hand.

Dear Haz– Temperly,

Sorry, I'm still not used to your real name yet. I think I will always think of you as Hazel in my head, hope you don't mind. Anyway, I'm writing because my mom always made me write thank you notes for my clients. For letting me investigate and stuff. She would probably want me to write one for you too, so here it is.

Thank you for reaching out to me with your questions and your trust. I apresh-appreciate the opportunity to investigate on your property, and I hope you were satisfied with the results.

Well that's dumb. Sorry. This is weird. I don't actually know what to say. I hope that you're okay. Me and Dad are staying with my Aunt Ruth right now. She has a ton of cats. One of them scratched me, but that's okay. I just avoid them. I'm not in school now. I might go back soon, I don't know. Dad and Aunt Ruth are always whispering in the other room about me. Like, what to do with me, whatever that means. They know I'm sad about Mom. And Isabella. I feel kind of lost without them, but I'll be okay. You'll be okay too. I'm not mad, if that's what you think. Sad, but not mad. Don't be mad at me either, okay? We just didn't know what would happen. It's nobody's fault. Okay? I wish I could talk to you, but Dad thinks it's best if we keep our distance, at least for a little while. I think he's just as sad as me.

I hope I can visit you someday, or that you'll come back to Fox Valley soon. I guess that's all I have to say. You can probably write me back if you want. You've been to my house, you know my address, right? If you forgot, just look at the front of this envelope. Talk to you soon. Be brave.

Jake

My chest heaves with sobs as I fold the letter up and slip it back into the envelope. My mouth hangs open in a silent cry – my world has blurred with tears. Such a sweet little boy – forgiving me, just like that? No blame? It's because of me he has no mother. And that is the worst feeling in the world. I should know.

I lay down in the fetal position on top of the bed covers, clutching the envelope to my chest.

* * *

I don't know how long I stay curled up on the bed, but my tears have long dried, leaving my face itchy with salt. I don't rub. It doesn't matter. The room is dark – the sun went down ages ago, dimming the window as it slipped from sight. This room faces the backyard, where there are no streetlights. Just grass. And a little garden I try not to think about. I wonder when things will stop reminding me of Keystone Mill. Maybe it will always be there. After what I've done, I don't deserve to forget.

Something shifts in the air. Something I wouldn't have noticed if I'd never spent time in that inn. It's not just the temperature that's changing, it's the energy, as Isabella would've called it. Movement in the corner captures my attention. It starts as a dim pinprick of light, hovering around the middle of the wall. The light gets brighter as the orb grows. I blink and then it's gone. A chill whispers across the room. The door's still closed and there's no movement to cause the breeze. I hold my breath and scrunch my toes against the bedspread as the cold air rises, touching my skin. It's soft but icy. I close my eyes and press my fingers against the lids for good measure. Is this really happening? Are the memories turning into sensory hallucinations? In my head, I count to three, complete with "Mississippis" to pace myself. I open my eyes.

Mom?

If this hadn't happened before, I'd believe that I've finally cracked, having some kind of psychotic break. She stands in the corner of the room, and I try so hard not to blink, frightened by the idea that if I do, she'll disappear. She's fading in and out, almost shimmering, but that could just be my eyes watering. I should be freaked, scared out of my mind. But how can I? It's Mom.

I wish she were solid.

It's hard to see her features, but I think she's smiling. Her light gradually dims, and I realize she's disappearing. It's too soon – I only had her for a second. "Please stay," I whisper. "You can stay. I want you to."

But she's already gone.

She can't stay. The voice isn't heard by my ears. It's more inside my head, as weird as that sounds. I can't place it, but it's like a warm, fuzzy blanket on a snowy day. And that's when I know. It's the only thing that makes sense. Isabella's using her gift on the other side. Just like she probably helped me connect with the victims, she's helped me see my mom. I imagine her guiding Mom across the spirit world to find me as a way of saying everything will be okay. My heart swells and my throat tightens. Everything's got to be alright because they're both okay, on whatever plane they're inhabiting. And I'll see Mom again, someday, now that I know she's out there. Maybe she'll be waiting to greet me with a cup of hot cocoa. I like to think there's plenty of hot chocolate on the other side. "Thank you," I say out loud, somehow knowing Isabella can hear me. Maybe Mom can hear me too.

I can't feel them anymore. They've drifted away, as I suppose spirits do. I stay curled up in bed, beneath the covers. The fabric of the pillow absorbs my tears. Maybe we're not supposed to feel them. That's why we're human – so we can lean on others for support. I think of Jake, telling me to write. I think of Brian. I wonder how he's holding up.

I get up and walk to the desk where my foster parents left a laptop for me. I've only used it to follow the news, but now I bring up various forms of social media and type in Brian's name. It takes a little bit of scrolling to find him, but there he is – his profile picture looking way more jubilant than the last time I saw him. I click on the messaging icon and pause, fingers hovering over the keyboard. What do I say?

Hey, Brian, I type. *It's me, Temperly.* I pause at first, but then my fingers take on a life of their own. Before I know it, I'm explaining everything to him, things I didn't get to say in that stuffy police building.

I tell him about the roller coaster of feelings I had, the guilt about lying, and my new foster home.

And that, ultimately, I'm okay.

Because it's true. Maybe not now, maybe not even next week. But someday, soon, I hope, I will be.

Acknowledgements

Many thanks to my editor, Kylie Lynne (@KylieLynne_Edit on Instagram) for your incredible story insight and plotting expertise.

Tracey and Alleyne, please accept my infinite gratitude for your endless patience, generosity of wisdom, and advice over the years. Those bookish weekends, conferences, and Wegman's meetups shaped me into the writer I am today, and this book would not be here if it weren't for you.

Rob, thanks for always believing in me and supporting my goals even when I'm a cranky witch knee-deep in edits. I'm forever grateful for your love, encouragement, and ready yesses to pizza.

My mom taught me how to read and write, and with that knowledge came a love of storytelling at a very young age. Thanks, Mom, for that. To you and Dad, thank you for your lifelong enthusiasm for my writing, even when it's not something you'd particularly want to read. Having you on my support team means the world to me.

And finally, without readers there would be no reason for books to exist. So thanks to *you* for taking a chance on me. Feel free to leave a rating and review on the platform of your choice, like Amazon, Goodreads, etc. I'd love to know what you think!

Kitt Creative

Heather lives in a charming but haunted little town in Virginia that's full of ghosts that keep her company and inspire her work. She is a member of the Horror Writers Association and has drafted one novel a year since 2002. When not writing, she can be found buying books faster than she can read them, practicing yoga, or eating her weight in thin crust pizza.

Catch up with her on social media:
@heathermihok

Find out more at www.heathermihok.com

www.ingramcontent.com/pod-product-compliance
Lightning Source LLC
Chambersburg PA
CBHW061233310726

48971CB00007B/2042